OBSESSED

A chilling mystery with a huge twist

PATTI BATTISON

(DETECTIVE MIA HARVEY THRILLERS BOOK 2)

JOFFE
BOOKS

Revised edition 2019
Joffe Books, London
www.joffebooks.com

Please join our mailing list for free Kindle crime thriller, detective, mystery books and new releases.
www.joffebooks.com

ISBN: 978-1-78931-208-9

FLYERS ACCOMPANYING LARCHBOROUGH EVENING NEWS

TURNTABLE MUSIC INCORPORATED

Presents

For 3 SPECTACULAR nights

27 - 29 JULY

YOUR ... ONE ... AND ... ONLY ...

JOHNNY LEE ROGERS

at

Stratton Manor, Larchborough

Tickets available at

Tourist Information Bureau, High St, Larchborough

or www.dreamfest.co.uk

* * *

Win tickets to see

JOHNNY LEE ROGERS ... LIVE!

At Stratton Manor on Sunday 29 July

Just answer one simple question

Where was Johnny Lee born?

Answers on a postcard to our Parliament Street address £5 per entry

All proceeds to go to the Rainbow Hospice fund

CHAPTER ONE

'This quiet spell'll be over quicker than that Rogers bloke can get a girl's knickers off,' Duty Sergeant Jim Levers growled into his morning coffee.

'Johnny Lee?' said Detective Sergeant Mia Harvey.

They were in reception at Larchborough's Silver Street Police Station. Mia had been heading for CID when Levers cornered her for a moan.

She laughed. 'I wouldn't mind a couple of hours with him, to be honest, Jim.'

Sergeant Levers looked aghast. 'You're joking. He's older than I am.'

'Maybe. But he still looks good.'

'Anybody can look good in a wig and make-up,' Levers huffed. 'Catch him first thing in the morning and he won't look so bright.'

'He wears a wig?' said Mia, appalled. She tutted, gave him a dismissive smile. 'I think you're jealous.'

Levers grinned, his small eyes bright with mischief. 'Wouldn't mind his money, that's a fact. And all those girls throwing themselves at him – well, middle-aged mums more like – wouldn't mind a bit of that either.' He sobered somewhat, a frown heavy on his forehead. 'These concerts though, Mia, they always attract the wrong sort. It's happened before and it'll happen this time. I've a funny feeling in my bowels, and they rarely let me down.'

'Glad to hear it,' she said, grabbing her shoulder bag. 'Anyway, can't waste the whole day chatting, Jim. The DCI's on one of his time-and-motion kicks.'

'So I've heard. Don't know how you work with him.'

'He's OK,' said Mia, heading for the lift. 'You just have to know the right buttons to press.'

She was about to summon the lift when the double doors leading in from the car-park were given a tentative push and two small children wandered into reception. The older child – a boy of around eight – was holding tight the hand of a thin scrap of a girl. She'd clearly been crying for tears had forged a clean path through the dirt caked on her face, and a blob of snot quivered precariously from her nostrils. Seemingly unable to move they looked towards the duty sergeant with expressions that told of unmitigated terror.

Levers lifted a flap in the desk and manoeuvred his considerable bulk through the limited space, a jovial smile stretching his lips. He approached the children carefully and dropped to his haunches while Mia rummaged in her bag for a tissue.

'Whatever's the matter with you two?' he said, dropping his voice a notch. 'You look like you've lost a shilling and found a thrupenny bit.'

'Our mum's gone and vanished, that's what it is,' said the boy. 'We need a copper to find her.'

The words were spoken firmly enough, but the boy's bravado was compromised by the constant trembling of his lower lip. Tears were little more than a breath away but he needed to stay strong for the girl.

Mia knelt beside her, clamped the tissue over her dot of a nose. 'Blow for me, sweetheart…nice big blow.' The girl duly obliged, all the while edging closer to the boy. 'That's better …' said Mia, viewing her critically, 'all nice and clean again.' In a fashion, she thought wryly. Neither of them had seen soap and water for some time. What sort of mother would let her kids roam around in that state?

Levers scratched his chin thoughtfully. 'Your mum's vanished, you say? How long's she been gone, son?'

The boy took in a shuddering breath. 'Since Wednesday.'

'Hmm, over two days. We'll have to do something about that. First things first though – I'm Jim, and this here's Mia. What do we call you two?'

'I'm Nathaniel … Nathaniel Beddows,' said the boy, all polite and serious. 'But you can call me Nathan, if you like.'

'Nathan,' said Levers, with a nod.

'And this is Amaryllis … Amy … she's my sister.'

Amy, deciding they could be trusted, favoured them with a gummy grin. 'Look, this is my new party dress,' she said, one hand holding out the dirt-streaked skirt while the other struggled to free itself from her brother's grip. 'It was my birthday and I'm going to have a party …' Her grin faded and more tears threatened. 'Only you've got to find my mummy first … I forgot.'

'Now you just cheer up,' said Levers. 'Didn't I already say we'd be sorting that out before you could shout yes to the offer of a cake? How old are you anyway?'

'Four. I'm a big girl.'

'Four, eh? Well, Amaryllis Beddows, we'll have your mummy back and you looking pretty for your party before you know it.'

Mia cast Levers a chiding look. It didn't do to make rash promises, especially to children. For all anyone knew their mother could be on another continent by now, enjoying the good life with an attentive lover; or at the bottom of a mine shaft, bloodied and abused, the life throttled out of her. No, it didn't do to make promises. Not in their line of work.

'Now, about that cake,' said Levers, struggling to his feet.

'Ooh, yes, please,' said Amy, jumping on the spot.

'What about Mum?' asked Nathan, his blue eyes huge and troubled.

Sergeant Levers wrapped an arm around the boy's skinny shoulders and pulled him close. 'You just leave your mum to us. We'll get it sorted. As for you two, well, you look like you could eat an elephant let alone a cake.'

'Two elephants,' squealed Amy. 'I'm really hungry.'

Mia moved closer to the sergeant. 'I'll go and tell them upstairs,' she said, keeping her voice low. 'Give us a bell when you've got the details and one of us'll come down.'

He gave her a swift nod and aimed a dazzling smile at the children. 'Right then you two – what sort of cake shall we have?'

'Chocolate,' yelled Amy. 'And lots of jam.'

They headed for the corridor that would take them to the police canteen, a rather solemn Nathaniel pulling up the rear. He stretched out a hand and tapped the sergeant's ample back. 'Sir…?'

Levers turned. 'Yes, Nathan, and what can I do for you, son?'

'I was just wondering … what's a thru'penny bit?'

She could hardly believe her luck. She'd won the competition. And what a prize! At last she'd see her beloved in the flesh.

It was just too incredible to think that a singer as great as Johnny Lee Rogers would want to perform in a boring backwater like Larchborough in the first place. But he did. And now she had two front row tickets to his third and final show. They'd be so near to each other, breathing the same air….

It was all too much and Lizzie Thornton sank on to the kitchen chair, put a hand to her chest, felt her thundering heartbeat.

Of course, everyone else would have said Johnny Lee was born in Los Angeles, but Lizzie knew every last detail of her handsome hero's life. She knew he was born in a trailer park in Michigan; but his parents, dirt poor and desperate, had moved to the City of Angels when their boy was barely six months old.

This was fate at work. It had to be. If she'd given the job of sorting through all the old books to Cathy Cousins – and Cathy should have done it because she was the most junior of the library staff – then Lizzie would never have come across that obscure biography written at the beginning of Johnny Lee's career and would never have learned about his inauspicious start in life.

The hands that held the letter were trembling. Indeed, her whole being was aflutter. Lizzie had loved the man ever since his first appearance on *Top Of The Pops*. September 1966. He'd sung *Travelling Back To You*, and he'd looked magnificent.

Soon he'd be travelling to her. They'd be only yards apart. So near.... If only they could meet. If only she could make him see they were meant to be together. Soulmates forever.

Lizzie clasped the letter to her sagging breasts, her eyes brimming with passion. She'd deliberately saved herself for Johnny Lee Rogers, had kept herself pure all these years for him.

Of course, the same couldn't be said of Johnny Lee. He'd endured three marriages. And three divorces too, thank God. But Lizzie didn't mind. She knew that all men were weak. And Johnny Lee's constant need for female company only highlighted a touching vulnerability that made him all the more attractive in her eyes. He was currently single, had been for a while. Lizzie grinned. But for how much longer?

The hall clock loudly signalled the hour. She must get ready for work; wouldn't do to be late. But first she'd read the letter again, properly this time.

Hunched over the kitchen table, a demented smile stretching the plumpness of her features, Lizzie's hungry gaze devoured the words ... *Miss Elizabeth Thornton ... lucky winner ... tickets to be collected from venue on night of performance ... fantastic prize ... but that's not all....*

Lizzie raised her eyebrows. There's more? She quickly turned the page and read on: *access pass to watch rehearsals ...*

dinner with the star … top class venue … just you and your partner, Miss Thornton, and the great Johnny Lee….

Lizzie gasped, clutched again at her breasts, and the letter fell from her fingers and fluttered to the floor. Thank goodness she was sitting down; a shock like that could have a girl off her feet.

Lizzie pictured the darkened restaurant: orchids floating in perfumed water between them, romantic music playing softly. Johnny Lee would take her hand and start to sing, his lustful gaze burning into her very soul. She could declare her love for him over the candlelight. She could persuade him to love her back. She'd always wanted a December wedding.

What a pity, though, that the prize consisted of two tickets. And who would she take anyway? Her aunt would hardly want to sit through a Johnny Lee Rogers concert. The music would be much too loud, even with her hearing aid turned off. Lizzie knew her aunt only too well, knew she'd moan constantly about the vibrations coming from the band and disturbing the very air around them. No, she didn't want Aunt Daisy spoiling her pleasure, especially over a romantic dinner.

But who could she ask?

Detective Inspector Nick Ford was in a quandary. Should he leave the small cushy division that was Larchborough where he was one of the main contenders for promotion, or transfer to a larger more hectic station and pander to the hierarchy? Main contender or small fish? A clear no-brainer in theory, but in practice….

Nick was bored. He'd served his apprenticeship on Manchester's mean streets, and he'd loved every minute of it. But after the sudden death of his pregnant wife, when his whole existence unravelled in an instant, Nick had sought the quiet sanctuary that Larchborough had had to offer, and he'd been glad of it.

He'd kept quiet about his past, preferring instead to play the silent, hard man. In Nick's view sympathy was an impossible meal to digest, so he chose to keep his own counsel and lick his wounds in private.

Nick pulled at his shirt collar and breathed in a lungful of thin air. It was so bloody hot. Funds for their small division couldn't quite stretch far enough for modern conveniences such as air-conditioning so they all had to sweat and stoically put up with the stink.

Just then the office door was pushed open too robustly and it bounced with a bang off the wall, dragging Nick from his thoughts. It was Mia, in a rush as usual.

'God, it's like an oven in here,' she said, dumping her shoulder bag on her desk. 'What's that you're reading?'

Nick skimmed her a look. 'What you left on my desk.'

She sidled up behind him, scanned the pink-sheeted vacancies list still clutched in his ample fist. 'You're leaving? Brilliant. When?'

'Get lost,' he said, tossing the pamphlet amongst the tangle of papers on his desk.

Mia sprayed deodorant inside the front of her blouse then sank into her chair, grimacing long and hard at the boring clerical work piled before her. 'Where's the boss?'

'No idea. Couldn't care less either.'

'We could have a missing-person soon, Nick. Two kids came into reception while I was talking to Jim. The mother's been gone since Wednesday. He's feeding them up in the canteen while they give him the details. He'll ring us when he's ready.'

'Thank Christ for that – a chance to get out of this bloody sauna.'

Mia snorted. 'Nice of you to worry about the poor abandoned children. Your compassion has been duly noted.'

Before he could come back with a stinging reply Detective Constable Jack Turnbull – the youngest member of CID – entered the office, shoulders hunched, face like thunder. Without a word Jack made for the coffee machine and poured himself a strong cup, downing it in one scalding gulp.

Mia stared at him, open-mouthed. 'Morning, sweetie. Did we get out of bed the wrong side this morning?'

'I'm never setting foot in that bed again,' he muttered.

'Oh? Why?'

'She's pregnant, that's why.'

'Who's pregnant?'

'Michelle. Who do you think?'

Mia grinned. 'That's great … isn't it?' She made a face at the despondent DC. 'You don't look very pleased.'

'I'm over the bloody moon … not.' He perched on the edge of Mia's desk, folded his arms with an indignant flourish. 'She rushes into the kitchen this morning and pushes the pregnancy test under my nose, dripping piss all over my cornflakes, saying, "look at the line, look at the line"….' He closed his eyes, swallowed loudly, reliving that historic moment.

'And?' said Mia, on the edge of her seat.

'I looked at the line. She's pregnant, all right.' He spread his hands, his expression one of sheer disbelief. 'And she actually wants to keep it.'

'What a strange girl she is,' said Mia, shaking her head. 'I can't understand Michelle, I really can't.'

'It's all right for you,' Jack huffed. 'You haven't got my responsibilities. You can please yourself.'

'Which might sound great from where you're sitting, sweetie, but I'd trade places with you any day of the week.'

He shot Nick an anxious look. 'Back me up, mate … please.'

'Leave me out of it,' Nick said, holding up his hands.

Jack sighed heavily. 'Cheers.'

He was heading for his desk like a condemned man on his way to the noose when the words, 'You'd better all be bloody working,' came travelling through the ether. It was Detective Chief Inspector Paul Wells calling from the corridor.

As Wells lurched through the doorway, all gangling limbs and hangdog features, his team was poring over statement forms and examining documents with an intensity that pleased him no end.

'Anything to report?' he asked, flinging his battered briefcase on to his desk.

'Jack's going to be a daddy,' said Mia, making a face at the young DC's prickly expression.

'Really, Jack? Well done, mate.'

Jack blushed, his cheeks clashing violently with the red of his highly gelled hair. 'Thanks, sir.'

'Only he's not very pleased,' Mia added.

'Why?' asked Wells, pouring himself a coffee.

'It's the shock, sir. We weren't trying and—' He finished the sentence with a helpless shrug.

Wells gave Jack a wink as he settled at his desk. 'I'll bet you the price of a pint you'll be hooked the minute you hold that baby. I don't know why but they get to you … here.' He made a fist and rapped it against his chest. 'And God help you if it's a girl, Jack, because you'll be well and truly scuppered then. I'd kill for my girls. I'd commit hari-kari.'

Nick shifted uncomfortably in his seat. His unborn baby was a girl. Sophie Violet. He needed to change the subject before his hurt made its way to his face, and was about to do so when Mia's phone buzzed.

It was Jim Levers. 'Mia, I reckon I've got all we need from those kids.'

'Are they OK?'

'Suppose. Anyway they've gorged themselves silly and now they want to go home.'

'Where is home?'

'A caravan parked on Heaven's Gate.'

'You're joking … they're travellers?'

'Yes.'

'Is there a father about?'

'No.'

'Who's been looking after them since Wednesday?'

'A Mrs Sheila Reeves … on and off. She's got another of the caravans.'

'What do you mean, on and off?'

'She's not always around to watch them apparently.'

'So they've been left to fend for themselves?'

'Looks like it.' Levers made a noise that strongly resembled a growl. 'That mother of theirs, she's a no-good addict. I'd bet a month's wages. I reckon she's taken a bad fix and keeled over. You start talking to the druggies, Mia, that's what I'd do. I've got a strong feeling about this.'

Mia couldn't help but smile, wondering whether that strong feeling originated in the sergeant's sensitive bowels. 'OK, Jim, I'll be down as soon as I can.'

'Anything we should know?' asked Wells, watching her intently.

'Two small children wandered into reception earlier today, sir. The mother's gone missing. Jim Levers says they're travellers parked illegally on those flood plains by the River Stratton. There's no other family so I'll need to arrange foster care.'

Wells raised an inquisitive eyebrow. 'Why's that then?'

'Because, well, they're on their own and they'll need looking after.'

'No, I mean, why do *you* need to arrange the foster care? Why can't you leave it to uniformed?'

Mia shrugged. 'I could, I suppose, but I was there when they arrived and I thought….' Her voice trailed off. She had no valid answer to his question. 'Would you rather I handed responsibility over to them, then, sir?'

Wells sat back and studied her, his piercing gaze bringing a redness to her cheeks and a disconcerting heat that only added to the film of sweat at the back of her neck. 'You're doing it again.'

'What, sir?' As if she didn't know. Wells hated them to show any initiative. She'd clashed with him on many occasions for daring to think for herself. But for a while now they'd shared a comfortable geniality, albeit tenuous, and she'd been lulled into a false sense of security. Not for much longer though by the look on her superior's face.

'Ever thought of social work, darling?'

'Sir, I—'

'Or the Samaritans? Now they do a lot of good work.'

'I know what you're getting at, sir, and—'

'Why do you keep doing it?' Wells scowled. 'Why do you feel the need to swan off and help everybody, like Mother bloody Teresa, when you're needed here?'

'But we've got nothing to do,' Mia hurled at him. 'We're just killing time 'til the next big case.'

Wells shot her a wounded look. 'Killing time, are we? Updating our filing system's no big deal then.'

'It's necessary, I'll admit, but….' She faltered. It was easier and far less stressful simply to give in to him. 'I should have asked you first, sir. I'm sorry.'

'That's more like it,' said Wells, with the hint of a smile.

'So can I go and help them?'

'Of course.' He motioned towards Jack. 'And take Casanova with you. He needs some practice with kids by the look of it and he might as well start now.'

CHAPTER TWO

'Whose idea was this goddamn competition anyway?'

Those words were expelled with force from the lips of Johnny Lee Rogers as he charged around like a hyperactive toddler, and they showed that he was not a happy man. He was in a sumptuous suite on the first floor of Stratton Manor – his home for the duration of the concerts.

The manor had seen many such events over the years, whenever its rooms fell below a certain level of disrepair. It was now Sir Nigel Stratton's turn to replenish the depleted coffers, and a weekend of rock and roll fitted the bill splendidly. And so, after a series of cautious phone calls between Sir Nigel and Bob Briscoe – the singer's hugely affable manager – a deal was struck.

Throughout the 1970s and 1980s Johnny Lee Rogers had been fêted the world over. Of course the musical tastes of a finicky public had changed vastly over the years, but his fans had remained loyal, even though he hadn't produced a hit for a long time. Any booking agent knew he'd be quids in with the ageing trouper. The man was a safe pair of hands.

He took nothing for granted though. Many performers better than he had had record deals snatched from their sweaty palms years ago. Johnny Lee was sixty-one now. He knew it wouldn't last for ever. So he watched his food intake constantly because slim sexy hips were not a man's God-given right once he'd passed his thirties. And he kept the wrinkles at bay by forking out a small fortune on anti-ageing treatments and spa sessions. Thankfully, his biggest fear – hair loss – had still to rear its ugly bald head, but that didn't stop Johnny Lee from brooding daily on the awful mechanics involved with keeping a toupee attached to the scalp whilst taking a pretty gal all the way to paradise with his tremendous – his goddamn *stupendous* – love pistol.

It was hard work being Johnny Lee Rogers but well worth the effort, especially at times like these. He almost skipped around the suite like a child in a toy store, eyes wide, expression incredulous, and his entourage were ready to expel a huge sigh of relief.

But then he found the competition flyer from the *Larchborough Evening News*. It lay, quietly innocuous, on a maple-wood writing desk positioned before a spectacular bay window in the master bedroom.

Win tickets to see JOHNNY LEE ROGERS … LIVE! All proceeds to go to the Rainbow Hospice Fund….

'Now ain't that great,' he said, rapping the flyer with his hand and grinning broadly. 'What's this Rainbow place – a hospital for kids or something?'

'A hospital for *dying* kids,' said Briscoe. 'Think of the publicity … Johnny Lee Rogers helps the kids beyond hope as a thank you to his loyal fans in … what's the name of this town again?'

'Larchborough,' said Sally Simms, Johnny Lee's personal assistant.

'Yeah, Larchborough.'

'Awesome,' said Johnny Lee, imagining the headlines.

'I've got the paparazzi and news guys lined up for a photo shoot at the restaurant,' said Briscoe, pulling at the front of his Hawaiian shirt so that air might circulate around his flabby waist.

Johnny Lee allowed the flyer to flutter back on to the desk as he turned puzzled features towards his manager. 'Restaurant? Photo shoot?' His lifted his shoulders. 'What you talking about, Bobby?'

'The meal you're gonna have with the prize winners,' Briscoe said, his smile tentative as he caught the coolness in his boy's tone. 'You'll want pictures for the papers, won't you?'

Johnny Lee spread his arms, his roving gaze taking in all persons: Sally Simms at the window; Lenny Price, his best friend and lead guitarist: and Briscoe, whose colour was fading fast in response to the look of quiet rage just beginning to distort the singer's famous face.

'Would somebody tell me what's going on here?' said Johnny Lee. 'Do I actually have to go eat with the winners like some kinda prize goddamn *monkey*?'

Briscoe, sensing a strop, rushed to his boy's side. 'Now, Johnny, wait a minute—'

'No, you wait a minute,' said Johnny Lee, pushing him away and starting to pace. 'Whose idea was this goddamn competition anyway?'

'Mine,' said Briscoe, chubby hands on barrel chest.

'Did you not think to run it past me first? Do I not work hard enough already, without having to give up my precious time to eat shit with morons, whilst grinning like a rabid dog for the goddamn paparazzi?' He fell on to the nearest *chaise-longue*, arms crossed, mouth a bitter line, like a small boy whose greatest wish had just been denied.

'Johnny ... baby ... you gotta listen to me,' said Briscoe, desperation turning his face a deadly puce.

'This ain't fair, Bobby. You should've asked me first.'

'Johnny, I emailed you details of the concept over a month ago, and when you didn't object—' He turned swiftly towards Sally. 'Didn't he get the message?'

Sally Simms had been Johnny Lee's right-hand girl for almost three years now and she'd had a ball. But she sure as hell earned her pay. He was such a high maintenance kind of guy. Every little hiccup was a huge drama; each small set-back a disaster. The man was so draining.

Stifling a sigh, Sally said, 'Yeah, I gave him the message, Bobby. Is it my fault if he doesn't listen? And what's so terrible anyway? All he's gotta do is stuff his face and make small talk for a couple of hours.'

'I don't do goddamn small talk,' Johnny Lee pouted.

It was Briscoe's turn to pace while his subconscious searched for a solution. Johnny had to turn up for that meal. If those two fans found themselves eating alone then he could kiss goodbye all that positive publicity he'd been working his guts out to secure. Johnny would make the papers all right, but for all the wrong reasons.

And then a soft rustling could be heard as Lenny Price manoeuvred himself into a sitting position within the shadowy depths of the four-poster bed. Lenny was a six-foot-five Texan, lean as a pole, with a quietness about him that spoke of hidden depths.

He'd known Johnny Lee since the sixties when, penniless and desperate for a meal, he'd hightailed it to Los Angeles, battered guitar strapped to his back. They'd found themselves busking on the same street corners and, later, on the same bills at music theatres little better than flea-ridden dives.

Lenny regarded his friend as a father would a difficult child. 'Hey, Johnny, you ain't thinkin' straight, man. Say one of these winners is a pretty little thing and she's just prayin' for Johnny Lee to give his all—' He snapped his fingers, struck by a sudden thought. 'Hell, what if they're both pretty little things – just as sweet as a peach – I can get me a piece too.'

Johnny Lee liked that scenario. He liked it a lot. 'Sweet as a goddamn peach, huh?'

Lenny grinned at Briscoe. Their boy was mellowing. 'You got it, man.'

Johnny Lee rose to his feet – that *chaise-longue* might look great, but its comfort score was close to zero – and he threw Briscoe an apologetic look. 'Maybe I'm being a little hasty here, Bobby. Maybe a meal with the winners might not be a bad thing after all. It's all good publicity for that Rainbow place – right?'

Briscoe was holding out his arms in a beseeching gesture. 'You'll do it, Johnny? You will?'

'Hell, yeah, I'll do it for the poor kids and I'll be glad to do it.' Johnny Lee wore a thick diamond band on his marriage finger and he fiddled with it relentlessly, his expression one of acute embarrassment. 'Hey, what I said … that crap about eating shit with morons … I didn't mean a goddamn word, Bobby. I was just sore, that's all, 'cause you didn't let me know.'

'Next time, baby, I'll email you twice,' said Briscoe, beaming at his boy.

Johnny Lee wandered across to Sally, wrapped a friendly arm around her shoulder. 'These prize winners, honey … do we by any chance have pictures of the sweet little things?'

Less than ten miles away, at Larchborough's main library, one of those 'sweet little things' was swilling her dentures under the cold tap in the toilets. Ruth had brought in a box of chocolates – leftovers from her birthday – and Lizzie had chosen one with a hazelnut at its centre. It was sheer agony once the bits got under her plate.

A toilet flushed behind her and Lizzie glanced up into the mirror to see young Cathy Cousins coming out of the cubicle, rearranging her trousers and staring straight back at Lizzie with an open smile.

Lizzie tut-tutted. 'I wondered where you'd got to, madam. I might have guessed.'

'Calls of nature must never go unheeded,' said Cathy, washing her hands briskly. 'That's what it says in *Bogart's Book of Proverbs*.'

'I'll bet it doesn't,' said Lizzie, all teeth now safely in her mouth. 'And I don't want you spending half an hour in here making sure every hair's in place either.'

'I wouldn't dream of it,' said Cathy, making a point of leaning against the washbasin, her back towards the mirror. 'I'd much rather hear your bit of news instead.'

'I don't know what you mean,' said Lizzie, her tone skittish. She took to patting and preening her own hair in the mirror to hide the faint flush creeping on to her moonlike features. The hair did need attention: great swathes of it had fallen from the loose bun at the back of her neck, its grey flecks matching exactly the colour of her prim woollen cardigan.

Lizzie's only concession to the summer heat was to replace her usual roll-neck sweaters with short-sleeved cotton blouses and cardigans in either grey or black. Today's good news had lifted her spirits to such an extent that funereal black wouldn't do at all; today she needed the recklessness of slate grey.

Cathy's laugh was a soft tinkling sound. 'You can't fool me, Lizzie Thornton. You've been bursting to tell us something all morning.'

And then Lizzie was laughing too. She patted her cardigan pocket. 'I've got a letter in here that's about to change my whole life.'

'Have you won the lottery?' asked Cathy, jumping with excitement.

'Better than that,' said Lizzie, forgetting her haughty persona. 'But not here – let's get back to the desk. I want Ruth to hear this as well.'

The library could hardly be called crowded. Old Mr Perkins was searching through the crime novels for an Ian Rankin he hadn't yet read. Two women were scanning the romances. And Fiona Wardle had brought in little Ryan for another half-dozen picture books. If only all mothers were like Fiona.

Ruth Findlay – the third member of their team – was at the desk trying to look busy when Cathy burst in, a delighted Lizzie close behind.

'Ruth,' Cathy whispered. 'Lizzie's got some news.'

'Really? What?' asked Ruth, as they huddled together.

Lizzie chuckled merrily. 'I've won two tickets to see Johnny Lee Rogers at Stratton Manor,' she said, excitedly handing the letter across.

Ruth read it with Cathy at her shoulder. 'How lovely,' she said, not at all impressed. Ruth was more of a Matt Monro girl. She couldn't stand the noise those pop singers made.

Cathy said, 'Is that it?' and tossed her shining blonde hair away from her face, catching her pretty reflection in the glass-fronted reference cupboard. 'I'm surprised you like him anyway. I'd have thought you'd be more into … what's his name … Pavarotti.'

'What do you know?' said Lizzie, tugging the letter from Ruth's grip.

'Don't you think he's a bit old to still be singing rock?' said Cathy, fast losing interest but loath to get back to work.

'Why stop when you're still on top of your game?' said Lizzie, who'd heard the phrase whilst watching a rather risqué drama on Channel Four. 'As a matter of fact, Cathy, I was going to offer you the spare ticket. But if you're not a fan….'

Cathy leant against the desk and searched her hair for split ends. 'When is it?'

'A week on Sunday … the twenty-ninth.'

The young girl wrinkled her nose as though the prospect of sitting through a Johnny Lee Rogers concert was repugnant. 'Sorry, Lizzie, I'm babysitting our Jasmine's Rowan on the twenty-ninth.'

'Ruth?' said Lizzie. 'Would you like to go?'

Ruth said, 'No thanks, I'm much too old for that sort of thing,' and then went red because she was three years younger than Lizzie and could see from her face that she'd put her foot very firmly in her mouth.

'What do I care?' said Lizzie. 'Johnny Lee Rogers is my hero – always has been, always will be – and now we're going to meet and I'm so excited you couldn't spoil my day even if you tried.'

'Who says you're going to meet?' asked Ruth.

'The letter does, over the page.' Lizzie held it up for them to see. 'I'll have a special pass for rehearsals *and* I'm going to share a meal with him.' She clutched the letter to her breast and heaved a huge sigh. 'Once we get to know each other anything might happen.'

'You're going to meet him?' said Cathy, split ends now forgotten. 'In that case I will come. He might be able to help with my singing career.'

Ruth laughed. 'What singing career?'

'I auditioned for *The X Factor* in Birmingham once and I nearly got through, only Sharon Osbourne didn't like me. I reckon she was jealous.' Cathy flicked the hair away from her face, gave them a beaming smile. 'Simon Cowell said if my voice had matched my looks I'd easily get into boot camp … only it sounded like fingernails being dragged down a blackboard. I think he was trying to let me down gently on account of Sharon. He did say I was the only one that day who'd set his teeth on edge, which was rather nice.'

'What about your Jasmine's Rowan?' asked Lizzie, not really caring about the boy but wanting to put a stop to Cathy's monologue.

Cathy frowned. 'What about him?'

'You said you were babysitting on the twenty-ninth.'

'Oh, yes.' She laughed. 'I'm a good liar, aren't I?'

Lizzie sighed and surmised that on the days when common sense and intelligence were handed out Cathy Cousins must have been loitering at the back of both queues, searching for split ends, her scatter-brained thoughts elsewhere.

Trouble was if Cathy did take the spare ticket then Lizzie would be stuck with her for hours. Could she cope with the girl's vain habits and silly conversation? It was bad enough during work, but at least then she was being paid to suffer. Unfortunately Lizzie knew she had little choice; she'd already offered it.

'I'll gladly let you have the ticket,' said Lizzie, sounding anything but glad, 'on one condition….'

Cathy said, 'What's that then?' Not that she was bothered. Her brain was already working overtime on the outfit she should wear for the meal. Her black strapless evening gown which simply oozed class? Or the pink satin mini-dress that made her look like a prostitute? – according to her dad anyway. Sometimes wealthy old men went for a bit of rough – like Richard Gere did in *Pretty Woman* – so maybe she should go with the pink.

Lizzie was sighing again and Cathy said, 'I am listening, Lizzie. What's the condition?'

'That you—' A coquettish giggle escaped her lips. 'That you make yourself scarce when the chemistry starts.'

'What chemistry?'

Scanning the library for eavesdroppers and continuing in a whisper, Lizzie said, 'The chemistry between me and Johnny Lee.'

'Oh, bloody hell, Ruth, did you hear that?' Cathy bellowed. 'Lizzie's hoping for a night of hot passion with Johnny Lee Rogers.'

Suddenly the library was so quiet a pin dropping in the far corner would have been heard by all. And when Ruth almost choked on a chuckle she grabbed her handkerchief and tried to make it sound like a sneeze.

'Bless you,' said Lizzie, dropping to her knees and searching with a sudden urgency for last month's order figures.

Down there, scrabbling amongst the dust balls and dead spiders, Lizzie attempted a mortified look, but faintly embarrassed was the best she could manage. Another giggle bubbled up from nowhere and there was nothing she could do to stop it. Why shouldn't she hope for … what Cathy had said?

Lizzie felt liberated, was ready to show a more earthy side to herself. But why, after all these years? Lizzie grinned at the threadbare carpet mere inches from her face. Wasn't it obvious? She'd waited almost a lifetime, but now, at last, her love was to be made manifest. And she could hardly wait.

Poor Johnny Lee; he won't know what's hit him.

You'd better watch out, you gorgeous man: Lizzie Thornton's coming to get you.

CHAPTER THREE

Amy Beddows thought her birthday had come again when she entered Helen Harrison's spacious semi-detached on the outskirts of Larchborough. There were toys *everywhere*. And Mrs Harrison said she could play with anything. They were all for her.

Nathan, rather more dubious, chose to keep his cards pretty close to his chest while those nice police officers talked to the woman. He did deign to stroke the coat of a small brown puppy that was there though. And he threw it a ball a couple of times. But they weren't getting any chat out of him – and no smiles either – as he sat, stony-faced, in the huge comfortable armchair. But then Mrs Harrison produced a Playstation from out of nowhere and bet him ten pence that he couldn't get to level three before teatime. He'd never owned a Playstation before and, well, it was pretty cool actually.

'They'll be fine,' Mia said to Jack as they buckled up in the car. 'Mind you, Helen's been fostering since you were in nappies so she ought to know what she's doing.' She shot him a sideways glance, hid a teasing smile. 'Talking of nappies, I bet she'll give you a few tips on child-rearing if you ask her. How to get sick stains out of your designer gear, stuff like that.'

Jack turned towards the side window and let out a low, dismal breath. 'Is this how it's going to be for the whole of the pregnancy – stupid jokes and innuendoes? Because if it is I'm putting in for a transfer.'

'You should be enjoying it. I know I am. I'm going to start knitting the minute I get home.'

'Don't you dare,' Jack warned. Another sigh. 'Where now? Back to the station?'

'Not just yet.' Mia started the engine and moved smoothly away from the kerb. 'I want a word with Sheila Reeves at that caravan site. Let's find out why those kids were home alone.'

Jack sucked in a long breath. 'Wells'll have a fit. He's already warned you about acting on your own initiative and, here you are, thinking for yourself again. You're a rogue officer, Mia Harvey.'

She shrugged. 'Their mother's already been gone two days. Who knows what sort of hell she's going through?'

'Oh, come on, she's a hopeless druggie. Whatever hell she's going through, the woman's brought it on herself.'

Mia tutted. 'You men and your stereotypes … Jim Levers said exactly the same thing.'

'There you go then.'

She gave him a disparaging look. 'Don't you think we should gather all relevant info before making wild judgements?'

'Not where druggies are concerned, no. They're too predictable to warrant having a lot of time spent on them.'

'But we don't know she is a druggie,' Mia said, finally exasperated. 'Those kids haven't seen the inside of a bath for a while, I'll grant you that, but they're too well adjusted and lovable to be neglected.'

'The lad was quiet … really sulky,' said Jack, determined to be right.

'Wouldn't you be quiet if your mum was missing and you were worried sick?' She turned off the dual carriageway and headed towards open countryside. 'No, I think you and

Jim are wrong. I think she's too good a mother to be high as a kite the whole time. There's a reason why that woman isn't there to see to her kids. A really bad reason.'

Eight long weeks without rain and Larchborough's countryside was parched. Hundreds of acres of crops lay ruined, stunted beyond repair. Dairy yields were the lowest for three decades. A state of emergency had been declared and even now pleas for remuneration from the county's farming community were winging their way towards the beleaguered Ministry of Agriculture.

The River Stratton was beginning to resemble a stagnant ditch. And that important waterway was so virile as a rule; a boisterous broiling mass. In fact, so often did the river burst its banks that emergency flood plains had been designated about six miles north of Larchborough's main drag. Those plains were known locally as Heaven's Gate because they led on to an area of outstanding beauty that was home to a multitude of fauna, wading birds, and notable botanical specimens. So important was the area in terms of conservation and pure aesthetic splendour that it had been featured many times in guidebooks for twitchers and ramblers alike.

Heaven's Gate was Larchborough's jewel in the crown. Or it used to be. Today the lush vegetation was all but reduced to brown stubble. And five caravans now stood where majestic herons and flighty kingfishers once drank their fill. The vans ranged from value-for-money cheap to full-blown gypsy. And four rusting estate cars formed a haphazard line nearby.

A communal area had been fashioned out of a flat piece of land about fifty yards from the caravans. Two wallpapering tables pushed together and covered with a white cloth formed a pretty impressive dining table that was surrounded by a collection of kitchen chairs, stools and foldaway seats, their legs deftly avoiding the hazardous fissures in the rock-hard ground.

Four adults sat around the remnants of a salad lunch. The older pair, probably in their fifties, had that joined-at-the-hip look of lovers who lived only for each other. The woman was feeding apple slices to the man as he stroked her long brown hair and gazed fondly into her eyes. They'd noticed the detectives' approach but were too wrapped up in themselves to wonder who the strangers might be.

The younger couple was silent, ill at ease, the man's cautious stare wholly on Mia and Jack; while the woman kept stealing quick glances towards three children – all under the age of five – who were labouring hard to create a break in the tall wooden fence that divided the flood plains from land surrounding Stratton Manor.

'Afternoon, folks,' said Mia, eyeing the food remains with genuine longing even though a swarm of blowflies was already tucking in.

When no words of welcome were forthcoming Mia took out her warrant card and waved it in front of the group. 'We're looking for a Mrs Sheila Reeves,' she said. 'We've reason to believe she lives in one of these caravans. Could somebody tell us which it is?'

The younger of the two men offered her a sneer. 'There's nobody of that name here,' he said, a slight Southern Irish twang causing his words to dance, 'so why don't you do us all a favour and piss off?'

Jack was in no mood for smart-arses. He took out his notebook in a threatening manner, pen poised over paper. 'Can I have your name, please, sir?'

'Why?'

'Because I like to know who I'm talking to.'

'Piss off,' said the man, waving a dismissive hand.

Jack continued to stare him out, pen still poised. Eventually the woman beside him could stand it no longer.

'My husband's name is Roy Barlow,' she said in a timid, almost inaudible, voice. 'And I'm Kelly … Barlow … obviously.' She was speaking too quickly, the panic in her words quite blatant. Swivelling in her chair to face the children, she went on, 'And this is our little family … Grace,

26

Owen, and Poppy. Stand up, children. Say hello to the nice man.'

Despite her pleading tone the children took not a shred of notice and continued to vandalize the fence. In desperation the woman shot a fevered glance towards the older couple, almost willing them to intervene. 'Our … our friends are Dick and Nancy Pantain,' she said. 'They're over from America … lovely people….' The words trailed off, her look of despair deepening.

Jack once more targeted the husband, reluctant to let his lack of manners go unchecked. 'My colleague was very civil to you just now, sir. Why the shitty tone?'

Barlow got to his feet, his chair toppling backwards. Kelly grabbed his arm. 'Roy, don't—'

He shrugged her off, staggered slightly. 'Because we're sick of being harassed by the likes of you. Constantly being moved on. I'm sick of it. Why don't you go after the real criminals? The murderers and the rapists and … God, I don't know … just piss off.'

'Why don't *you* stop breaking the law,' Jack replied, heatedly. 'If you kept to the designated sites you'd have no trouble from us.'

Grabbing Jack's arm Mia gave him a firm look of admonishment. It was enough to shut him up. In the ensuing silence a subdued Roy Barlow retrieved his chair and sank into it, elbows on the table, face in his hands. And he stayed that way, gently rocking, a low continuous groan escaping through his long delicate fingers.

His wife looked decidedly fragile, close to tears. Without taking her anxious eyes off Jack she slid a protective arm around Barlow's neck. 'Roy isn't well, I'm afraid. You'll have to make allowances.'

Jack's pointed stare settled on the two empty wine bottles standing beside Barlow's plate. 'Let's hope he feels better soon then. But he could get time inside for failing to help us with our enquiries. Perhaps he should remember that.' Jack scanned the group. 'Perhaps you should all bear that in mind.'

Nancy Pantain lit a cigarette, blew smoke in Jack's direction. 'What exactly are those enquiries?'

Mia considered the motley group, her insides seething. Those poor Beddows kids could have met with all kinds of disaster during their hike into town and these weirdos were too busy feeding their faces and downing the wine to give them a second thought.

'We just want to talk to Sheila Reeves,' she said, attempting a civil tone. 'Could you tell us where she is? Or do we have to drag the information out of you at the nick?'

Kelly Barlow's stricken look intensified. 'Sheila's in that gypsy caravan right at the end,' she said, pointing.

Mia managed a smile. 'Thank you, Mrs Barlow.' Her gaze fell on the Americans. 'See, that wasn't too difficult, was it?'

The caravan had a stable door, its top half already open. Mia rapped on the fine mahogany wood, saw that its varnish was bubbling in the intense heat.

'Mrs Reeves, are you in there?'

A woman came into view, talking on a mobile phone. She held up a hand for them to wait, a gesture that did little to quell Mia's rising impatience.

'Now, please. We haven't got all day.'

The woman was around forty, short and well-padded, her huge bosom hardly contained within a red cheesecloth top. Her long hair was the colour of nicotine-stained fingers, her features plump and jovial – and wrinkle-free too, apart from the frown that had formed at the sharpness of Mia's tone.

'Hold on a minute, Phil.' She lowered the phone and glared. 'What do you want?'

Mia held up her warrant card. 'Are you Sheila Reeves?' The woman nodded, her eyes taking on a haunted look. 'We need to talk to you urgently about Nathan and Amy Beddows.'

And then the woman crumpled, made a grab for the bottom half of the stable door, her face completely without colour. 'Have you found them? Are they dead?'

'They're fine, no thanks to you.'

Sheila Reeves hurriedly pushed open the door and moved back to allow them entry. The interior was surprisingly roomy, all dark wood and red velvet upholstery, its air cool and serene.

The woman sank on to one of the window seats and motioned for them to sit. 'Phil, you can stop looking,' she babbled into the mobile. 'They're all right. Yes, the coppers are here. Come straight back.'

Once again Mia thrust forward her warrant card. 'I'm DS Harvey, Mrs Reeves, and this is DC Turnbull. We shouldn't keep you too long.'

'The kids – they're really OK?'

Mia nodded and took a seat opposite the woman while Jack leant against the tiny sink, arms folded. 'They turned up at the station this morning. They're being looked after by a foster carer.'

'Am I in trouble?'

'Probably not.' Mia took out her notebook, found a clear page. 'Why were you looking after them in the first place, Mrs Reeves? Where's their mother?'

The woman spread her hands, her expression one of utter confusion. 'Don't know. I've been worried sick, and then when the kids disappeared….'

'What's the mother's name?'

'Sky Beddows.'

'That's her name … Sky?' said a sceptical Jack.

The woman nodded briskly.

Mia said, 'How long have you been here?'

'About three weeks. Sky wasn't keen to stay, said we ought to keep moving, but the others wouldn't have it.'

'Why didn't she want to stay?'

'No idea.'

'Where was she going on Wednesday when she disappeared?'

'Haven't a clue. She said she'd got an errand to do and would I mind keeping an eye on the kids.'

'You don't know what that errand was?'

'No.'

'Has she left them with you before?'

The woman's eyes took on a guarded look. 'Yes, but never for this long. Sky loves her kids. She wouldn't leave them for days on end.'

'Where did she go those other times?' asked Jack. Sheila Reeves remained tight-lipped. 'Where did she go, Mrs Reeves?'

Suddenly rolling her eyes in defeat, she said, 'Oh all right, she goes off to buy a fresh stash now and again, but she only uses it herself. It's not like she's selling it or anything.'

Jack flashed Mia a triumphant look. 'Mrs Beddows goes off to buy drugs?'

'Only weed. Sky only smokes weed. And only when the kids are in bed.'

Jack snorted. 'That's all right then. Kids never get sick after bedtime, do they? She can happily drift off into her own little world knowing they'll be quite safe … I don't think.' He let out a disgruntled breath. 'When did you notice the kids had gone?'

'This morning, about seven,' she said, brushing her damp fringe away from her eyes. The woman clearly had a problem with the heat. Her every movement sent the sweet stench of body odour wafting towards the detectives.

Mia, itching to offer her a deodorant spray, said, 'So you put them to bed last night only to find that sometime before morning they'd done a runner.'

Sheila Reeves turned away briefly, the shake of her head decidedly hesitant. 'No, you see, I've got a little boy, Billy. He had a bad fall last night. There's crevices opening up all over the place and he got his foot stuck. It started to swell really bad so we took him to A & E. We were there all night, what with waiting for X-rays and having it plastered.'

'We?' said Jack.

'Me and my dad. He lives with us. I asked the others to keep an eye on the kids. I didn't expect to be away so long. But it turns out Billy's leg's fractured in two places. Bloody council, I've a good mind to sue.'

'Where's Billy now?' asked Mia.

'Still in the hospital. He's got a bit of a temperature so they're keeping him in for a while. Dad stayed with him and I came back to see to Nathan and Amy.' Her eyes started to brim. 'I felt really bad about leaving them. But what could I do?'

Mia put a hand on hers, squeezed it gently. 'No harm done. Just as well though – I've an idea that lot out there wouldn't be much help in a crisis.'

The woman plucked a tissue from a box on the windowsill, dabbed at her eyes. 'They didn't know the kids were missing.'

Mia frowned. 'Why keep it to yourself?'

'Phil thought it best to say nothing. You've seen what they're like. The Pantains live on a different planet. And that Roy Barlow's a nasty head-case. He's already turned his wife into a wreck and he's halfway towards doing the same to the rest of us, Sky especially.'

'What's he got against Sky?' asked Mia.

Sheila Reeves laughed, the sound holding little humour. 'Nothing. Just the opposite. Roy thinks he's in love with her. Stupid bugger.'

'But his wife, those lovely children … is that why he's in such a state, because Sky's gone missing?'

The woman shook her head. 'He's convinced she's just gone off to think things over.'

Mia looked puzzled. 'And leave her kids?'

'Roy couldn't give a stuff about his own kids, so why should he worry about Sky's?'

Jack said, 'What's she supposed to be thinking over?'

'Roy's proposition – that she becomes wife number two and they all live happily ever after.'

Jack considered this. 'Is Barlow a Mormon?'

'No, Roy's just Roy, thinks he's God's gift. If he wants something he usually gets it. Well, he wants Sky, doesn't he? Only he didn't bargain on her having such a strong will.'

'She's turned him down?'

The woman nodded.

'What about his wife? She doesn't look the type to go along with a threesome.'

Sheila Reeves let out a cynical snort. 'Kelly hasn't got the strength to fight him. I told you, she's a wreck. Roy's been in a right state since Sky took off. Drinking too much. Picking fights. He goes away for hours at a time. Poor Kelly gets frantic, but the camp's a nicer place without him. I'm just sorry when he comes back.'

'Who's Phil?' asked Jack.

'Phil Hunt.' She managed a smile. 'He's one of the good guys, been with us for about four years. Phil's been watching out for Sky ever since her old man buggered off. He's been looking for the kids all morning. Treats them like his own, he does.'

'Are they an item, Phil and Sky?'

'Couldn't say. You'll have to ask Phil.'

'What's her husband's name?' asked Mia, turning to a fresh page in her notebook.

'Scott Beddows.'

'What's he like?'

Mrs Reeves wrinkled her nose as though a bad smell had passed beneath it. 'Good for nothing. Same as mine.'

'Why did he leave?'

'He's allergic to responsibility. Same as mine.'

'Did he stay in touch?'

'Shouldn't think so.'

'She couldn't have gone off to meet him?'

'Scott was in Liverpool last I heard, doing time for assault and battery.'

Mia fell silent, allowed her gaze to fall upon the acres of burnt farmland flanking the caravans on two sides. Stratton Manor stood in the distance, resembling a child's discarded fort, sunlight glinting off its many windows. It was a stunning view, but one that held little hope in light of their enquiries. Sky Beddows could be in any one of those fields, long dead or grasping precariously to life by a thread. But where to look first? Even with tracker dogs it would take days to cover it all. And what if Sky couldn't last for days?

Mia let out a plaintive sigh. 'Why are you all here, Mrs Reeves?'

'For the concerts. We go where the crowds are. But we thought we'd get here early, have a bit of down time. It's a nice place.'

'How do you make a living?'

The woman pointed to her clothes, the rich red of her blouse clashing horrendously with the bold cerise of her voluminous skirt. 'I'm Madam Sheila, fortune-teller to the stars. I read palms, angel cards, rune stones – you name it, I can see your future in it.'

'What about the others?'

'Phil's a clairvoyant, a real one; not like me, making it up as I go along. His folks are seers as well. They all share the next caravan along. Kelly and Roy are sketch artists – do your face in charcoal for a tenner. The Pantains are writing a book about their travels through Europe. We met them at Land's End about nine months ago and they've been with us ever since.'

'What about Sky?'

'She makes ethnic jewellery … hippy stuff.' Mrs Reeves shifted position, pulled at the folds of her skirt in an effort to cool herself. 'We'll soon be setting up our stalls outside Stratton Manor. There'll be a small fortune to be made on the days of the concerts, and a fair bit before then, probably. People have already started milling round the manor and there's still more than a week to go.'

'Really?' said Mia. 'I hadn't realized.'

'Me and Sky took the kids to have a look on Sunday. They'd already started building the outdoor stage, positioning the chemical toilets, things like that. Quite a few fans around as well, all hoping to catch a glimpse of somebody famous. Silly buggers.'

'Did you get talking to anybody?'

Sheila Reeves stared into space, her frown thoughtful. 'There was a bloke. Dressed real nice he was. Told Sky he was the estate manager. Really took to her. Couldn't keep his eyes off. When Sky asked if we could maybe pitch our stalls inside the grounds on concert days he said he'd make enquiries and let her know.'

'Did he let her know?'

'She went back the next day – the Monday – but he hadn't got an answer. Needed a bit more time, he said. I think he was leading her a dance because he wanted to see her again.'

'Did he give his name?'

'Bulmer, I think it was. Andrew Bulmer.'

'That'll be easy to check,' said Mia, making a note. 'Did Sky see him again?'

'She was planning to get a definite answer on the Wednesday. We'd make a real killing if we could work inside the gates. Captive audience, you see. Only she never came back, so I'm not sure whether she did.'

'What time did she leave on Wednesday?'

'After breakfast. About nine.'

'Did she take a car?'

'A Vauxhall Estate. Dark Blue. P Reg.'

'OK,' said Mia, glancing at her watch. 'We'll need a description of Sky.'

'I've got a photo.'

Mrs Reeves edged past Jack, who surreptitiously turned his face away from her ripe scent, and selected a gold-edged photograph frame from a number of others on a thin ledge. She returned to her seat and handed the photograph to Mia.

It was a coloured snapshot, about three inches square, showing a young girl sweetly feigning shyness for the camera, her long golden hair pulled back by a thrusting wind to reveal delicate features. Sky Beddows was beautiful, her smile quite mesmerizing, eyes the most delicate of blues.

Mia experienced a faint stirring of envy as she stared at the girl's exquisite features. 'How old is she?'

'Twenty-five.'

She passed the photo to Jack. 'I can see why men fall for her,' he said.

'She's a stunner,' said Mrs Reeves, nodding.

'What I can't understand,' said Jack, still staring at the snapshot, 'is why you didn't report her missing. You said you were worried.'

A flicker of anxiety showed in the woman's eyes. 'Ask Phil,' she snapped. 'It's nothing to do with me.'

Jack fixed her with a suspicious look. 'No, I want you to tell us.'

'Ask Phil,' she repeated, avoiding their eyes. 'I've answered your questions. I'm saying nothing else.'

In the space of a second the woman's demeanour changed. She wanted the detectives out, shooing them towards the doorway, all niceties forgotten.

'But, Mrs Reeves—' said Mia, attempting to hold back.

'You think I've got something to hide, don't you? Suspicious buggers.' She almost hurled them down the metal steps, her strength quite astonishing. 'You want to know anything else about Sky … ask Phil.'

'We thought you two had gone under a bus,' said DCI Wells, his tone deceptively pleasant. 'You only had to drop two kids off. How difficult was that?'

They'd returned to the office to find Wells and Nick drowning under piles of old files and case notes, the computers idling behind their screensavers. The DCI preferred paper and pen; he loathed all things technical.

Jack was allowed to escape Wells's hostile glare as he edged towards his desk, but Mia was caught full-on. She was rummaging in her bag, mouth opening on to silence. But Wells still had her in his sights. She needed to say something.

'Sorry we've been so long, sir, but after we dropped the kids off we went to see Sheila Reeves at the caravan site.'

Mia risked a look in his direction, her stomach rolling in response to his furious expression. 'I know our orders were to head straight back, but bearing in mind their mother's been missing for two days I thought—'

Her words stuttered to a halt when Wells held up a hand for silence. 'I told you not to go off on your own.'

'You did, sir, but—'

'Which part of "ask me first" don't you understand?'

Mia knew she was well and truly in a hole. But she knew, too, that Wells was only being shirty because he was bored. He hated having nothing to do; it made him irritable. Give him a case to solve and he became an altogether different bloke. Mia was certain she'd taken the right course of action. All she had to do now was convince him.

'Sir, we were already halfway towards that unapproved caravan site. Coming back here would have been a waste of time and petrol.'

'Ever heard of the telephone?' he snarled. 'And there's even *mobile* phones now. Completely wireless. You can use them anywhere.'

'To be honest, sir, I didn't ask for permission because I didn't think you'd give it.'

'I see.' He ran a thoughtful hand across his jowls and then turned to Nick. 'From now on, mate, you'll be partnering Miss Marple. Let's see if you can keep her in line.'

Mia's jaw dropped. Nick was a miserable prat at the best of times. She couldn't possibly work with him. 'But, sir—'

'No buts.' The DCI clapped his hands together smartly. 'Now tell us what you found out from Sheila Reeves.'

Still reeling, Mia related the encounter with meticulous accuracy, Jack interjecting now and again with his own pearls of wisdom. If he was going to be stuck with the DCI then he'd better show willing.

Wells stared into space, his mood thoughtful. 'What makes you think there's anything dodgy about her disappearance? Perhaps she met a bloke with enough dosh to keep the drugs coming and she's buggered off with him. She wouldn't be the first addict to abandon her kids.'

Mia glanced beyond Wells to where Jack was punching the air, his grin triumphant. She looked away quickly, rolled her eyes. 'You're not the only one who likes that scenario, sir. But Sky Beddows wouldn't abandon her kids. I *know* she wouldn't.'

Wells gave a wry smile. 'Female intuition?'

'If you like,' said Mia, bristling.

'OK, I'll trust your judgement for now.' He retrieved his pen from the desktop, took to tapping it against the mountain of files. 'Let's get ourselves organized. A search of the girl's caravan had better be top of our agenda. If one of those loonies she's hitched up with has anything to do with her disappearance they'll have wiped it clean days ago – supposedly. But there's always something that's missed. All we've got to do is find it. We'll make that tomorrow's first job, Jack.'

'Why wait 'til morning?' said Mia. 'A lot can happen overnight.'

'Because my car's having a new alternator fitted and Nick's taking me to pick it up.'

'Then let me and Jack do it. We won't miss anything.'

'I'm sure you won't, but I want you to have a go at Andrew Bulmer at the manor. Did he actually make enquiries about them setting up their stalls, or was that just a line he threw because he fancied the pants off Sky?' Mia looked ready to interject, but the DCI shouted her down. 'And I want it done in the morning. Christ, are you ever going to learn?'

'Sorry, sir.'

Wells reached for his briefcase and glanced at his watch. 'It's five-thirty now so let's get off, Nick. We all meet back here tomorrow, eight o'clock sharp.' At the door he turned back to point a stern finger. 'And remember, kiddies, I mean eight o'clock. One minute later and I turn into that nasty man who shouts a lot.'

CHAPTER FOUR

'Nobody's been in here since the kids buggered off,' said Wells, leaving the door to Sky's caravan wide open.

The air inside reeked of stale incense, so strong it took their breath. Jack collapsed in a fit of coughing while Wells glanced around at an immaculate interior where everything matched. The caravan was clearly loved, from the sandalwood fittings polished to within an inch of their lives to the curtains and upholstery whose colours had obviously been chosen with care.

'Here,' said Wells, flinging a pair of latex gloves at his DC. 'We'll start at either end and meet in the middle.'

In control of his lungs once more Jack approached a slender built-in cupboard sandwiched between the dining area and a shower cubicle.

'Mia seems certain Sky wouldn't leave her kids, sir.'

'I know, and that bothers me. We've no extended family to go at, no girlfriends she goes clubbing with. All we've got is a bunch of tossers like that one out there.'

He nodded towards a tiny window above the sink, through which he could see a painfully thin young woman clutching an unwashed and quarrelsome child while two more reached up their grubby fingers and grappled with her waistband, their words lost behind the glass but their faces speaking loudly of want.

Wells found the woman strangely naive for the twenty-first century with her plain brown, ankle-length skirt and chaste white blouse; world-weary face free of make-up; dark-brown hair tumbled halfway down her back, unhindered apart from simple hair grips positioned above both ears. As he stared at her tragic profile he was reminded of an Amish woman, or the wife of an American settler whose job it was to fashion a home out of nothing while her intrepid husband fought off the Indian threat.

Jack let out a humourless laugh. 'If anybody looks ready to take off and never come back, she does.' He shouldered through a small doorway leading into the van's only bedroom and found not a thing out of place. 'She's not taken her cannabis, sir, or her purse. They're here on the bed. And what's this? I thought Roy Barlow was supposed to be in love with Sky – obsessed, even.'

Wells turned to find Jack holding up a piece of canvas stapled to a plywood frame. Measuring around two feet by three it held an image painted in oils. The image was a caricature – an extremely cruel caricature. It showed Sky in the guise of an abomination from Hell peering forlornly towards the heavens. They recognized the girl because the exquisite eyes were clearly hers, as was the pretty nose, the sensuous mouth. But the rest was the work of a morbid imagination goaded apparently by a fiendish hatred for its subject. In the bottom left-hand corner Roy Barlow had signed his name with a bold flourish.

Wells said, 'Bloody hell, there's all kinds of obsessions but that's not healthy, mate.'

'I told you he was a strange bloke.'

'You also said he was used to getting his own way,' said Wells, stroking his jowls. 'And that Sky wouldn't play ball.'

'He's definitely not the sort who'll take no for an answer.'

Wells nodded, his gaze still on the painting. 'I wonder how far Barlow's prepared to go to get what he wants.'

'Looking at this, sir, the possibilities are endless. Her eyes – they're so desolate, like she's given up, like she feels worthless. Some pervs like that; they need to dominate in order to feel virile. And the fact that he's given her an unearthly image is interesting as well. It shows Barlow doesn't acknowledge her humanity. And it's a fact that psychos can only get pleasure and fulfilment from their crimes by seeing their victims as objects rather than human beings.'

Wells was watching Jack closely, his jaw slack. 'Who's been watching the *Cracker* reruns then?'

Jack gave an embarrassed laugh. 'I'm interested in criminal psychology, sir.'

'So am I, and I'd say that assessment's spot on. But is it the right one? People have some funny ideas about art, Jack, and paintings a lot stranger than that change hands for small fortunes in the London galleries. So, is Barlow a psychopath or a future Turner Prize winner?' Wells peeled off his latex gloves and headed for the door, nostrils quivering like a dog on a scent. 'Bring the picture, mate. Let's see what our man's got to say about it.' He grinned, his dark eyes showing menace. 'I just love listening to nasty bleeders talking themselves out of a hole … or further into one, if we're lucky.'

'Hey, who let you two in? Get lost. *Now.*'

'Nice to meet you too, Mr Bulmer,' said Mia, approaching the man with her warrant card held aloft, a bored-looking Nick trailing behind.

They were making their way to the hulking structure that was Stratton Manor from the south side, across an asphalt forecourt that even at this early hour felt tacky with the heat. Indeed the only shade from an incessant sun came courtesy of a circle of ornamental trees at the centre of the forecourt, their thirsty leaves hanging limp and already turning a curious yellow. Only a vigorous monkey-puzzle tree towering like some bizarre sentinel to the right of the main doors showed any signs of vitality in its growth.

Peace reigned supreme – the manor was closed for the day on account of the music rehearsal – and the surrounding quiet offered an aura of gentle calm that Mia found wonderfully soothing despite the heat.

But not for long. Andrew Bulmer, hugely annoyed by their continued approach, began huffing loudly and proceeded to block their path. 'Listen, madam, whatever it is you're selling, we don't want it….' His words trailed off as the detectives came close enough for him to read the wording on Mia's card. 'Oh, you're the police. What makes you think you know me?'

'I took a wild guess, sir.' Mia pointed to the identity pass dangling from his neck on a length of brown cord. 'Seems like I was right.'

Bulmer aimed a disarming smile at Mia. 'Sorry about the unorthodox welcome, DS Harvey, and—' He turned to Nick, brows raised.

Nick said, 'DI Ford, sir,' and brought out his own warrant card.

'DI Ford … right … only Sir Nigel expects me to keep the riff-raff out and you can't be too careful nowadays. Not that I'm saying you're riff-raff. It's just….' He fell silent, held up his hands in a gesture of defeat. 'I'll shut up, shall I? I'm only making matters worse.'

Bulmer had a slight and wiry build, his height only marginally topping Mia's five-foot-seven. His unruly hair was dark blond; his upper-class features sharply defined but indisputably pleasant. He wore his blue Italian suit with an elegant ease and looked quite at home in the lavish surroundings where his clipped speech and rounded vowel sounds fitted in perfectly. Mia had him down as a small-brained toff. Quite dishy though.

Nick said, 'We're conducting a missing person inquiry, sir, and we need to ask you a few questions.'

'Me? Why?'

'The missing person is a young lady called Sky Beddows, sir. We've been led to believe that the two of you met here earlier in the week.'

'Sky Beddows … Sky Beddows,' he said, staring into space. 'No, sorry, can't remember the girl.'

But Mia knew he was lying. She saw only too clearly the flash of desire that expanded his pupils and instantly darkened the pale blue of his eyes when Nick mentioned the girl's name, a name that Bulmer uttered with obvious relish.

'Perhaps we should talk in your office,' she said, her manner brusque. 'Lead the way, Mr Bulmer.'

The man's body language was hardly willing as he ushered them through the main doors into an immense gloomy hall whose tiny porthole windows and attractive marble flooring created an oasis of almost icy chill. After the tiring heat of outdoors the low temperature was a pleasant relief.

Bulmer was leading them diagonally across the hall to a small doorway hidden from the main area by the clever positioning of a display case packed with leaflets praising the many joys to be found during a guided tour of the manor. The door opened on to his private office, a large musty room with several other doors leading off.

Its central area was occupied by an elegant oak desk which was home to a flat-screen computer monitor and keyboard. In front of Bulmer's chair sat a desk diary – closed – and an antique pen caddy fashioned out of an old oil lamp. His 'In' and 'Out' trays sat in careful alignment with the top left-hand corner of the desk. In fact, everything on the desk was just so. A definite obsessive/ compulsive trait, Mia thought wryly. He'd be hard work after a while.

Against three of the walls stood a variety of oak cupboards aimed at matching the desk. The fourth was covered floor-to-ceiling with dark wood shelving upon which hundreds of leather-bound volumes resided. Portraits of minor Strattons fit only to grace an employee's office looked down on the group as they took seats around the desk.

Mia fished out her notebook and aimed an interrogatory look at the man; saw the panic in his eyes; the nervous twitch of his right eyelid; the way in which he fidgeted constantly with a stapler plucked from the desktop. All of these, she knew, were manifestations of anxiety. But why should Andrew Bulmer be anxious? Did he have something to hide?

Nick was evidently thinking the same. He said, 'Care to tell us why you lied about not knowing Sky Beddows, Mr Bulmer?'

'Oh God, you people,' he said. 'I've already told you I can't remember meeting her and that's the truth. Have you any idea how many people I see in this job? Hundreds come to look around every week. I can't be expected to remember every one of them.'

Mia said, 'You allegedly met Sky Beddows on at least two occasions, Mr Bulmer. She's a very beautiful girl, not easily forgotten. She sells jewellery from a roadside stall. You were supposed to be making enquiries into whether or not she and her colleagues could set up their stalls in the grounds of the manor on the days of the rock concerts.'

Bulmer stopped fidgeting with the stapler and took to aligning it carefully with the right side of his diary. In the ensuing silence it was almost possible to hear the cogs of his brain working on a suitable reply. When he eventually looked up, Bulmer's manner had undergone a startling change. The panic was absent, the anxiety expunged. In their place was a warm smile meant for Mia alone.

'Nothing's coming back, DS Harvey. But if she is beautiful – as beautiful as you – then I can't see how I could possibly forget her.'

Mia flushed at the unexpected compliment, and she was about to cover her delight with a harsh retort when a faint noise cut through the silence. It sounded like a high-pitched mewling, was similar to the warning an old cat might utter to a potential threat in the dead of night. It was a plaintive sound. And it seemed to be coming from the wall of books.

'What the hell's that?' asked Mia.

'What's what?' said Bulmer, acting the innocent.

Mia swivelled in her seat and glanced at the bookshelves. From her present position she could see that a section of them was hinged. A hidden doorway. She also saw that the door was slightly ajar.

'I didn't notice that when we came in.'

'Me neither,' said Nick.

'It only leads down to the cellar and a load of junk,' said Bulmer, his tone dismissive.

And still the pitiful sound continued.

'That noise … it seems to be coming from the cellar,' said Mia, already on her feet and striding towards the doorway.

But Bulmer got there first. Slamming it shut with the heel of his hand he leant against the door and faced the detectives.

'It's only Rosie, one of our feral cats. They're a bloody nuisance, but we can't get rid of them for love or money. Rosie had a litter of kittens in the cellar barely a week ago and like every good mother she's very protective of them. Honestly, you can't go down there without being hissed at or worse. She's probably warding off a rat or something.'

Mia frowned. 'She sounds very distressed to me. I think we should go down and have a look.' She searched around for means of releasing the lock but could find nothing. 'Would you open this door, please? I want to see if Rosie needs help.'

But the man remained with his back to the door, his features stoical. 'I can't allow you to do that, DS Harvey, for reasons I've already listed.' He moved towards Mia, his hot breath on her neck. 'I don't want her to hurt you. I wouldn't want you ever to be hurt.'

Mia meditated on his words, revelled in the way they were said. And then she contemplated the possibility of rats in the cellar. 'Perhaps you're right,' she said, heading back to her chair.

Nick had been following their flirtatious volleys with a quiet desperation, but he could stomach no more. 'Let's get back to Sky Beddows,' he said, curtly.

Bulmer sat down and let out a long breath. 'But I've already told you, I can't remember the girl.'

'She was with a group of kids and an older woman called Sheila Reeves. Mrs Reeves was probably dressed like a fairground fortune-teller. She'd be hard to forget.'

Bulmer shook his head. 'No, can't remember.'

'If Sky did ask permission to put her stall in the grounds,' said Mia, 'what's your procedure for things that need Sir Nigel's approval? Do you write them down in a log? Is there a form to be filled in?'

'I'd make a note, obviously. I have loads of queries and problems to deal with in my job and if I didn't write them down I'd forget.'

'Where do you write them down?'

'In here.' Bulmer pushed the diary towards Mia. 'Have a look. I've nothing to hide.'

The diary allowed one page for each day. Mia turned to Sunday 15 July – the date of their first meeting with Bulmer according to Sheila Reeves – and found the page littered with notes hastily scribbled in blue ink. All routine stuff. No mention of Sky or her request. Nothing on Monday's page either. And Tuesday and Wednesday were equally as blank. Mia slid the diary back to Bulmer, her dejected sigh all that filled the lull in their conversation.

Nick got to his feet, eager to be gone. 'Thank you for your time, Mr Bulmer. I can't see any reason to disturb Sir Nigel for the moment so we'll be making our way back to the station.'

'Just as well. He stayed long enough to welcome that pop singer into his suite yesterday and then made a hasty retreat to his villa in France. Can't say I blame him either. Those concerts are going to be sheer hell.'

Mia's eyes widened. 'Johnny Lee Rogers is here?'

'Oh God, don't say you're a fan,' said Bulmer, managing to hide his disgust behind a genial smile.

Mia grinned. 'It's not every day I get to be so near to a genuine star.'

'Perhaps I can arrange a meeting,' said Bulmer. 'Nothing's too much trouble for a pretty lady.'

Nick stomped towards the door, his patience exhausted. 'I hate to break up the party,' he said, 'but I've got better things to do than listen to inane chatter that basically adds up to a big fat zero in the greater scheme of things.'

Mia gave him a look that wouldn't quite kill but could possibly cause serious harm. She rose from her chair. 'My colleague is right, of course. We'll be getting back to the station.'

Bulmer tried for a sorrowful pout. 'It's a shame we won't meet again. I do like you, DS Harvey.'

Mia started to blush once more. She felt awkward, like a schoolgirl ignorant of the rules of sexual banter; was aware that something needed to be said but was unable to form a sentence.

Nick's tongue was anything but tied. 'We'll be back, don't worry. You might have satisfied DS Harvey, but you've done nothing to convince me of your innocence.'

Bulmer baulked at Nick's harsh tone. 'I wasn't aware you thought me guilty of anything.'

'That remains to be seen.'

Glaring steadily at Nick, the man said to Mia, 'I've no wish to be further accused of inane chatter, DS Harvey, but could I possibly have a number I can reach you on? I'd hate to ring the station with something important and be put through to your partner here.'

Mia passed across her card with an apologetic smile and followed Nick out of the room.

Once alone, a trembling Andrew Bulmer slumped into his chair. How could he have been so stupid as to leave that bloody door open? And what if the ugly bitch had taken a look beyond it?

Dragging in deep breaths to subdue the nausea threatening his stomach Bulmer saw all too clearly a likely future should his carefully orchestrated plans go awry. Diligence was called for, he told himself sharply. Diligence and forethought. Otherwise he could be facing a long stretch and that was unthinkable.

Had they believed him? Was his performance convincing enough?

'Damn Sky Beddows,' he muttered, thumping the desktop and sending his pen caddy toppling. 'Damn the bitch.'

CHAPTER FIVE

They eventually found Roy Barlow sheltering within the shade of a huge hawthorn tree a fair distance from the caravan site. The tree was set upon a steep rise that allowed for a panoramic view of the surrounding farms and woodlands.

The vista spread before him was, as a rule, a frenzy of varied greens, yellows, and the darker browns and swarthy tones of meandering hedgerows and ramshackle farm spreads. Months of fierce sunshine had, however, burnt it all to a near crisp and today its beauty was of a different kind. It resembled the crude labours of a child whose only choice of colours was in the brown-to-orange range.

Barlow was sitting on a foldaway chair, legs apart, a thin brush behind one ear, a cream straw hat pulled low to cover his face. In front of him and slightly to his left was an easel holding a canvas similar to the one found in Sky's bedroom. He clutched a palette of oils, his intense gaze flitting between the canvas and his spectacular subject as he jabbed a short-bristled brush laden with burnt orange at his unseen creation.

It would have been an idyllic scene but for the three small children causing mayhem behind him. Barlow's wife was trying her utmost to exert some level of control over their play but for the moment her efforts were proving to be quite fruitless.

The children were pouring water on to a mound of freshly dug earth and heaping the resulting mud into small seaside buckets with the intention of creating their own fairytale castle. So far, so good. But it would seem that all three were determined to use one spade in particular – a garish design in fluorescent pink and green – and not one of them was willing to budge an inch.

Kelly Barlow, her finely boned features flushed pink with a sort of resigned misery, was quietly reciting the virtues of the other spades and digging with a desperation all too obvious in order to show those virtues. But the children were having none of it. One in particular was remonstrating loudly that the spade should be his because he was the oldest.

Suddenly Roy Barlow let out an aggressive growl and hurled his paintbrush into the still air. 'For God's sake, Owen, shut the fuck up or I'll—'

'Or you'll what?' asked Wells, as he and Jack entered the man's line of vision.

Barlow lifted the brim of his hat and regarded the detectives through narrowed lids. 'Who are you?' he asked, leaning back into the seat.

They took a few steps towards the group, all the while brandishing their warrant cards. 'Your worst nightmare, probably,' said Wells, staring at the man over the rim of his sunglasses.

'Oh, I remember you,' said Barlow, sneering at Jack.

Jack shrugged. 'I'm hard to forget, sir.'

Wells nodded an acknowledgement towards the wife, surprised to find she was the same downtrodden woman he'd spotted from Sky's kitchen window. Now he could see why she carried with her an aura of weary acceptance. Her husband was clearly one of those deep, unfathomable types lacking in all the finer feelings that set human beings apart from everything else that drew breath. Roy Barlow wouldn't be an easy man to live with – a fact all too evident in his poor wife's face.

Kelly Barlow fell back on her heels and brought a hand to her mouth, her gaze fretful as she watched them in silence.

Her children continued to dig, but without the bickering; daddy had shouted, so now was not the best time for them to push their luck.

'What do you want now?' asked Barlow, reaching down into the dust for his paintbrush. 'Am I not allowed to enjoy your countryside because I happen to prefer the freedom of a caravan as opposed to the solid security of bricks and mortar? Are you persecuting me because I'm a traveller? Or have you and your team decided it'd be fun to make me look like a spineless twat in front of my family?'

Wells pretended to hide a smile. 'You don't need us for that, sir, you're managing just fine on your own.' Before Barlow could retaliate Wells took the painting from Jack and held it up for the man to see. 'We've come to ask you about this picture actually, sir. We'd like an artist's interpretation, if you wouldn't mind.'

Barlow considered Sky's likeness for the merest of moments and then dropped his gaze, but not before Wells caught the flicker of pain that flashed across his face. Kelly Barlow stared long and hard however. She even got to her feet and inched towards the painting, her eyes transfixed.

While the woman scrutinized the painting Wells scrutinized her. He'd seen only her profile earlier in the day and found now that she possessed a delicate oval-shaped face with a fine bone structure; huge almond eyes with long black lashes, and a pale complexion made lighter still by the waves of dark hair framing those features. She displayed a fine Irish beauty that was slowly but surely being diminished under the heavy burden of her life.

Wells retrieved Sky's snapshot from his jacket pocket and considered it briefly. Kelly Barlow was lovely, yes, but she was no match for Sky. Very few women would be.

Wells held out the snapshot. 'You're closely associated with this woman, Mr Barlow, or so we've been told.'

Without a word Barlow grabbed his straw hat and slung it aside as though it were the cause of his annoyance and not the two detectives considering him with unguarded amusement.

'Where did you get that?' he asked, his hostility barely concealed. 'And more to the fucking point, where did you find that painting?'

'In Mrs Beddows's caravan,' said Wells.

'What were you doing there?'

'Searching for clues, sir.'

'Why?'

'Because she's gone missing and we're trying to locate her.'

Barlow frowned, tilted his head to one side. 'Missing?' he said, as though acquainting himself with the word. 'What on earth makes you think that?'

Wells removed his sunglasses, dropped them into his breast pocket. 'Oh, the small fact that her kids turned up at the police station yesterday morning, half-starved and filthy.'

Barlow's laugh held little humour as he glanced from Wells to Jack and back again. He was trying for light-hearted nonchalance but his brown eyes showed mild panic. 'You're out of your fucking minds. Sky's not missing: she's just gone away for a while. The girl's got a lot to think about.'

Wells made a face. 'And she's left her kids to fend for themselves? I don't think so.'

Barlow heaved a sigh. 'You clearly don't know anything about life on the road. We're one big family. We look out for each other. Those children are safe enough without their mother.'

'You didn't even know they were gone,' Wells huffed. 'How bloody safe is that?'

Barlow lifted a shoulder. 'I just assumed they were behaving themselves. Nobody told us they'd gone, did they, Kelly?'

The woman made no reply. She simply continued her visual exploration of Barlow's painting. As a fellow artist it was likely she saw meanings within the brush strokes that the detectives had missed. And Wells could only assume that those meanings were cutting her to the quick because her face suddenly contorted with rage. Pummelling her husband's shoulders, she yelled, 'I hate you, Roy. I hate you—'

The assault stopped as abruptly as it had started. Kelly Barlow, tears coursing down her cheeks, aimed one last look of hatred at her astonished husband and returned to the children. Ignoring their loud protests, and failing to retrieve the buckets and spades, she scooped up the smallest two and fiercely directed the third to follow her closely. With that they trudged off along the well-trodden path that would eventually lead them back to the flood plains. Roy Barlow could only watch them go, a hand to his neck, his mouth gaping open.

'Not Mr Popular today, are you, sir?' said Wells, handing the painting to Jack.

'She'll be back with her tail between her legs, begging for my forgiveness,' he said, his tone hardly matching the bravado of his words.

'You seem very angry,' said Jack. 'I sense a lot of angst in you. Why, sir?'

Barlow shrugged. 'Misery and depression go hand in hand with creative ability. I doubt I'd be much of an artist if I was a happy fellow.'

'You'd class yourself as a good painter then?'

'Inspirational,' said Barlow, his cool stare challenging the detectives to disagree.

Jack held up the painting. 'So you reckon this is good?'

'Don't you?'

It was Jack's turn to shrug. 'I don't know much about art, sir. I don't understand it. I mean, Sky Beddows is a lovely woman and yet you've made her look like this. What's behind the concept?'

Barlow let out a long breath, rested the palette and brush on his lap. 'All my working life is spent capturing images in charcoal. Smile, if you will … a few deft strokes … there you go, that'll be ten pounds, please.' He gave a rueful shake of the head. 'It's soul-destroying, it really is. So, when I paint for pleasure – in the hope of one day selling my creations – I like to go beyond the norm, think outside the box.' His eyes crinkled into a smile. 'If you're assuming I painted Sky in that way because I hate her then think again. That's a fine painting, a fine celebration of a woman's beauty. In that painting I caught the girl's essence. I captured her very soul. That's why my wife reacted the way she did. She's always been jealous of Sky.'

Paul Wells wandered to the edge of the shaded area and peered towards the horizon. 'She's got good reason to be jealous from what we've heard.'

Barlow displayed an oily grin. 'Oh, let me guess … Madam Sheila's been blabbing again.'

Wells turned his back towards Barlow, eyes narrowed against the bright sunshine. 'The lady's been helping with our enquiries, yes.'

A sharp look of hatred replaced the grin. 'And if she told you of Tuesday night's slight debacle then don't believe a word of it. Sheila wasn't there. It's all hearsay. And anyway Sky forgave me. She knows I've a problem with the drink.'

A slight debacle on Tuesday night?

Wells cast Jack a sly glance. 'She did actually, sir. Mrs Reeves told us all the ins and outs, and very informative it was too. Still, if you say she's got it all wrong then here's your opportunity to set the record straight.'

Barlow put a hand to his forehead, a look of despair distorting his features. 'I can't, it's all too hazy.' He looked up at the detectives, his wide eyes earnest. 'You don't understand what it's like. I can't eat. I can't sleep.'

'You can drink though,' Jack cut in.

'And you can mock,' said Barlow, lips pulled back. 'But that doesn't change the fact that I'm fucking dying here. That woman's killing me.'

Jack feigned incomprehension. 'But you said suffering and despair made you a better painter. Surely all that pain's going to make you a star. You'll be quids in.'

'Everyday problems and superficial despair, maybe. But my hurt, my feelings for Sky, they go way beyond that. I'm being consumed by a jealousy so profound I could—'

'What, sir? Kill?' asked Wells. 'Could you kill, Mr Barlow?'

'I could kill myself. And I will if she doesn't stop taunting me with that … that … *prick.*'

'Which prick might that be?'

'Philip Hunt,' Barlow snarled. 'Hunt the fucking cunt….'

'And where exactly does Mr Hunt fit into the picture?'

'He's after Sky. He says he isn't – he thinks I'm a fool – but I've seen the way he looks at her. I've seen the way he undresses her with his eyes. A fucking blind man could see he's fallen for the girl as surely as I have.'

Wells unbuttoned his jacket and paced, hands in trouser pockets, before the man. 'OK, let's go back to Tuesday night. How was Hunt involved in your … slight debacle?'

'I don't know.' Barlow ran impatient fingers through his hair and sighed heavily. 'He was there … the bastard was there because we had an argument about Sky. But as for later … I told you, I was drunk, I can't remember. Two of your officers turned up and slapped our wrists – I remember that – but as for the rest, nothing.'

Jack said, 'You told us you were consumed with jealousy, Mr Barlow. Have you any reason to be? Is Sky involved with Mr Hunt?'

'I fucking hope not.'

'And what about you?' asked Wells. 'Have you managed to get into her knickers yet?'

Barlow let out an impatient sigh. 'I'm not after sex, for pity's sake. Sky's my muse. She inspires me. I'm in love with the girl. I ache with love for her. She's never out of my thoughts. I would die for the beautiful Sky Beddows.'

Wells gave a derisive snort. 'And you wonder why your missus is jealous.'

'Leave Kelly out of this,' was Barlow's curt reply. 'Sky's got nothing at all to do with my marriage.'

'What about your kids?'

'What about them?'

'They're hardly growing up in a stable environment, are they? There's you mooning over Sky Beddows day and night – consumed by … what did you call it, Jack? … oh yes, *angst* – and their mother's so affected by it she's starting to resemble a bloody zombie.'

Barlow grinned at the heavy sarcasm in the DCI's words but said nothing. With slow and deliberate movements he pulled a dirty piece of cloth from the breast pocket of his yellow linen shirt and proceeded to wipe the small mounds of paint from the palette on his lap.

Wells's hackles rose sharply as the man continued to grin. 'You couldn't give a damn about that missus of yours, could you, Mr Barlow? She knows her place and that's all that matters. But what about Sky? She's not so easy to manage, is she? She's got a mind of her own. She doesn't think you're God's gift – nowhere near it, mate. She'd rather have Phil Hunt with the big prick. No, hang on, he *is* the big prick. That's what you said, isn't it, sir?'

Barlow's grin widened as he refused to be goaded. 'Are you such an expert on matrimony, Chief Inspector? Did you leave your wife all warm and satisfied in bed this morning? Lucky you, if you did. You must give me a few tips. Show me where I'm going wrong.'

'I'm no expert, sir, far from it. But I'll give you one tip: if you're going to be a naughty boy, don't do it on your own doorstep because somebody's likely to get hurt.'

'Thanks, I'll bear that in mind.' Barlow reached behind his chair for a canvas holdall into which he packed the palette, brush, and dirty rag. Then he got to his feet, reached for his straw hat, and folded up the chair. He turned back to the detectives. 'Are you two still here? What are you waiting for, a fucking autograph?'

Wells folded his arms, stood with legs apart. 'Sky's location would do,' he said, with a glint in his eye.

'I've already told you, she's gone off to consider our future. She'll be back soon enough. Besides, it isn't in me to hurt anybody. I couldn't even harm a fly.'

'There's more than one way to cause harm, Mr Barlow. Psychological abuse is just as bad as the physical in my book, and I reckon you'd be a natural at that.'

Barlow skimmed him an evil look, but his tone remained level as he said, 'Of course I'll expect a public apology when Sky does come back because you see, Chief Inspector, I'm not involved. And there's no abuse involved either, physical or psychological. She needs time to herself so she's taken it – simple as that.'

Wells raised a dubious eyebrow. 'You know what I think? I think she wants Phil Hunt. I think she's going to live happily ever after with Phil. She's not taunting you, Mr Barlow, she loves the bloke. I think an ice cube's got more chance of surviving the fires of hell than you've got of ending up with Sky Beddows. You'd better face it, mate, you ain't gonna get her.'

Barlow let the holdall drop as he rounded on the two men. 'That bastard's never going to get her either. Not while I've got breath in my body.'

Those words produced a powerful adrenalin surge in Wells's solar plexus. 'What are you planning to do, sir?'

'Go fuck yourself,' Barlow said, retrieving the holdall and making an aggressive grab for his work-in-progress. Tucking the canvas under his arm, unmindful of the still wet oils, he folded up the easel and turned towards the detectives, his stance determined. 'You've completely ruined my session for today, but you've got a job to do and I'm a fair man so I'll let it go. If, however, you continue to harass me I'll put in a formal complaint.' He inclined his head, favoured them with a tight smile. 'It's been a pleasure talking with you both, but it's a pleasure I don't want repeated. Go and annoy somebody else.'

They watched him tread an uncertain path towards the flood plains, his heavy load slowing his progress.

'Nasty bloke, isn't he?' said Wells.

'Complete nutter,' said Jack, wandering across to pick up the discarded buckets and spades.

'Is he capable of violence though?'

'He's angry enough, sir. I reckon he could easily go too far when he's had a few.'

'Me, too,' said Wells. 'OK, now we've got the next two entries on our "Important Things To Do" list. We get the report from Tuesday night's little set-to. And we have a word with Philip Hunt. We'll do Hunt first because I'm missing our Mr Barlow already.' He buttoned his jacket and straightened his tie as if preparing for the fray. 'Right, Jack, let's go. It's time for a bit of Barlow-baiting.'

CHAPTER SIX

Saturday. 10.45 a.m.

Security was tight at Stratton Manor. Down by the main gates Johnny Lee's bodyguards were keeping out all those unable to provide bona-fide invitations to the so-called rehearsal. And a number of hefty individuals – two-way-radios at the ready – were positioned at the end of a wide gravelled pathway which connected the rear of the manor to the huge area of meadowland housing the stage.

It was all completely over the top and so unnecessary. But Bob Briscoe had been in music management for a good many years. He knew that if their boy was seen to be living the superstar lifestyle then the CD-buying fans would perceive him as such.

And inaccessibility was no bad thing. Johnny Lee had stayed in the public eye for so long because of Briscoe's look-but-don't-touch strategy. He knew you couldn't fool all the public all of the time, but you could sure as hell get rich trying. Sex and mystery had always been a winning combination. You only had to look at Elvis. Bob Briscoe was no Colonel Parker, but he'd done a fine job so far.

Lizzie Thornton was sharing a bench with Cathy Cousins a short distance from the stage, her expression one of huge distaste as a number of unkempt individuals scurried around, checking power points, testing sound levels, and generally taking care of business.

'You'd think they'd dress more appropriately,' she said to Cathy. 'Johnny Lee always makes an effort so why can't they?'

'They're the roadies,' said Cathy, rolling her eyes. 'They're not paid to dress up.'

'Even so, soap and water doesn't cost much.'

In front of them a small swarm of journalists stood with notebooks at the ready, hand-held tape machines all set to go. With them were a number of photographers, one of whom was approaching the women with surreptitious steps, his gaze supposedly fixed on the lighting gauge at the back of his camera. About three yards short of the bench he snapped off a shot.

The flash caught Lizzie in the eyes. 'For goodness' sake,' she said, blinking rapidly.

'Didn't mean to blind you, babes. Didn't realize the flash was on,' he said in a rich Cockney lilt. 'I wanted a shot of your lovely granddaughter.'

Lizzie scowled and Cathy had to swallow a giggle.

The photographer smiled at Cathy and she smiled back because he was a handsome boy and because she wasn't fussy as a rule. She liked his tall lean frame, the blond highlights that gave his brown shoulder-length hair a sun-kissed, beach-boy look.

'Are you one of the paparazzi?' she asked.

'Suppose I am, yeah. I'm Rick,' he said, all perfect white teeth and suggestive eyes. 'What do I call you, sugar lips?'

'Oh, please,' Lizzie said, grimacing. 'Her name's Cathy, if you must know, and you can sniff around her all you like when the rehearsal's finished. But for now, kindly go away. I can smell your testosterone from here, you disgusting boy.'

'Lizzie,' Cathy pouted, while Rick beat a hasty retreat back to the scrum.

'I don't care. You're here for me, don't forget. Once that important moment of fate has been realized and my future is passionately entwined forever with Johnny Lee's then you can mess around with … Rick … as much as you like. Until then let's just concentrate on me, shall we?'

Cathy's pretty forehead folded into a frown. 'Your future's passionately what?'

'Shut up, Cathy, it's almost eleven o'clock.' Lizzie grabbed the girl's arm and, grinning, shook it boisterously. 'He'll soon be here. Quick, how do I look?'

Lizzie was wearing a pair of black polyester slacks bought yesterday from a 'Final Reduction' rail in Marks & Spencer. She'd matched them with a pale-grey silk blouse with three-quarter sleeves and buttons right up to the white lace collar. She'd kept the top two buttons undone – Lizzie's equivalent of strolling around the high street naked – and around her neck could be seen a thin black velvet choker on to which was pinned a cream and brown cameo brooch. Her sandals were black leather and open-toed so that Johnny Lee would be treated to a tantalizing glimpse of her American Tan tights. And to complete the look aimed at tempting her sweetheart, Lizzie had piled her hair into a frizzy bun on top of her head, leaving only a wisp of fringe with the gargantuan task of covering the deep furrows on her forehead.

'You must be bloody roasting,' was all that Cathy said.

Cathy wasn't roasting. Nowhere near. Her pert bra-less breasts were only just covered by a canary-yellow halter-neck T-shirt which kept bare her highly-toned midriff. And that tiny top was teamed with an equally diminutive black mini-skirt which showed off to perfection the long, tanned and beautifully shaped legs from which Rick was struggling to wrench his gaze. She'd left her blonde hair hanging loose so the sunlight could catch its gorgeous sheen every time she tossed it away from her face. Cathy Cousins hadn't been lost in a cloud of mindless thoughts when intelligence and common sense were handed out. She'd been right at the front of the vanity queue.

'You could have smartened yourself up,' said Lizzie, nose wrinkling.

For one devastating moment Cathy worried that her outfit might be unsuitable after all; but then she peered across at the tight group of men in front of the stage and saw that the handsome photographer was still looking her way – indeed the majority of his companions were openly watching her every move too – and she was able to relax again.

Within minutes a shout went up. Johnny Lee Rogers was in the vicinity. Johnny Lee Rogers was making his lazy hip-swinging way towards them. And Lizzie was so excited. She jumped to her feet and grabbed Cathy's arm again, almost yanking her off the bench.

'This is it,' she whispered. 'My husband-to-be is almost here.'

Cathy was studying Lizzie with a look of utter perplexity – an oh-my-God-she's-really-lost-it-now type of glance – when a hint of startling blue showed itself on the periphery of her vision.

And there was Johnny Lee skirting around the stage, a living dream of sexual charisma – in Lizzie's eyes at least – surrounded by his usual mob of black-suited security. The man had prepared well for the concerts with not an ounce of spare flesh showing on his five-foot-nine frame. His tight blue shirt – a mass of glitter and frills – was slit to the waist, revealing hard pectorals. His black, bell-bottom trousers looked as though they'd been painted on to his slim hips.

'I thought he'd be taller than that,' said Cathy, unconsciously striking a pose for the man: right hand behind her neck, breasts pushed forward, legs slightly apart. 'And his hair must be dyed. Nobody his age has hair that black. What do you think, Lizzie?'

But Lizzie said nothing and Cathy turned to see that her mouth was moving wordlessly as if in silent prayer, eyes damp with emotion. Lizzie raised a hand, waved it enthusiastically in order to catch the singer's attention, her expression filled with hope. But those efforts came to nothing: his attention refused to be caught.

Johnny Lee was too busy swapping quips with the journalists, grinning for the cameras, and generally showing his commitment to 'them poor kids at that Rainbow place, the Good Lord bless their souls'. As a daddy himself – he'd had one child with each wife – he said he was mighty thankful for the opportunity to make his own small contribution to such a worthy cause.

Bob Briscoe had been keeping to the side, watching his boy and checking the time periodically, monitoring the roadies and making sure his musicians were where they should be. Finally he strode across to Johnny Lee, hands in the air, palms forward.

'OK, I'll be calling it a day now, boys. Thank you all for your time but Johnny's gonna be singing for the delight of your ears in a minute or two so you'd best be giving him some air.'

The men slowly dispersed in a hum of satisfied conversation, their wide smiles signalling that a profitable time had been had by all. Briscoe led Johnny Lee towards the lucky prize winners while the bodyguards closed in around them like flies on a hog-roast.

'Johnny, these are the lovely gals who won the tickets to Sunday's show,' he said, putting a hand to Lizzie's elbow. 'This here is Miss Elizabeth Thornton….'

What the fuck…? Johnny Lee flicked a withering glance at his manager but Briscoe refused to acknowledge it, searched instead for imaginary flecks of cotton on his baggy chinos. The singer was just glad he'd replaced his sunglasses. At least the woman couldn't see the horror in his eyes.

Nevertheless Johnny Lee – ever the showman – reached for her hand and held it briefly. 'Miss Thornton,' he said, with that dazzling smile.

Lizzie couldn't reply. Lizzie couldn't even open her mouth. The warm fingers of her beloved were actually touching hers – the first in a lifetime of caresses – and rampant desire just grabbed her vocal chords and ran.

'And her pretty little companion is Miss Catherine Cousins,' Briscoe went on blithely.

This was more like it. Catherine Cousins. So that's the little gal's name. During the slow amble across to the interview area Johnny Lee had been secretly enjoying Cathy's superbly nubile body behind his sunglasses and he bowed deeply now, his heavily bejewelled hand clutching hers for slightly longer than was officially acceptable.

'Pleased to meet you, Miss Cousins. Pleased to meet the both of you,' he drawled, his lustful gaze centred on Cathy's breasts.

Lizzie grinned and plucked at the collar of her blouse. Over at the side Bob Briscoe was thanking the Lord for he could sense a strong chemistry between his boy and the trashy blonde. And he was heartily pleased because that meant nothing but good for the forthcoming meal and the positive publicity that was sure to follow.

Heaving a sigh of relief, Briscoe said, 'Johnny, these gals are big fans of yours and you'll be enjoying the pleasure of their company for dinner at the Fox and Hounds Hotel on Wednesday night, you lucky sonofabitch.' He quickly inclined his head. 'If you'll excuse my mouth, ladies.'

Cathy's face lit up. 'The Fox and Hounds? Bloody hell, that's fantastic.'

Good job she'd accepted Lizzie's offer of a ticket. It was widely known that the Larchborough rugby team used the Fox and Hounds as a regular watering hole and they were all so *hunky*.

It was decided then. She'd definitely wear the pink satin mini-dress. She might not get another chance to eat at such an expensive place so she needed to get it right first time. There were plenty of sumptuous rooms upstairs apparently and, if she played her cards right, well, she'd heard their full English breakfasts were fantastic.

Lizzie couldn't have cared less about the Larchborough rugby team; or any other rugby team for that matter. She was completely enraptured by the delicious Johnny Lee and her hungry gaze took in every inch of the man as he stood before them, hands on slender hips, shirt gaping open to reveal a slight sheen of perspiration on his smooth solid chest. He smelt of wild strawberries and musk, a perfume that set Lizzie's large nostrils twitching, her skin prickling with desire.

She moved a step closer, arms spread wide, head cocked to the side in what she hoped was a seductive manner, while her dentures hid behind a devilish pout. It was a pose that screamed: *take me, lover … make me sizzle and burn*!

Unfortunately, Johnny Lee failed to notice because he was still ogling Cathy. And he sure as hell liked what he saw. He was about to start his sweet-talking – what Lenny Price called his 'Ten Thousand Watt Gal-Trappin' Technique' – a sexy grin already forming, when Lizzie lunged into his arms.

'At last, Johnny Lee, at last,' she moaned.

'Hey, steady on there, ma'am,' he said, grabbing her shoulders, keeping her safely at arm's length.

And, as Cathy looked on in disgust, her grossly underused brain cells suddenly cranked into overdrive. What on earth was she thinking? Of course she'd dine at the Fox and Hounds again. When she was a big singing star – no, when she was the *biggest* singing star on the planet – she'd only ever eat at upmarket establishments like the Fox and Hounds. And measly rugby players wouldn't even get a look-in.

At that moment she no longer saw Johnny Lee Rogers as that old has-been who was only three years younger than her granddad. Now she saw him as her very own Simon Cowell – sort of – and that all-important key to her singing career. One favourable word from Johnny Lee and fame and fortune would be hers.

Therefore as Lizzie attempted to mount the man in full view of everyone Cathy quickly struck up her butter-wouldn't-melt-in-my-mouth pose: legs crossed at the ankles, shoulders slightly raised, hands clasped in front of her pubic mound so breasts were surreptitiously pushed together by upper arms, and chin lowered to give the full effect of her huge blue eyes as she looked at the singer and willed him to look back.

But Johnny Lee was incapable of looking back. He was too busy grappling with the love-struck Lizzie Thornton who even now was trying for a handhold on the back of his neck in order to shorten the distance between their lips.

'Kiss me,' Lizzie murmured.

Johnny Lee's laugh was cautious as he cast a nervous glance towards Briscoe. 'But, ma'am, kissin' a lady on first acquaintance just ain't done,' he said, managing to free himself from Lizzie's steely grip. 'My old mammy taught me that, so I know it to be the solid truth an' all.'

Oh, how sweet. The man was simply divine. 'You're such a gentleman in public, aren't you, my darling?'

Johnny Lee took to fiddling with his rings while his mind raced. Trust my goddamn luck, he thought ruefully. Still, her buddy's a luscious little baby-doll, so one outa two ain't bad. Johnny Lee gave a low, lascivious chuckle – he was imagining the startled look on Lenny's face when he spied his prospective date for the night – and Lizzie mistook it for consensual lust and started to give him the come-on again.

Johnny Lee's stomach executed a nauseous flip, and a furtive raising of his eyebrows gave the bodyguards unspoken permission to intervene should the madwoman make another grab for him.

Bob Briscoe quickly stepped into the breach and did what he did best – he talked deal. Taking Lizzie by the arm in an attempt to lead her away from his boy, Briscoe said, 'Perhaps we'd best leave Johnny to prepare for the rehearsal … huh, Miss Thornton? Wouldn't do to take all his strength – what d'you think? How about I arrange for an autographed picture to be mailed to your address first thing on Monday morning? First thing, mind. How about that?'

Smiling benignly, as though Briscoe was soft in the head, Lizzie shrugged off his hand. 'Can't you recognize true love when you see it? We were meant to meet today. God wants us to be together.'

She made a quick dash towards Johnny Lee and, while he sidestepped, his bodyguards moved in *en masse*, expressions determined, muscles flexed for action.

Lizzie simply laughed. 'Tell them how you feel, my darling. You must have dreamt about me. You must have sensed me getting nearer.'

Johnny Lee slipped off the sunglasses because he wanted her to see the truth in his eyes. 'Fact is, ma'am, I didn't sense nothing. And I got too much respect for you as a woman to lie and say I did. I believe a guy and a gal should get better acquainted – if you know what I mean – before they start talking about love and stuff.'

Lizzie gave another lilting laugh and held out her arms. 'I couldn't agree more. So come here and let's get acquainted.'

The bodyguards were highly amused, their stiff grins showing more gold than a jeweller's main window. But Cathy was livid as she watched from the fringes. Tossing her hair away from her face and sighing crossly she stamped her high-heeled sandal most firmly on the sun-baked earth. Johnny Lee hadn't glanced at her in ages. And why was Lizzie getting all the attention? It was so unfair.

She was about to remind Johnny Lee of her existence when a blue-suited man came running towards them, a bundle of papers under one arm, Sally Simms following.

'Hello again, Mr Rogers,' was the man's breathless opener. 'The name's Andrew Bulmer, Sir Nigel's estate manager. Remember me?'

'Sure do, Mr Bulmer. Good to see you.' Johnny Lee treated the man's hand to a hearty shake. Then with wild hope, one eye still on Lizzie, 'I'm supposing you want a word or two. Yeah?'

'Not with you, sir, no. It's Mr Briscoe I've come to see.' Bulmer turned towards the manager. 'The programme proofs have just arrived by special courier, Mr Briscoe, and we need your final approval of the design. It is rather urgent though. The courier's waiting to take them back.'

As Bulmer led the others across to the bench, Johnny Lee was left unarmed – apart from half a dozen black-belted bodyguards – and vulnerable while Lizzie continued her sustained attack.

And it was then that Cathy's rage finally erupted. 'Well, thank you for *nothing*, Lizzie Thornton – bringing me here and *totally* humiliating me in front of Mr Rogers.'

Lizzie reeled around in surprise, watched with horror as Johnny Lee attempted to pacify the distraught blonde. Cathy in turn made a show of melting under the weight of his softly-softly touch. But not too quickly; he had to work for his reward. As she watched the mating game progress, adrenalin pumped through Lizzie's system and warned her to beware.

'Leave her, Johnny Lee,' she said, making a grab for his arm. 'This is our time now. Haven't we waited long enough?'

But she was ignored. Cathy drew nearer, laid a hand on Johnny Lee's hairless chest. 'I'm a singer just like you. I love to sing.'

Johnny Lee covered her hand with his own. 'You do, honey? Maybe we can make time after sundown. Maybe you can sing for me then.' He gave her a wink before replacing his sunglasses. 'Maybe.'

Lizzie was distraught. It was all going wrong. *She* was the love of his life. *She* should be embracing him after sundown. 'Johnny Lee,' she cried.

Cathy giggled and was curling an arm around his slim waist in an attempt to raise the stakes when a shout went up from the stage and the energetic strains of an electric guitar filled the still, heat-baked air.

It was Lenny Price. 'Hey, Johnny, how about comin' up here to do some singin' before we all pass out from the freakin' sun?'

Johnny Lee raised a hand, yelled an affirmative. Then his lustful gaze returned to Cathy. 'The first song's called *There'll Be Some Good Lovin' Tonight*. I'll be singing it for you, honey.'

'No … no …' Lizzie whimpered. She was preparing to throw off Cathy's insidious grip when the nearest bodyguard grasped tight her upper arms and held her steady.

'I can hardly wait,' said Cathy, blowing him a kiss.

'Johnny Lee,' Lizzie called as she grappled with the guard.

But he seemed not to hear. He was ambling towards the stage, running fingers through his glossy hair and turning occasionally to wave at the little blonde who'd surely give as easily as a broken step. A meaningless treat with which to fill the empty hours after midnight. Lizzie Thornton was forgotten; an ugly inconvenience that had momentarily slipped his mind.

Still slumped in the arms of the bodyguard Lizzie called again to Johnny Lee, pleaded with him to look her way, begged him to give her a sign that their destiny had been reached. But his only response was to raise a hand, his back still towards her, as if to say: 'Whatever, ugly bitch.'

That brittle gesture, that cold rebuff, was enough to break her fragile heart in two. It was a defining moment – and in a way her destiny *had* been reached – for it was then that Lizzie Thornton's dark thoughts turned to vengeance.

CHAPTER SEVEN

'Where are you now?'

'In the car park at Stratton Manor,' Mia said into her mobile.

'Any luck with Bulmer?'

'No, sir, he can't remember meeting Sky Beddows on any of the dates we mentioned, and we believe him. Plus, there's nothing in his office diary to suggest a request was made to put up stalls, and that's where he'd have jotted it down.'

'OK,' said Wells. 'Me and Jack are heading to the caravans for a word with Phil Hunt. It shouldn't take long. We'll all meet back at the office. I want posters done of Sky's photo. They'll need to be distributed around town asap. And we need to get a piece in tonight's *Evening News* if it's not too late.'

'You're taking her disappearance seriously then, sir?'

'Suppose I am.' Mia heard him exhale sharply. 'The tasty Sky Beddows seems to bring out the worst in men, and I've a feeling things have got out of hand. We'll just have to wait and see whether she's already paid the ultimate price.'

'What do you want us to do?'

'Concentrate on the husband. Is he still inside? If not, what's he been up to lately? And we need to put a trace out for the girl's parents. Start that off, will you?'

The line went dead and Mia glanced across at Nick slumped in the passenger seat. They were still in the car park because Nick had turned on her the instant they'd left Bulmer's office, the resulting argument still going strong as they buckled up in the car. He'd accused her of flirting with a potential suspect; she'd urged him to get his arse out of his hands and grow up. He was still brooding, staring out of the side window, refusing to appear curious as to what Wells might have said.

In order to break the tension, Mia said, 'The DCI smells a rat, Nick, so it looks like we've got ourselves a case.'

Nick's fleeting glance was ripe with annoyance. 'What's all this "we-believe-Bulmer" crap? I don't believe a word the smarmy bastard said.'

Mia sighed heavily. 'Why not?'

Nick held up a hand, marked the points off on his fingers. 'Why should Sheila Reeves make up that story about the stalls? How come Bulmer reacted the way he did when I mentioned Sky's name? Why wouldn't he let you take a look in the cellar?' He turned again to the side window, his fingers tapping an irritable tattoo on the dashboard. 'I tell you, Mia, if Sky's down there and she winds up dead it'll all be down to you.'

'Oh, really?' she spat. 'You were there. You've got a voice. Why didn't you make him open the door?'

'And keep boss's little favourite from falling in the shit?'

'God, not this again,' she huffed. 'If I'm his favourite why does he jump down my throat every time I open my mouth?'

'Why did he just phone you?' he fired back. 'I'm the senior officer. He should be talking to me.'

Mia moved to pat his shoulder. 'Is Nicky jealous? Is he feeling left out?'

He shrugged her off. 'I've a bad feeling about Bulmer, that's all.'

Mia didn't respond immediately. She didn't know what to say. Yes, Bulmer did come across as fishy. But lots of people appear evasive when talking to the police, innocent or not. It was something to do with the collective guilt of mankind and more often than not had no connection with the case in hand. Yes, he denied everything told to them by Sheila Reeves, but did that mean he was lying? Couldn't Sheila have been handing them a load of bull? Who should they believe? The educated employee of Sir Nigel Stratton? Or the fake fortune teller who robbed the public blind every time they crossed her palm with silver? No contest in Mia's eyes.

She turned to Nick, her frown thoughtful. 'OK, when you mentioned Sky there was a second or two when I thought … oh. I don't know. I couldn't see him hiding anything though.'

'That's because you were looking at him through the eyes of the smitten.' Nick changed his tone to match Bulmer's. 'You're so beautiful, DS Harvey. I do like you, DS Harvey. Perhaps I can arrange for you to meet Johnny Lee Rogers as a special treat. Would you like that? Would you give me a treat if I did?'

'Don't,' she said, shoving his shoulder. 'I'm not that easy.'

Nick skimmed her a look. 'You're desperate enough.'

Refusing to be pulled into a conversation about her sex life – or lack of one – Mia started the engine and eased the car towards the EXIT sign.

Meanwhile, on the opposite side of the car park Andrew Bulmer was watching their steady progress as the courier mounted his motor bike. And he continued to stare at the exit long after the car and the motor bike had disappeared from view.

The caravan site was deserted apart from the Barlow clan causing a rumpus at the fence. They were joined now by a small, mixed-race boy who, although appearing older, was following the younger kids' lead rather than instigating their play himself.

'They'll grow up to be overbearing bullies like their dad,' Wells told Jack.

The atmosphere was heavy, the air still and silent as the grave. No birdsong, no insects buzzing…. It felt as though the whole of humanity was waiting with bated breath. But waiting for what exactly?

While Jack returned the buckets and spades to their rightful owners and replaced the oil painting in Sky's caravan DCI Wells had a look around. And he was about to offer Jack another pearl from his wisdom box when Sheila Reeves emerged from her gypsy caravan and called smartly for Billy to 'get back here now, little man, or I'll lather your backside 'til it's redder than a Man United strip on the first day of a new season'.

At that moment Wells realized two things: first, that Jack's description of the woman was absolute perfection: she really did move like a parched and bloated buffalo desperate to get to the water's edge. And the second revelation – one that held not the slightest hint of humour – was that simple fear was causing the hush. Fear had stilled the breeze, stolen the birdsong. Fear hung heavy overhead. Those simple folk, those inveterate law breakers, were *scared bloody rigid*. It was as clear as the nose on his face. But, why?

'Mrs Reeves, a word in your shell-like,' Wells said, holding up his warrant card.

She gave it a cursory glance and continued towards the children. 'I told your lackey to talk to Phil,' she said, scooping up her boy. 'I'm having nothing more to do with it.'

Wells caught sight of the pink plaster cast on Billy's leg, and he couldn't help but wince at the look of pain that clouded the boy's angelic face when his mother almost threw him to the rock-hard ground in front of her caravan steps.

'It's Phil we want to see, love. Where can we find him?'

The woman pointed to her right. 'Along that path. He's picking blackberries with his old ma.'

'Thanks, love, appreciate it,' said Wells, about to move off. 'One thing though before we go.' His amiable grin transformed itself into a hostile stare. 'You ought to take better care of that kid's leg, darling, 'cause if you don't I'll have you down the station so bloody quick your crystal ball won't even know I've done it.'

As she watched them disappear along the path Sheila Reeves muttered morosely and gripped tight the shoulders of her strangely silent son as he attempted to lose himself within the ample folds of her gypsy skirt.

Her heart was heavy with worry. The hospital nurses already thought she was the cause of Billy's injuries. They hadn't said as much but she'd seen it in their eyes. And now that mouthy copper had witnessed her being rough with the boy. She'd have to be careful or they'd take him away – for good, this time. And then where would she be? Up shit creek without a paddle, that's where.

Sheila Reeves might not be a natural clairvoyant, but, as she listened to the kindling wood crunching loud beneath the detectives' determined steps, she was certain of one thing: only tragedy lay ahead of all this. Tragedy, and the disbanding of their little troupe.

She glanced around at the familiar line of caravans with growing dismay. They'd had a good innings, no doubt about it. They'd earned well and laughed a lot. But for how much longer? Sooner rather than later the shit was going to hit the fan and they'd be left with an awful lot of mess to wipe away.

And who would be to blame when it finally happened? The beautiful Sky Beddows, of course – every man's precious sodding fantasy.

Sheila Reeves lifted her son into the cool interior of the caravan and followed him in.

I hope Sky is dead, she thought, scowling as she closed the stable door. *And I hope it was a slow and painful death as well.*

The path was little more than a furrow edged both sides with shoulder-high plants and grasping brambles that pulled at their clothes and scratched hands and faces at every opportunity.

'Bloody things,' muttered Wells, freeing his trouser leg from a particularly thorny bramble shoot. 'Look at this suit … ruined. This is going on my expenses sheet, mate.'

'Joys of the countryside,' said Jack, brushing delicate seed heads from his dark-grey sleeves.

Wells was still complaining when he noticed two figures up ahead. They were standing where the path meandered along a wider ridge, plucking berries from surrounding bushes and lobbing them with gentle accuracy into a number of colanders and deep tubs around their feet. The detectives took a moment to observe them, to weigh them up – the man especially.

Philip Hunt was of average height; his dark cropped hair thick but receding. He wore light-blue jogging bottoms below a slight paunch, and his darkly tanned chest showed the beginnings of man-boobs.

'No Mr Universe, is he?' said Wells.

Mrs Hunt was the first to catch sight of them. 'Breathe in, Phil, strangers passing,' she said, smiling as she hugged the bushes to the side of the path.

She had a mass of silver hair that stood out at angles, and her pleasant features bore the heavily ingrained lines of a sun worshipper. That hair and those lines gave her an ancient look, like a wizened troll. But she was sprightly enough; in fact she moved with the effortlessness of a woman half her age. And her pale-blue eyes were quite amazing; they shone with an energy the DCI's had never quite managed.

Those eyes wouldn't miss much, Wells surmised, filing the fact away for future reference. However, by the time names had been exchanged and warrant cards shown Mrs Hunt's gaze had lost much of its sparkle.

'You must think we're wicked picking these berries while Sky's goodness knows where,' she said, mopping sweat from her face and neck with a wad of tissues. 'But they're early … the blackberries. If we don't get them now they'll go over and that'll be such a waste. Don't you think? It's the weather … global warming … everything's so blasted early.'

Hunt laid a gentle hand upon his mother's shoulder. 'How about heading back to the van, Ma? You look all in. I'll have a quick word with the coppers and then I'll be ready for one of Pop's beers. You could get a can out the fridge, have it ready.'

His mother gave a loud huff, her amused glance skimming the detectives. 'No need to go round the houses, Phil. Tell me to clear off and I will.' She nodded towards the tubs littering the ground. 'You can bring the berries. I dare say they'll be too much for me being as I'm all in.' She aimed a conspiratorial wink at Wells and began to make slow progress along the clogged pathway.

'Nice lady,' Wells remarked.

Hunt nodded, his eyes boring into her back. 'Ma's the best. I don't want you upsetting her with your questions.'

'I wasn't planning to question your mother, sir. I'm not thinking any further than you for now.'

Hunt's stance was easy, his expression open. And Wells was impressed with the man's ability to deceive. For deceiving them he was. And the DCI knew it because his eyes told a different story as they scanned the surrounding hedgerows, focusing anywhere but on their expectant faces.

The silence was growing awkward and Wells decided to break it. 'So, sir, you talk to dead people.'

Hunt skimmed them an irritable look. 'I talk to the spirits of dead people. There's a difference.'

'I've been wanting to ask about that,' said Jack. 'Why can't you get these spirits to tell you where Sky is? It'd save a lot of time.'

Hunt sighed heavily, hands bunched into fists at his sides. 'Let's get all the talking-to-ghosts bullshit out of the way first, shall we? Then maybe we can have a near decent conversation.' He folded his arms and for the first time looked Jack in the eye. 'My guides, and the souls who take the trouble to contact me, aren't there to be spiritual crime-busters or know-all oracles. And even if they did have information they probably wouldn't tell because we're in this life to learn, to progress. We shouldn't be asking them for shortcuts or easy ways out. We should be working things out for ourselves, whether it's the solution to a crime or the road out of a broken relationship. We have to work it out for ourselves.'

Wells made a face. 'But what if Sky's not dead yet and one word from above could get us to her before she is? Don't they care about saving a life, these spirits? Couldn't one of them be forced to do the right thing? We're not asking for a bloody name, mate, just a nudge in the right direction.'

'When it's your time to go there's nothing anybody can do about it.'

Wells's eyes widened. 'Not even God? Bloody hell, if the bloke in charge can't make things happen, what chance have I got?'

Hunt wiped his sweaty palms on his jogging bottoms and let out a tired sigh. 'Take the piss all you like. It's my job to give evidence of life after death, and as far as I'm concerned I do it well. I help a lot of grieving people, mend an awful lot of broken hearts, so take the piss all you like, I don't care.'

Wells glanced at Jack and gave a shrug. 'That's put me in my place.' He returned his amused gaze to the indignant man. 'OK, Mr Hunt, if we're to get zero cooperation from your friends on the other side you'd better tell us all *you* know. Now, Roy Barlow says you and Sky are as tight as this.' He held up his right hand, the index and second fingers entwined.

Hunt's laugh was clearly forced. 'You shouldn't believe a word Barlow says. That prat's got massive rejection issues and he's been taking it out on me ever since Sky told him where to go.'

'Why do you think that is?'

'Search me,' said Hunt, shrugging.

Wells undid his jacket and thrust his hands deep into his trouser pockets. 'OK, why did Sheila Reeves also point us in your direction?'

Hunt shook his head. 'Dunno. You'd better ask her.'

Wells began to pace, careful to avoid the containers of berries. 'Let's see if I've got this straight, Mr Hunt. We've so far interviewed two of your fellow travellers and both have hinted quite strongly that you and Sky Beddows are more than just friends. But for some reason they're both leading us up the wrong tree. Is that what you're saying?'

'That's about right.'

Wells twisted round to face Jack. 'Are you getting all this down, DC Turnbull? Don't forget, we need to be spot on for the court case.'

Jack held up his notebook. 'Every word, sir. My shorthand's pretty exceptional.'

Hunt's worried gaze flitted between the two men. 'Why would you want me in court? I don't know anything.'

Wells said, 'You might be an expert when it comes to ghosts and ghoulies, mate, but talk about detecting signs of guilt from body language and they don't come much better than me. You've been lying through your teeth throughout the whole of our chat. Oh, apart from when you said your old mum was the best – I dare say she probably is. Anyway, I want to get all these lies down pat for when we have you in the witness box. Don't want to balls it up, do we?'

Hunt shot them a bitter glance. 'I've got nothing to say. I'd tell you if I did.'

'Of course you would.' Wells started to pace again, tugged at the knot of his tie. 'OK, what have we got so far? You've never had anything to do with Sky Beddows. You've never even spoken to the woman.'

'I didn't say that,' Hunt muttered.

Wells lifted an eyebrow. 'What *did* you say?'

The man let out a breath. 'Look, it's not like me and Sky ignore each other. We get on all right. We have a laugh.'

'Are you giving her one?' asked Wells, grinning. 'Are you parking your Ferrari in Sky's garage?'

'Huh, I wish.'

'You do fancy her then? For a minute there I thought you might be gay.'

'Yes, I fancy her. Who wouldn't?'

'But she doesn't fancy you?'

The man peered down at himself, arms spread. 'I'm no Adonis, am I?'

Wells caught his gaze again. 'Is that why you killed her – you wanted Sky but you couldn't have her?'

Hunt snorted. 'Come on, Chief Inspector, you'll have to do better than that.'

'You wouldn't be the first bloke to be overcome by his emotions. And crimes of passion carry a lighter sentence so it's not all bad news.'

'I'm treading a spiritual path. Murder isn't on my agenda.'

'You'd be surprised how many murders are committed by decent, hard-working blokes like yourself, Mr Hunt, when their urges – sexual urges more often than not – push them that little bit too far and instinct takes over.'

'I dare say, but that's not what happened this time.'

'What did happen this time? Do tell 'cause we're dying to know.'

'So am I.'

Wells pulled at his tie again. The weather was too hot for playing silly-buggers and his patience was wearing thin. 'When was the last time you saw Sky?'

Hunt gazed up at the sparse cloud, his eyes narrowed. 'About eight o'clock on the morning she disappeared. She was having a cuppa on the steps of her van. I was taking my car in for a once-over. The brakes weren't biting as well as they should.'

'How did she seem to you?'

'Fine,' he said, shrugging. 'We chatted for a few minutes, about the kids mostly. She never mentioned anything about going off to see somebody.'

'What makes you say that?' asked Wells. 'About going off to see somebody?'

'That's what Sheila told me. She said Sky had somebody to see. But she never mentioned it to me. I expected her to be there when I got back from the garage. We'd arranged to share a bottle of wine at lunchtime. I was looking forward to it. I got the wine on the way back. It's still in my caravan.'

'Sheila Reeves was wrong then?'

'Seems like it.' He leant towards them, lowered his voice to a conspiratorial whisper. 'Sheila's not the sharpest knife in the box.'

Wells plucked a large blackberry from the bushes and chewed it thoughtfully. 'Mrs Reeves told DC Turnbull here that Sky's relied on you quite a bit since her hubby did a runner. Is she wrong about that as well?'

'Yes,' he said with a definite nod. 'That would indicate a closeness that simply wasn't there. Sky does ask for my help occasionally – they all do – because I'm handy with a hammer. But I wouldn't say she relies on me.'

Wells decided to change tack. 'Did you have much to do with the husband?'

'Not much, no, I thought he was a lout.'

'You know Sky's kids are in care?'

'Yes, Sheila told me.'

'Do you like her kids?'

'What's not to like?'

'Would you say they look on you as the father they've never had?'

Hunt gave the DCI a bewildered grin. 'I wouldn't think so. What are you getting at?'

'I'm not sure,' said Wells, frowning. 'I just can't understand why you're dead against us knowing you're flavour of the month to a gorgeous girl like Sky Beddows.'

'But it's not true,' said Hunt, exasperated.

'Why did Mrs Reeves go straight to you when the kids went missing?'

'I happened to be around at the time.'

'Are you always such an early riser?'

The man gave a derisory snort. 'Just because I don't work nine-to-five in a nice suit like yours, Chief Inspector, doesn't mean I spend all day under the sheets like some layabout. I like the early morning as it happens. I like the peace. It helps with my meditation.'

Wells gave a pinched laugh. 'Not much peace around here, though, is there? Pretty girls disappearing into thin air, young kids going missing … it's more restful at the bloody cop shop.'

'Really?' said Hunt, showing little interest. He was gingerly touching his shoulders and the back of his neck. The skin felt burnt, was extremely hot to the touch, and he silently chastised himself for not bringing a T-shirt. 'Have you nearly finished? Only I'm frying here and I'd like to get covered up.'

'Let's start walking back,' said Wells, stepping aside and motioning for Hunt to go ahead. 'DC Turnbull can bring the berries.'

While Jack hung back to juggle the various tubs, Hunt followed the path in front of Wells. His step was light, his demeanour easy. He looked like a man who'd recently negotiated a treacherous path and was thankful to be at the end of it. Along the way he showed his knowledge of all things natural by pointing out the various species of birdlife to the dedicated townie that was Paul Wells and trying to acquaint him with the multitude of wild flowers and medicinal herbs that littered the hedgerows. Wells managed a few timely grunts and the occasional, 'Oh yes?' but looked on the whole like a man distinctly out of his element.

Back at the caravans all was quiet. Even the tiny Barlow thugs had disappeared. All that could be heard was the persistent call of a wood pigeon to its mate. The tantalizing aroma of hot steak and kidney pie wafted through a nearby window and teased the DCI's nostrils.

'Hmm,' he murmured, eyes closed, 'somebody's got a nice dinner to look forward to.'

'Me, actually,' said Hunt. 'I told you my old ma was the best. You can join us if you like. She always makes way too much for the three of us.'

'Thanks for the offer, sir, but we'd better get on.'

Jack arrived then, balancing the tubs and colanders with all the skill of an artless contestant on a seventies television game show. And his thanks were heartfelt when Hunt helped to relieve him of his load.

Hunt stacked the berries beside his caravan and after an airy, 'Let us know when you hear anything,' he started up the steps.

But Wells was quick to stop him. 'Just a couple of things before you disappear....'

The man made his smile sincere as he returned to the detectives, but not before Wells caught sight of his tiny huff of irritation, the impatient roll of his eyes.

'What now?' he asked, amiably.

'You don't seem too anxious about where the beautiful Sky might be. I just wondered why that was.'

Hunt gave the detectives an incredulous look. 'Of course I'm anxious. We all are.'

'Why did nobody report her missing?' asked Wells, lifting his sunglasses from the breast pocket of his jacket. 'A lot of water's gone under the bridge since she disappeared. A hell of a lot of pain could have been inflicted.' He put the glasses on, made a show of getting them just right. 'God knows what the poor girl's been going through these last few days. I'm worried, Mr Hunt, I really am. And if you'd witnessed some of the sights we've seen over the years you'd be worried too.'

Hunt was shifting his weight from one foot to the other, his quick glances spanning the open countryside; gestures that showed he longed to be elsewhere; anywhere other than standing before the DCI where his strong feelings of guilt could so easily cause his downfall.

When Wells prepared to go on Hunt held up a hand. 'All right, all right, I get the picture.'

'Good. Why did nobody report her missing?'

Hunt took in a breath and held it, hands spread wide, his expression beseeching. On the long exhalation, he said, 'None of the others knew she was missing. Only Sheila and me. Oh, and my folks.'

'That means half your little group was aware she'd disappeared. I'll ask again: why wasn't it reported?'

Hunt sighed heavily. 'Because I thought she'd taken a shine to that Bulmer bloke up at the manor. The others thought the same. I guessed he'd probably made Sky an offer she couldn't refuse and she'd taken him up on it. He's got a lot to offer, after all. Plenty of cash. Introductions to lots of big names. That Johnny Lee Rogers for a start. He's staying at the manor apparently. How could I compete with that? How could any of us compete?'

The DCI's frown was thoughtful. 'You knew she was planning to see Bulmer that day?'

'Yes, we were all hoping he'd have some good news.'

Wells's frown deepened. 'You said earlier that Sky wasn't planning on seeing anybody. You were going to share that bottle of wine.'

Hunt swallowed loudly. 'I should have said she wasn't going anywhere *apart* from the big house to see Bulmer.' He nodded in the general direction of Stratton Manor. 'I'd have a word with him if I were you, Chief Inspector. And that singer as well – everybody knows he's a sucker for a pretty face. Sky could be with him. His "current squeeze" I think they call it in the celebrity mags.'

'Why haven't you been up there yourself if you're so certain that's where she is?'

'Can't really see the point. If that's where she wants to be, nothing I say'll ever change her mind.'

Wells said, 'Hmm,' and turned to gaze at the scorched farmland.

'Is that all, Chief Inspector? I'd really like to cover up this sunburn.'

'What?' said Wells, pretending to be preoccupied. 'Sorry, sir, I was just thinking….'

'About what?' asked Hunt, his grin apprehensive.

But Wells didn't speak immediately. He stood pondering for a moment, his fingers worrying the dark stubble around his chin. Presently he turned back to Hunt. 'I was thinking about Sky's kids,' he said.

'What about them?' asked Hunt, sweaty palms finding jogging bottoms again.

'We've had reports from the social worker and foster carer involved in their case and both have said how great the kids are, very well adjusted, bright for their ages… even my DS has fallen overboard for them, says they're fantastic, she could cuddle them to death.'

Hunt let out an impatient breath. 'I told you they were great kids. What's your point?'

'My point is that those kids are being brought up well, which means that Sky Beddows must be a good mother.'

'She is. She's a very good mother.'

Another frown marred the DCI's forehead. 'And yet you think she'd go off with that singer just because he can show her a good time? I don't think so. Good mothers don't usually put themselves first, Mr Hunt. And they don't abandon their kids on a whim.' Wells shrugged. 'So there's your theory straight down the pan.'

Hunt adopted a bored expression. 'Can I go now? My shoulders are really stinging.'

'Sorry, sir, 'course you can. And thanks for your help.'

Hunt made for the caravan, careful not to rush. It wouldn't do to exhibit signs of stress. Not at this stage in the game. He thought he'd done pretty well throughout Wells's interrogation, left him quite satisfied.

As he prepared to climb the steps Hunt turned to wave at the detectives, his face showing an open smile. And that was when Wells said, 'By the way, where did you take your car, sir?'

'Sorry?' said Hunt, smile quickly fading.

'Your car. You said the brakes were a bit sloppy. On the day of Sky's disappearance.'

'Oh yes.' Hunt put a hand to his forehead. 'It was … oh God, I can't think what the garage's called now. It's definitely in Larchborough.'

'Was it Handy's Car Repairs?' said Jack. 'That big modern place right next to the cattle market … round the corner from the railway station?'

Hunt gave a triumphant laugh. 'That's the one. Handy's Car Repairs.' And then he disappeared inside the caravan.

As they began the short walk back to the car, Jack said, 'The cattle market's nowhere near the railway station, is it, sir? And Handy's Car Repairs is about twenty miles away in Milton Keynes.'

'I want surveillance on that bloke. Get one of uniformed to keep a surreptitious watch.' Wells gave his DC a wry look. 'And let's hope his spirit guides don't tip him the wink.'

CHAPTER EIGHT

By Monday morning two thousand MISSING PERSON posters had been distributed and Sky's likeness was attached to every lamp-post, every shop window, and the walls of every public building in Larchborough and surrounding villages. Her disappearance had been highlighted on the front page of the *Larchborough Evening News*, and was being mentioned on the hour in every local radio and television news report.

DCI Wells had deliberately opted for saturation coverage because he knew that time was crucial and procrastination the enemy in an inquiry of this type.

Sky Beddows was beautiful; she would easily stand out in people's memories. But memories could be fragile and life was full of worries. If anyone had seen Sky on that fateful day then the police needed to prompt those memories now, before they were crushed beneath the thousands of careless thoughts that cluttered our minds on a daily basis.

Meanwhile Scott Beddows was proving to be a difficult man to track. They had so far ascertained that his last prison term – nine months for aggravated burglary at Her Majesty's establishment in Winson Green, Birmingham – had come to an end the previous January. That particular stretch had finished two months early due to prison overcrowding and

Beddows was let out clutching a small wad of cash with which to begin his new journey along the straight and narrow.

Luckily for Mia his early release had come with a proviso: Beddows was required to sign on every week at his local nick for the remainder of his original term. A quick phone call to the duty sergeant at Marsh Green police station revealed that Beddows had actually managed to uphold that requirement, his address at the time being a ground floor flat in the immediate area.

And that was where the trail went cold. When Mia spoke to the landlord of the flat he stated that Beddows had handed in the keys on 19 March. He was hitching to Rugby to 'kip on a mate's settee for a bit and see what's what'. Straightaway Mia put out a trace in the Rugby area and was now waiting with nail-biting frustration for the results to materialize.

The whereabouts of Sky's parents were still a mystery, along with the rest of her life prior to taking to the road. Her name wasn't in the computer system, which would prove at any other time that their quarry was an upstanding and law-abiding individual (or the possessor of too much good luck to be caught). But they were far from certain that 'Sky' was indeed her legal name, and that scepticism kept a big fat question mark hovering at the backs of their minds.

The team was in the CID office with heads down and all talk restricted to the matter in hand. Each one was genuinely fearful for Sky – her death was becoming more of a probability with each passing day – and they were pulling together as never before for the one lucky break that would smash the case into a thousand pieces. Not only was the life of a young girl at stake, but also those of two small children pining for their mother. They needed to get some sort of momentum going for their sakes too.

Mia took a sip of her lukewarm coffee and grimaced. She said, 'I'm worried the public aren't going to care about finding Sky. She's a traveller after all and they're a waste of space to most people.'

Wells was over by the window, peering down at the bustling street. 'I know what you mean, darling. What's the travelling community good for as a rule? Wherever they settle, they bring chaos. And what's left when they finally bugger off? A couple of tons of litter and a list of burglaries as long as your arm. That's the public's perception at least. And I ain't far behind them, to tell you the truth.'

There was a no-nonsense knock on the door and a young uniformed officer hurled himself into the room and thrust a slim file into Wells's hand. 'The report you wanted, sir,' was all he said before turning smoothly and gliding out of the office with hardly a pause.

Jack sniggered the moment the door closed. 'I reckon he was roller-blading, sir. Isn't that against station regulations?'

Wells said nothing, his attention wholly on the report. 'Gather round, kiddies. This is the story of Roy Barlow's "slight debacle" on Tuesday night.' He returned to his desk, made himself comfortable. 'The wine flowed freely that night – too freely. Barlow started coming on strong to Sky. Only she didn't want to know and told him so. But Barlow wouldn't listen. He started pawing her, pulling her about, and that's when things got nasty. Sky was crying. Barlow's missus was crying and trying to pull him off. Philip Hunt had kept quiet 'til then. He was in his caravan – communing with the spirits probably. But when he heard the women crying he rushed out and confronted the dastardly Barlow.'

'A bit like Batman,' said Jack.

'No, mate, nothing like Batman. Hunt wanted the girl and Batman only fancied young lads in tights. According to this, Hunt threatened to fight Barlow if he didn't back off, but that only made him worse. He was shouting about – if he couldn't have Sky then nobody would.'

'Like he told you last week,' said Nick.

Wells's nod was vigorous. 'And when Hunt asked him what he meant Barlow pointed to the girl. "She's dead", he said.'

'Christ,' said Nick. 'Bit over the top.'

'They started fighting, fists at first, but then Barlow pulled out a knife and everything changed. His missus tried to reason with him – got a nasty cut on her arm for her trouble – but it was Sky who finally got through to the bastard and made him calm it.'

'How, sir?' asked Mia.

'It doesn't say.' Wells fell silent while he read to the end of the report. And then he looked up, his expression incredulous. 'The bastard raped her.'

'Who? Barlow?'

Wells nodded. 'As good as. He got away with it an' all.'

'Who was attending?' asked Nick.

'A couple of bloody idiots by the look of it. Sky wasn't willing to press charges, but even so they should've hauled him in.'

'What exactly happened?' asked Jack.

'It was later on. The fight was forgotten, things had quietened down. Barlow was drinking with that American couple, getting nicely pissed. Sometime after midnight he decided to end it with Mr Chardonnay and was treading an unsteady path home when he saw Sky having a quick ciggie outside her van and he dragged her away from the site. The first anyone knew he'd done it was when Sky came running back to the Pantains, clothes ripped and numb with shock. Barlow turned up a few minutes later full of apologies. But when he tried to approach Sky she went berserk, couldn't be consoled, started screaming. That's when uniformed was called. But as penetration hadn't been achieved and Sky wasn't willing to take it any further, the dopey bastards thought it best to tell Barlow he was a naughty boy and leave it at that.'

Just then Mia's mobile phone started to vibrate in her jacket pocket. A surreptitious glance behind her desk told her she had a text message. It read: *Johnny Lee Rogers a no-no, I'm afraid ... but I'm a definite YES. Could we meet? Maybe go for a quick drink? Please call. Can hardly wait to hear your voice. Andrew.*

Mia read and re-read the words, her eyes unbelieving. Andrew Bulmer wanted to take her out? He could hardly wait to hear her voice? Mia frowned. It was a wind-up. It had to be. But what would he gain from it? She thought back to their chat in his office. He had seemed rather keen. Even Nick had said as much in the car.

While the DCI droned on in the background Mia surmised that a text might be better than a phone call. A text could sound confident when the sender was anything but. And he wouldn't hear the excitement in her voice, put there because he was the first decent bloke to ask her out in a long time.

Yes, she'd text him; keep it business-like in case she'd misinterpreted his motive. But when would be the best time to meet? That evening was out because she visited her mother on Mondays. Barbara Harvey had suffered a massive stroke three years ago and was now a permanent resident at St Stephen's Nursing Home. Barbara didn't actually recognize the 'nice lady' who visited every Monday, but Mia felt guilty for not going more often as it was and couldn't bring herself to cancel, even though a drink with Andrew Bulmer was an altogether more attractive prospect. Anyway she'd deliberate no longer in case she talked herself out of answering at all.

With fingers that trembled slightly Mia tapped out a reply. *Would enjoy another chat. Any new info most welcome. Tomorrow? 8pm? At Stratton Manor? Mia.*

Mia was hitting the SEND key when she sensed a hulking presence behind her right shoulder. It was Wells peering at her mobile.

'Tell me, darling, what's more interesting than listening to actual proof that one of our suspects has been threatening and physically assaulting our victim?'

'Pardon, sir?'

Before he could fully get into his rant, the phone on Wells's desk buzzed. He snatched it up, his venomous glare still fixed on Mia's mortified features. And as he listened his own expression softened with each passing moment.

'OK, keep it secure. We'll be right there.'

Three pairs of eyes were fixed on Wells as he gazed at the receiver still resting in his hand. Eventually he dropped it back in its cradle and slowly buttoned his jacket.

'Looks like we might be too late,' he said, running angry fingers through his hair. 'A body's been found … a young girl's body.'

While Roy Barlow's sadistic leanings were being systematically dissected by the CID team, the man himself was silently bemoaning the meaningless drift of his futile existence.

He was seated at the tiny dining table in his caravan, head in hands, legs bent almost double because there was no room to spread out. No room for *anything*. His painting equipment wedged out of sight in the van's only cupboard. His ambitions squashed to nothingness. His dreams….

He glanced around at the infant paraphernalia covering almost every inch of the confined space: towelling nappies – grey from overuse – piled along the window seat; potties and picture books; baby bottles and plastic dishes; miniature outfits awaiting the iron; fishing nets, coloured buckets, gaudy spades; teddies and dollies and pink bloody skipping ropes … signs of puerile fucking rubbish everywhere he looked.

How the *hell* did he get here? What was he *thinking*?

He'd left the Art Academy with so many dreams, so much ambition … so much *passion*. He was going to rock the world of portrait art; knock it off its fucking hinges. But what did he do instead? Succumbed to the first pretty girl who'd put up with him and spawned his devil brood instead.

And then there was Sky. One moment in her dazzling presence healed his battered soul. One tiny glimpse of her sent his fractured spirit soaring. Sky inspired him. Sky made him whole.

She was hurting now. He knew that. But there'd come a day when she'd see that his way was the right way, the only way. They were meant to be; their tangled love all-encompassing, all-embracing, all there was. The rest could go fuck itself.

He should be painting now, creating, flexing his artistic muscle. But he hadn't the heart. Kelly and the brats would be back soon. All hell let loose.

He needed his fix, needed it badly, before he drowned in the pool of despair that was his life. Gathering his things together swiftly Roy Barlow let himself out of the caravan and prepared to meet once more with his salvation.

'And what can I do for you, sir?'

'*You* can do nothing, Sergeant. Get me one of your senior officers. And straight away. Time's money.'

Jim Levers leant on the reception desk and regarded the man with distaste. Levers had seen his sort before: tall, silver-haired, well-dressed, smug expression. Professional type with no manners and plenty of aggression. Not a minute to breathe and no time for the little people. There were plenty like him in the legal profession.

'You a solicitor, sir?'

'That's hardly your concern,' the man said, eyeing Levers as though a dog had just done him in the gutter.

'Fair enough,' said the sergeant, pulling the duty roster towards him with deliberate slowness. He made a show of searching the pages, taking his time. And then he glanced up, eyes smiling. 'Looks like all our senior officers are unavailable at the moment, sir.'

The man tut-tutted, wiped a bead of sweat from his temple. The persistent heat did little to quell tempers at the best of times and Levers had had to deal with quite a number of scurrilous individuals that summer. This man, though, he'd be touchy in a snow storm. Here was a man used to getting his own way – quickly, because time was money – and the alternative wouldn't be considered.

'Surely there's somebody?'

'No, sir, just me.' Levers lifted a mug from behind the desk and took a long drink. Replacing it, he said, 'What can I do for you, sir?'

The man let out an irritable breath, was considering leaving, his cold blue eyes flicking towards the double doors. Instead, depositing his slim-line briefcase on the desk, he said, 'All right, I've come to report a theft. My car's been broken into and a number of items are missing.'

'Oh dear,' said Levers, selecting a form from the pile at his elbow. 'Let's get some details down, shall we? Name, sir?'

'Mandley. Robert Mandley.'

'Of course,' said Levers, hitting his forehead with the heel of his hand. 'You're the bloke who got Sir Nigel Stratton off that money-laundering charge.'

'There was no charge to answer,' Mandley said, nostrils quivering with annoyance. 'The case was thrown out of court, as you well remember.'

'Oh, you're clever, sir … ran rings around the prosecution.'

'Just doing my job.'

'You are a solicitor then.'

'A defence lawyer, Sergeant.'

'Same difference,' said Levers, returning his attention to the form. 'Address?'

'The Old Rectory, Stratton Heights.'

'Very nice too,' said Levers, eyebrows raised. 'Fruits of your labours, eh, sir?'

But the man's attention was elsewhere. A uniformed officer had emerged from the bowels of the building and was pinning a poster to the large noticeboard next to the double doors. Robert Mandley edged slowly towards the poster, studied it closely, all aggression spent.

Sky's laughing face blown up to eighteen inches by fifteen.

Have You Seen This Woman?

'But that's … that's her,' said Mandley, shock whitening his complexion to match the silver hair. 'That's my daughter.'

Lizzie Thornton wasn't happy. Top to toe in black, hair piled on her head like a ragged halo, she resembled a Sicilian widow after a mobster's bullet had taken her man.

'Going to a funeral?' Ruth had asked first thing.

Lizzie hadn't replied. In fact Ruth had hardly got two words out of her all morning. Just as well though; work had been steady with no time to chat.

It was lunchtime and the library was empty apart from a couple of students busy on the Internet. Ruth and Lizzie were eating their sandwiches over by the large-print biographies, one eye on the desk.

'I wonder why Cathy hasn't phoned in,' said Ruth. 'Do you suppose she's all right?'

Lizzie raised a listless shoulder. 'Too busy wrestling under the sheets with Johnny Lee Rogers to think about work.'

'Lizzie!' said Ruth, horrified.

Ruth stole a glance at her colleague. Lizzie was hardly touching her lunch and that was so unlike her. 'Voracious' was the word to describe Lizzie's appetite as a rule. Voracious … or hoggish.

They'd worked together for over twenty years and Ruth still knew little about Lizzie Thornton. She shared a home with an elderly aunt. Had no friends. No hobbies as such. Not even a dog to take for walks. An empty life dragging on towards a lonely death.

The fact that Lizzie had feelings for a promiscuous rogue like Johnny Lee Rogers had come as quite a shock to Ruth. Still, everyone had their secrets, little fancies that went against the grain. Ruth was partial to the raunchy novels of Jackie Collins, but she'd never admit to it; buying the forbidden fruits from Waterstones during her regular jaunts to Milton Keynes rather than borrowing them from the library which would make more sense.

To push the conversation along as much as anything, Ruth said, 'How was he then … your Johnny Lee Rogers? Live up to expectations, did he?'

'The man was a complete animal,' Lizzie rasped, picking at the crust of her sandwich and crumbling it into her lunchbox. 'Pawing me constantly. Begging me to be his. The bodyguards had to pull him off in the end, Ruth. It was all so *undignified*.'

'And what did Cathy think?'

'Of course I knew there'd be a connection between us,' said Lizzie, ignoring the question now she'd got into her stride. 'I'd sensed it quite keenly. And I was looking forward to a future with Johnny Lee, I really was.'

'But?' said Ruth, trying hard not to smile.

Lizzie put her lunchbox to one side, laid a hand on Ruth's shoulder and leant closer. 'I couldn't have put up with the sex. The man would have been at me all the time. I'd have had no peace.' She gave Ruth a knowing look. 'No woman would want that.'

'And Cathy?'

'She was so jealous,' Lizzie gushed. 'Turned up half naked … breasts on show … bare legs … and all for nothing because he wanted me.' She grinned widely, the sudden movement dislodging her dentures.

'Did she sing for him?' asked Ruth, thoroughly enjoying the bitchy turn their chat was taking. She'd never liked the brazen Cathy. Bare legs indeed.

Lizzie sniggered. 'Fingernails down the blackboard, you mean … as Simon Cowell supposedly said?'

'Exactly,' said Ruth, almost choking on her peach.

'Quite probably,' said Lizzie, with a sudden catch in her voice. 'After sundown.'

'Sorry?'

'Oh, nothing.'

'You won't be going to the meal on Wednesday then?'

Lizzie shot her a surprised look. 'Of course. Why shouldn't I go? I won the competition. I've every right to be there.'

'I just thought….'

'Well, think again, Ruth. Lizzie Thornton doesn't give up without a fight.'

Ruth stared at Lizzie's insipid profile, totally confused. What was there to fight *for*? Wasn't Lizzie cured of her infatuation now that the singer had shown his true lecherous colours? Not that she believed a word.

Ruth knew from Jackie's novels that the love lives of the rich and famous could get quite messy. But none of the books had so far included the character of an old and ugly, small-town librarian spinster. So she could strive as much as she liked but Lizzie was never going to win *this* particular fight.

Lizzie's expression had suddenly become maudlin and Ruth was about to ask why when she said, 'Oh well, can't sit around chatting, Ruth, best get on.' Then snapping the lid on her lunchbox she grabbed her shopping bag and lunged towards the staff entrance. 'Just powdering my nose. Won't be a minute.'

'Should I call Cathy? See what's going on?'

'Why not?'

Alone in the toilets Lizzie dabbed her face with water and stared at her reflection in the mirror. There, she'd done it. She'd finally spoken of Saturday's events. Her version, of course; a version guaranteed to steer Ruth away from the truth.

Cathy Cousins. Dirty cat. Trying to steal her man. Giving him the come-on in front of her very eyes. Johnny Lee Rogers was hers, and no one would deny Lizzie Thornton her destiny.

No one.

CHAPTER NINE

'She's been stabbed, Paul.'

'And that's the cause of death?'

'I'd put money on it. Come and have a look.'

Wells had arrived at the crime scene with Jack to find the police doctor, Donald Moore, about to get into his car, the routine job of confirming death having been completed.

They were in a small lane adjacent to Stratton Manor, the doctor's car standing approximately 200 yards north of the main gates. Opposite the gates was a sturdy hawthorn hedge about six feet in height, bordering a field of around five acres. The field had been home to a wheat crop, but the wheat had fallen victim to the summer's blistering sun and had proved to be unusable. So the farmer had cut his losses and ploughed the whole crop back into soil which now lay fallow.

Donald Moore steered the detectives towards a break in the hedge and all three trudged across the hard-baked earth – careful not to contaminate any future evidence – to where a uniformed police officer stood guarding the victim. A second man dressed in dark-blue overalls and black baseball cap was dithering a short distance away, his back towards the corpse. Further along the field stood a small orange tractor, its engine quietly idling.

Wells nodded a greeting to the uniformed officer and stared down at the naked body of a young girl, her glossy blonde hair splayed in an arc across the neat furrows. She was on her back, legs and arms lying at angles to the tanned torso.

'Christ,' Wells muttered on a long breath. Jack merely swallowed loudly.

The girl had been stabbed repeatedly in the chest and groin areas, but those wounds were not the cause of the detectives' distaste: it was the almost total annihilation of her features that had them scowling softly. That and the scores of blowflies making a meal of her torn flesh.

Moore said, 'Damage to the face was almost certainly caused after death. Not much blood around, you see. Either that or the crime took place elsewhere and the body was dumped here.'

Wells gestured towards the overalled man. 'He found her?'

A nod from the uniformed officer. 'Martin Thorpe, sir. Farm labourer. He was working in the area when he came across her.'

'Get his statement, Jack, then he can go,' said Wells. 'Poor sod needs a stiff drink by the looks of it.'

'I'll be off myself,' said the doctor. 'Things to do. 'Bye all.'

While Donald Moore gingerly negotiated the furrows back to the lane Wells delved into his jacket pocket for the snapshot of Sky Beddows. It was hard to identify the smiling face with that of the corpse, the features battered as they were. The hair was similar though; a trifle lighter than in the photograph but that meant little; hair colour could change over the years.

The body had been beautiful: highly toned and slender; designed to send male libidos into a frenzy of desire. Exactly like Sky's.

Wells put a hand in his trouser pocket and jiggled the small change found there. His fingers were fidgety and he wished, not for the first time, that he hadn't abandoned his thirty-a-day smoking habit.

His gaze took in the vast field. 'We need to secure the scene, but where does it start and where does it bloody end?'

'I've stayed as still as possible, sir, so as not to corrupt any footprints that might be about. And I cautioned Mr Thorpe to do the same.'

'You've done a good job, mate. I'll be sure to let your guv'nor know.'

'Thank you, sir.'

Jack was heading back, treading softly so as not to scuff his expensive Italian shoes. The witness, however, in a rush to get away, was bounding towards his tractor when Wells shouted, 'Mr Thorpe, leave the tractor, please, it's part of the crime scene. Collect it when we've finished. We'll let you know. OK?'

The man raised a hand and killed the engine before quickly heading for the break in the hedge.

Jack said, 'He was using the field as a short cut when he noticed the flies, sir. Thought they were on a dead fox or something.'

'He had a bloody shock then,' said Wells, staring down at the girl. 'He didn't notice any discarded clothes on his travels, anything suspicious?'

'Nothing, sir, only the body.'

'Pity.' Wells let out a heavy breath. 'OK, Jack, what do you reckon? Is it our Sky?'

'Hard to say, sir. Could be.'

Just then Wells's mobile rang out. 'Wells.'

He listened, eyes widening, lips pulled back in an excited grin. 'I don't believe it. OK, we'll be right there. Thanks, mate.' He pocketed the mobile, ran those fidgety fingers through his hair. 'You'll never guess – the old man's turned up.' Jack gave him a frown. 'Sky's dad. He's at the station.'

Jack looked gobsmacked. 'Who is he?'

'Robert Mandley. Larchborough's renowned lawyer and philanthropist.' Wells waved a hand towards the body. 'Jack, meet Rachel Mandley ... we hope.'

'That's her. That's Rachel,' said Mandley, hastily replacing the white sheet over the girl's wrecked features.

Paul Wells watched the man closely, noted the sheen of sweat glistening on his ashen face, the tremble of his hand as it brushed back the silver hair.

'You're sure, sir? I mean, the injuries…. Have another look. We need you to be very sure.'

Wells moved to pull the sheet away again but Mandley stopped him. 'It's definitely my daughter, Chief Inspector. I don't need another look.'

They were in a side room at the mortuary, the stench of formaldehyde strong in the cool air. Wells nodded his thanks to the hovering attendant and led the distraught Mandley outside into the still scorching heat.

Their cars were parked in the only spot to offer shade. Wells leant against his bonnet and surveyed the bereaved man with dismay.

'Were you aware that your daughter was the mother of two children, Mr Mandley?'

The man was about to open his driver's door, but those words caused him to spin round. 'What?'

'Nathan and Amy. Eight and four respectively.'

Mandley shook his head, unbelieving. 'I'd no idea.' He gave Wells a beseeching look. 'My wife and I hadn't heard from Rachel for nearly nine years.' The beginnings of a smile immediately altered his harsh look. 'Grandchildren? I can't take it in. The girl's four, you say?'

Wells nodded. 'And the boy's eight. They're with local foster carers at the moment.'

'We'll have them, of course,' said Mandley in a rush. 'My wife … she needs to know.'

Wells said, 'There was a falling out?'

'What?'

'Between you and your daughter.'

'You would think that,' said Mandley, lip curled. 'I worshipped my daughter. She was—' He stopped abruptly, got into his car and made to slam the door but Wells wouldn't let him.

'What happened?'

'Read the report, Chief Inspector. There was a huge search when Rachel went missing. Get your facts from the report.'

'We'll need you at the station, sir. Official identification needs to be recorded.'

'I've forgotten more about English law than you've ever learned,' Mandley huffed, yanking the door from Wells's grip. 'Don't lecture me, there's a good chap.'

The car pulled smoothly on to the road and Wells watched it disappear into the line of traffic.

'No wonder she did a runner,' he muttered.

*

Andrew Bulmer read Mia's text message and immediately panicked. Why did she want to meet *here*, for Christ's sake? She was supposed to phone. He was supposed to seduce the fat bitch over the *phone*. Now what was he to do?

Bulmer was heading back to his office from the upstairs suite. That bloody pop singer had been nothing but trouble ever since he arrived. Demanding specific meals from their superb chef and sending them back if they weren't exactly to his taste. Grumbling that the sheets weren't soft enough, the water wasn't hot enough, the air wasn't cool enough. For God's sake….

In his office Bulmer closed the door firmly and started to pace. Perhaps his text had been a mistake after all. But he'd reasoned that getting to know Mia Harvey on a personal level might be a smart move. *Jump into bed with the police and you could get away with murder*. If that wasn't an ancient proverb then it bloody well ought to be. After all if you're slap bang in the middle of a crime, where was the safest place to hide? Under the detective sergeant's duvet, of course. Who'd think of looking for the guilty party there?

Bulmer crossed to his desk and fell into the chair, repositioning his crooked diary without thinking. The office was stifling. How could he come up with a plan in this heat? There was a jug of still water on the desk, the ice cubes long since dissolved. Bulmer filled his mug and drank deeply, ran the back of his hand across his mouth. He needed to calm down. He needed to focus. He had until eight p.m. tomorrow. He needed to think fast.

Bulmer snatched his mobile from the desk and tapped out a number. But the phone at the other end was switched off. *Fuck*. He'd have to try the lodging house. Another traceable call.

'Hello?' A woman's voice.

Bulmer let out an irritable breath, his fingers making circular movements on his perspiring forehead. He had no choice. He'd have to do it.

'Could you do me a favour?' he asked, affecting a friendly tone. 'Could you give door number twelve a knock…on the first floor? I'd be so grateful.'

'Number twelve?'

'That's right. The chap's named Beddows. Scott Beddows. If he's there could you tell him I need a word … urgently?'

'He's viewed the body already?' said Mia. 'How did you wangle that, sir?'

Wells made a face. 'Procedure goes right out the window when you're "*the* most notable advocate of the town" – his words, not mine.'

Jack said, 'I'm surprised he recognized her at all the state she was in.'

'That worried me,' said Wells. 'But Mandley's adamant it was his daughter so….' He shrugged.

They were in the CID office. Wells had called his team together to discuss strategy now the body had been formally identified. The large sash windows were gaping open, allowing what little air there was to circulate. Trouble was that same air brought with it sounds of a busy high street – traffic noise; voices made fractious by the heat; loud music drifting from shops whose doors and windows were also propped open – and they were finding it difficult to hear themselves think.

Wells moved to the far corner where a large whiteboard stood. On the board was one of the MISSING PERSON posters showing Sky's smiling face. Taking the top off a black marker pen he started to write.

SKY BEDDOWS = RACHEL MANDLEY.

'For the purpose of the investigation I suggest we carry on calling her Sky. Anybody disagree?' Nobody did. Wells turned to Mia. 'What was Sky wearing when she disappeared?'

Mia simply stared back, shrugging her shoulders. 'I don't know, sir?'

Wells frowned. 'What do you mean you don't know? You were bloody quick to rush off – *against my orders* – and quiz Sheila Reeves. Didn't you think to ask what she was wearing, one of the first things you're taught in police training?'

That look was on his face again and Mia's stomach lurched. What could she say? She hadn't asked, simple as that. Dare she point out that Wells had interviewed Roy Barlow *and* Philip Hunt? Had he thought to ask them?

'I'll find out, sir,' was her lame reply.

'You'd better make it your first job,' he scowled. 'Uniformed are about to search the area. It'd help if they knew what they were looking for, don't you think?'

'Yes, sir.'

Wells wrote VICTIM STABBED on the whiteboard. 'The post-mortem's already underway so we'll soon know what sort of knife was used in the attack. Also what was used to batter the face, hopefully.'

Wells's phone buzzed and Nick rushed to answer it. 'DI Ford … OK … yes, thanks.' He replaced the receiver. 'They're having a job to find the file on Rachel Mandley's disappearance, sir. They just wanted you to know they're on it and you'll get it asap.'

Wells nodded. 'Mandley told me he and his missus had heard nothing from Sky for nearly nine years which means she was probably up the duff when she did a runner. Was that the reason she disappeared? Or was it something else altogether? Mandley wouldn't go into details so I'm hoping the case notes might throw some light on it.'

'It's good that the kids have got rich grandparents to look after them,' said Mia. 'I know it's not the same as having their mum, but it'll be better than foster care.'

'Probably,' said Wells with a grimace. 'I was with Mandley for ... what? Twenty minutes? That was twenty minutes too long, believe me. I wouldn't want to live with him.' He brightened. 'Talking of kids – how's the missus, Jack?'

'Still pregnant,' said the sullen DC.

Just then the monotonous strains of hip hop music drifted through the windows, the base tone so loud its vibrations caused everything on their desks to judder and move.

'Bloody hell,' muttered Wells. He lurched towards the windows and jerked them shut, but not before yelling another expletive towards two young men in an open-top sports car waiting at the lights. 'Who needs oxygen anyway?' he said, returning to the whiteboard. 'OK, we've got a dead girl. Who do we drag in?'

'Roy Barlow,' said Jack.

'Absolutely.' Wells wrote the name under his SUSPECTS heading. 'I'd give Barlow good odds if I was a betting man. Right, who else?'

There was a sharp rap on the door and Wells muttered, 'Peaceful here, ain't it?' as Duty Sergeant Jim Levers entered the office.

'Sorry to disturb, Paul, only we've just had a couple in. The daughter's been missing since Saturday night. They've given us a photo and I thought you'd better take a look at it.'

Wells took the framed portrait from Levers, said a gentle 'Fuck', and handed it to Jack, who stared at it, open-mouthed.

'God,' he said, 'she could be Sky's sister. Same hair, same gorgeous body....'

'More to the point,' said Wells, taking the photo back, 'she could be our dead girl.'

'That's why I thought you'd better see it,' said Levers.

'You did good, Jim. What's her name?'

'Cathy Cousins. Twenty-three. Works at the local library.'

'What was she wearing when last seen?' Wells asked, his brittle gaze directed at Mia.

Levers took a sheet of foolscap from his trouser pocket and studied it for a brief moment. 'Not much as it happens. Yellow T-shirt with one of them straps that goes round the neck—'

'Halter-neck,' said Mia, trying to be helpful.

'That's it,' said Levers. 'And let's see … a black mini skirt, black high-heeled sandals, and black lace knickers.'

Wells was writing it all down in a shorthand notebook. 'Thanks, mate. Keep us informed.'

As Levers quietly closed the door Wells lifted his telephone receiver. He said to Nick, 'Who's the quack doing the PM?'

'John Lloyd, sir.'

Wells punched out a number and waited. 'Hello? Yes… DCI Wells here, Larchborough CID. Listen, John Lloyd's doing a PM for us right now and it's important we get the victim's blood type, dental match—' He took the receiver from his ear and glared at it. Listening again, his tone chilly, he said, 'I wouldn't dream of teaching your grandmother how to suck eggs … just give Lloyd the bloody message.' The receiver was slammed down. 'Tosser.'

No one spoke while Wells stomped back to the whiteboard, his gaunt features made longer by a scowl. 'OK, until we're told otherwise that's still Sky's body on the slab. So let's bring in Roy Barlow. And we keep the murder under wraps for now.' His thin mouth showed the start of a smile. 'When you're fishing for clues, kiddies, it's best to let the worm wriggle a bit.'

CHAPTER TEN

Next morning Jack had the CID room to himself and that suited him just fine. He felt fired up, raring to go. He'd actually looked forward to coming in today and that was a definite first.

He found himself relishing the challenge of partnering Paul Wells. When the DCI had first dropped that particular bombshell Jack had felt his world falling in on him, but it was working out all right.

He'd been paired with Mia for a long time and he'd enjoyed it. But he saw now that he'd merely been an appendage, a buffer to bounce her ideas off while his own were dismissed, more often than not, without a second thought. Wells listened to his theories though, made him feel worthwhile. It was a nice change.

He was even looking forward to the baby now. Michelle had come home last night with a load of bumf about the building society's maternity policies and they were pretty generous to say the least. All thoughts of eating bread and cheese by the light of a solitary candle were now banished to the hinterland of his mind. They were going to be OK. All three of them.

This newfound enthusiasm for the job brought with it an eagerness to prove to the DCI that he was sergeant material. DS Jack Turnbull. Yes, that sounded pretty good.

First though he needed to get some results; and not in a half-baked way like Mia. Jack allowed himself a smile as he thought back to last night. Wells had been going on again about Mia's failure to get a list of Sky's clothing. But that small rumble of discontent was nothing compared to the explosion following her admission that she hadn't thought to take a mobile number for Sheila Reeves.

Mia was at the caravan site now, getting the relevant information. With Nick carrying on where Wells left off no doubt. Wells had gone to the mortuary to ascertain the true identity of their corpse. And to lambast the assistant who'd been rude on the phone probably.

Roy Barlow was languishing in the cells. He'd been hauled in last night, so drunk he could hardly stand, and Wells had thought a night staring bleary-eyed at four graffiti-stained walls might help to focus his mind. Jack was to sit in on Barlow's interview as soon as Wells got back and he was looking forward to it. In the meantime he wanted to gather together as many details relevant to the case as he could muster.

He'd already discovered that Sky's car had been found dumped on waste ground approximately two miles away from Stratton Manor – a little under one mile from the caravan site – and he'd immediately instructed forensics to give the vehicle a good going over.

He'd put in a call to the constable tailing Philip Hunt, only to be told that nothing untoward had been spotted so far. The constable would of course ring back should circumstances change.

And he'd contacted the Jobcentre in Rugby to ask whether Scott Beddows had been in looking for work. It was a long shot, he knew, but Beddows would have to show a willingness to find some sort of employment if he were to pocket the Jobseeker's Allowance. The helpful clerk had revealed that Beddows wasn't among their list of new clientele, but said she'd search through their back files for the past four months and ring back.

Jack was pouring himself a much-needed coffee when his telephone buzzed. He grabbed the receiver. 'DC Turnbull.'

It was the girl from the Jobcentre. She'd located Scott Beddows. Yes, they had found him employment and, yes, he'd taken the job. She gave Jack all details of the firm; even the name of the bloke in charge of human resources. He couldn't thank her enough and told her so, only without his usual smatterings of *double entendre*. He had a pregnant wife to consider now.

Jack was feeling pretty pleased with himself. He sat savouring his coffee and staring at the sheet of paper. Plexis Chemical Appliances. Based in Corby. Well, that was local enough. Twenty minutes away in a car.

Jack dialled the number and asked to be put through to their HR department. Not a bad morning's work. The DCI should be well pleased.

'Hello? Mr Dangerfield? Oh good … DC Turnbull here, Larchborough CID. I'm hoping you'll be able to help us with our enquiries….'

An hour later Paul Wells had returned from the mortuary and was studying the whiteboard on to which Jack's findings had been neatly added.

'Nice to know somebody's on the ball,' he said.

'There's more, sir.' Jack consulted his notebook. 'Plexis Chemical Appliances is a small local firm that supplies mobile toilets to all kinds of events. And they're currently involved with the Johnny Lee Rogers concerts at Stratton Manor.' Jack was expecting a display of unparalleled delight but Wells merely nodded. 'And guess what, sir…Scott Beddows was one of the team erecting the toilets. How about that?' Jack tossed his notebook on to the desk and sat back. 'The net's closing in. Beddows killed Sky for whatever reason and dumped her body in that field. I'd bet you anything.'

'I wouldn't if I were you: the body's not Sky's.' Wells lifted a shoulder, his face glum, and headed for the coffee percolator. 'John Lloyd's adamant. He checked and double-checked.'

'It's the other girl? Cathy Cousins?'

'It bloody better be,' Wells muttered. 'Lloyd's sent for the dental records. We'll know more this afternoon.'

'Robert Mandley was wrong then.'

'Obviously.' Wells lifted the percolator, queried if Jack wanted a cup but he declined.

Jack sat puzzling. 'Why would Mandley lie, sir?'

'Who said he lied?' Wells took the coffee mug and slumped in his chair. 'Mandley hadn't seen his daughter for years. People change. He made a mistake, that's all.'

'So what do we do about Scott Beddows?'

'Did you get his address?'

'Yes, he's got a bedsit in Corby.'

'We'll get uniformed to drag the lad in, see what he's got to say for himself.'

'What about Roy Barlow, sir? He's still in the cells.'

'This changes nothing as far as Barlow's concerned. Sky's still missing and he's still our number one contender.'

Jack brightened. 'So we'll go ahead with the interview?'

'Oh yes.' Wells took off his jacket and hooked it over the back of his chair. 'Forensics are going over Sky's car you said?'

'Yes, sir.'

'We'll fingerprint everybody at the site and see what comes of it.' Wells drained his coffee and glanced at his watch. 'Nearly twelve … where's Nick and Forgetful Sal? They been back yet?'

'No, sir.'

'Jesus,' Wells huffed. 'A bloody snail'd get the job done quicker.'

'Shall I give them a ring?'

Wells nodded. 'Tell them to get their arses back here. They'll be interviewing Barlow.'

Jack pouted. 'But I thought we were, sir.'

'Can't. Mandley's collecting his grandkids in less than an hour and I want us to be there.' He made a face. 'We can give him the good news at the same time.'

'What a fucking waste of a morning,' said Nick, flicking away his cigarette butt and getting into the car.

Mia gazed out of the passenger side window, decidedly down in the mouth. 'You think?'

'We should have been back ages ago.' Nick skimmed her a look as he fired the engine. 'You're in for another bollocking.'

'I've made your day then.'

Nick shrugged. 'Just trying to make conversation.'

'Well, don't.'

They were heading back to the station, Mia's sense of despondency growing by the second. It had been a bad few hours and she'd felt at a disadvantage from the start. Not only had DCI Wells made it painfully obvious that she was a total waste of space, but she also had a grumpy DI to contend with. Nick was far from happy with his 'baby-sitting duties', as he put it, when there were more important tasks to perform, so she hadn't expected much cooperation from him. And she'd been right.

Sheila Reeves had been hugely disagreeable from the off, refusing to answer questions and hurling abuse at the beleaguered DS. Nick had merely stood by, arms folded, a wicked smirk on his face. Mia did eventually manage to prise the required information from the fortune teller, but only after threatening her with an obstruction charge.

And it was then that things got messy. Throughout Mia's clash with Mrs Reeves, Kelly Barlow had been ensconced inside with her family of hoodlums. When she spied the detectives returning to Nick's car, however, Kelly had sped down the caravan steps and launched herself at Mia, demanding to know the whereabouts of her husband.

After much coaxing Mia managed to calm the girl, with an amused Nick looking on. And it was then, back in the caravan while the children were creating havoc outside and Mia was preparing a cup of camomile tea, that Kelly had keeled over in a dead faint.

Mia briskly manoeuvred her into the recovery position while Nick dialled the emergency services. The ambulance was hardly prompt and Nick – an anxious frown now replacing his childish amusement – had taken to checking his watch at intervals. Once there the paramedics wasted little time and an ashen Kelly was soon sitting at the tiny table, gratefully sipping the tea.

'Missed any periods, love?' one of the paramedics asked.

In answer Kelly burst into tears, nodding wretchedly. 'Two,' she managed to get out.

So Kelly Barlow was pregnant again. Mia had inwardly cringed. Four children under the age of six. How could any woman cope with that? Especially in a caravan, when the father was a psychotic prat like Roy Barlow.

When the paramedics took their leave Nick had been desperate to go, but Mia was adamant they should stay with Kelly until she'd settled down. So it was nearly half eleven when they finally got to Nick's car.

The atmosphere on the drive back was heavy with recrimination. Mia thought Nick should have been more supportive instead of sniping her constantly, while he was blaming her for the wasted hours and the dressing down from Wells that was sure to follow.

Both were silent as the scorched countryside sped past their open windows. And then a yell tore through the air. They immediately looked to where a large number of uniformed officers were slowly poring over an area of ploughed field in the distance.

Mia said, 'That must be where the body was dumped.'

'Looks like they've found something,' said Nick, taking a sharp right. 'Let's have a look.'

They parked behind a row of police vans and made for the uniformed sergeant reclining in the passenger seat of the nearest, its door hanging open. He was logging the contents of various evidence bags in a hard-backed ledger, the bags in a heap on his lap.

Nick said, 'Hi, Dave, what have we got?'

'Nothing much, pal.' The sergeant lifted a few of the bags. 'Half an earring, severely tarnished, so it's probably been here a long time. A few buttons, a bra strap, a pair of prescription glasses … national health. Nothing that's gonna set the case on fire.'

'We heard a shout,' said Mia. 'We thought you'd found something relevant.'

'That was Tony. Don't know what it is yet. I'm waiting to be amazed.'

And then Mia's mobile buzzed. It was Jack. 'Where are you?'

'At the crime scene. Why?'

'You're needed back at base. Wells wants you to interview Barlow, like, now.'

Mia tut-tutted. 'OK, keep your carroty hair on.'

'He's in a mood, so you'd better be prepared.'

But Mia didn't answer immediately. She was looking to where a uniformed officer was hurling himself through the gap in the hedge. In front of him, on the end of a thin tree branch, was a small yellow garment.

'Struck gold, sarge,' said the officer, grinning. 'Yellow T-shirt. Will that do you?'

'Halter-neck,' murmured Mia.

'That'll do nicely,' said the sergeant.

'Oh shit,' said Mia.

CHAPTER ELEVEN

'The missus isn't with you?'

Robert Mandley gave Wells a truculent look. 'Your powers of observation never cease to amaze me.'

'Just thought she would be,' said Wells. 'Important moment, meeting your grandkids for the first time.'

'Things to do at home. She's getting their rooms ready.'

'Oh, right.'

They were approaching the foster mother's house along a short pathway bounded by deep flower beds in which ragged marigolds were putting on a brave show. The earth around them was damp and a child's purple watering-can stood on the first of two steps leading to the white double-glazed door. Jack was waiting in Wells's car at the kerb, the mortuary their next stop. Mandley's car stood behind it.

The lawyer reached up to press the doorbell, but Wells stayed his hand. 'Before we go in, sir, there's something you need to know.'

Mandley huffed and turned to him, his face expectant. 'Well?'

'The dead girl ... she's not your daughter.'

Mandley made no reply for a while, simply stood rigid on the step. 'This changes nothing,' were the words he finally uttered as his finger found the doorbell.

'Knew you'd be pleased,' said Wells.

The door opened on to a large homely hallway and the warm maternal smile of the foster mother.

'Mrs Harrison,' said Wells, thrusting forward his warrant card. 'This is the kids' grandfather, Robert Mandley. You're expecting us, I believe.'

'Oh yes, come in,' she said, pulling wide the door. 'It's all been a bit of a rush. Things don't usually move this fast.'

Wells gave a wry smile. 'Mr Mandley's a famous lawyer. Normal procedure doesn't apply to him.'

They followed her across the hall and into a large living-room. Nathan was sitting straight-backed in an armchair, the puppy on his lap. Amy was on the sofa, legs tucked beneath her, colouring in a picture she'd drawn on a large sheet of paper.

Mrs Harrison motioned for the men to sit, and said, 'Look who's here, children. It's your granddad. Say hello.'

They didn't. Both simply stared at the strange man who'd made himself comfortable on the opposite end of the sofa to Amy, his smile sitting slightly awkward on the stern features, but genuine enough as far as Wells could tell.

Mandley was watching the girl, taking in every sweet detail. 'You must be Amy,' he said. 'You're even prettier than I'd imagined.' He was keeping his distance, taking it slowly, waiting for her to come to him.

And she did. Uncurling her legs she edged hesitantly along the sofa, holding out the picture for him to see. 'This is for you,' she said in a small voice.

'For me?' Mandley took the picture. 'Why, it's beautiful. Did you do this?'

'Yes,' she said, shyly. 'Is it good?'

'It's brilliant.' He looked at her and frowned. 'You didn't really draw this all by yourself...?'

With a quick glance at the foster mother Amy jumped off the sofa and stood by her grandfather, one small hand on his knee. 'Yes, I did.' She started pointing to the matchstick figures in the picture. 'Look, there's me and Nathan. And there's you....'

'Who's this?' asked Mandley, motioning towards the fourth figure.

'That's my mummy.' Amy paused, suddenly serious. 'Are you really her daddy?'

'I am,' said Mandley, his eyes showing delight in the lovely little girl. 'And I'm your granddaddy. Aren't I lucky?'

'My mummy's gone away for a bit but she'll be back soon.'

The words were spoken bravely but her voice held a tiny quiver that alerted Mrs Harrison to the tears even now forming in the girl's huge eyes. She was swift to intervene.

'Amy, why don't you introduce Nathan to his granddad?'

The tears were forgotten now that she had a mission and Amy skipped across to the boy's chair and said with high excitement. 'This is Nathan. He's my brother. He's older than me.'

'Pleased to meet you, Nathan.'

The boy was fondling the puppy. When Mandley extended a hand he ignored it and muttered a grudging 'Hello' before returning his attention to the dog.

He'd been told the man was their grandfather. But what if he wasn't? What if Mrs Harrison was just fed up with looking after them and wanted rid? Nathan had decided before the man arrived that he'd go along with their plans but keep his own counsel until their mother returned. And he saw no reason now to change his mind, even though his sister appeared to be already smitten. He'd really miss the dog though.

DCI Wells studied the boy. So, he wasn't partial to Mandley either. Very astute for an eight year old. Not for the first time Wells wondered why Mrs Mandley hadn't shown her face. Surely she'd want to be there. Was the great Robert

Mandley so controlling that his own missus had to fall in with his wishes? If so, what chance would two small kids have in his clutches?

Still, that wasn't his worry. He had problems enough with their mother. The body wasn't hers so she was still out there somewhere, alive and suffering, or dead and beyond pain. And he wasn't going to find out which sitting there in Mrs Harrison's cosy living room.

'I'll be off then,' he said, getting to his feet. 'We'll call you, Mr Mandley, as soon as there's any news.'

He said his goodbyes and made to go, surprised to find the man hot on his heels. In the hallway Mandley pulled the door to and said in a lowered voice, 'There's still the small matter of those items stolen from my car, Chief Inspector. I expect something to be done, you know.'

'Then you'd better get on to uniformed,' said Wells, heading for the front door. 'My team hasn't time to spend on paltry little thefts. Not even for the likes of you.'

In the car, Jack said, 'How'd it go, sir?'

'It went,' said Wells, buckling up.

'I spoke to Mia, sir. She was at the crime scene. They've found a yellow T-shirt matching the one Cathy Cousins was wearing.'

'Good.' He started the engine. 'They'll be grilling Barlow, I hope?'

'Should be doing that now.'

Wells pulled away from the kerb.

'We going to the mortuary, sir?'

'Yes, mate, the preliminary report should be ready. John Lloyd's already told me he found semen in the girl's vagina and no signs of a struggle, meaning she agreed to the sex. So now we need to find out who Cathy Cousins was shagging on Saturday night.'

Cathy's mother was also eager to retrace her daughter's steps on that fateful day; a quest which brought her to Larchborough's main library and Lizzie Thornton.

Susan Cousins was an attractive forty-five year old, but a night without sleep was already blighting her pleasing features, and she walked with the slow inertia of a broken soul.

The library was busy that morning, the two queues at the desk quite substantial, and Ruth and Lizzy were working in wordless monotony. But the moment Ruth caught sight of Mrs Cousins she abandoned her customer and rushed to the woman's side, leading her gently towards the nearest chair and pledging to bring her a cup of strong tea in the quickest time possible.

So Lizzie was left with her worst nightmare seated mere feet away. Straight away her pulse started to race, a pink sheen covering her usually pallid complexion. Ever since Cathy's disappearance was made public knowledge Lizzie had dreaded any meetings with her family. She'd wanted the girl gone from the moment Johnny Lee's eyes had locked on to her lascivious body. And now she was. But what was Lizzie to do next?

In no time at all she found herself stamping the last of the books to be taken out. There was nothing else for it; she would have to confront Cathy's poor mother.

'Mrs Cousins, how are you?' Lizzie asked, sweeping around the edge of the desk and falling to her knees at the woman's side.

She shrugged, her eyes bright with unshed tears. 'I've come to ask … have you any idea where Cathy might be?'

Lizzie gave a sigh, her face etched with concern. 'I haven't. I'm so sorry.'

'But she was with you at the rehearsal. Did she say anything, give any clues where she might be going?'

Lizzie's thoughts raced. She had to be extremely careful. Any mention of Johnny Lee might get him into trouble with the police and quash all hopes she had for a December wedding. Besides, there was the meal to look forward to at the Fox and Hounds tomorrow night. Nothing must spoil her plans now.

Lizzie tried a reassuring smile. 'She's probably off enjoying herself somewhere. Youngsters today, eh? – thinking only of themselves.'

'That's more or less what the police implied,' said Mrs Cousins, rummaging in her handbag for a tissue. 'Just because Cathy's pretty and likes to show off her figure they think she's a slut, I'm sure they do.'

Lizzie thought back to Cathy's state of undress that afternoon and decided that the word 'slut' fitted the picture admirably.

'There was a boy at the rehearsal. A photographer. He was really keen on Cathy, and she seemed to like him. Rick, I think his name was. Or Mick.'

Mrs Cousins suddenly brightened. 'Do you know who he works for?'

'I don't, I'm afraid. Of course, if I'd known it would end like this I'd have taken more notice.'

Ruth came back with the tea, but Mrs Cousins eyed it with distaste and Ruth set it upon a nearby table beside a display of family sagas.

'How are you bearing up?' she asked.

'Miss Thornton's just been telling me about a photographer Cathy liked at the rehearsal,' said Mrs Cousins, hope loud in her voice. 'I think it might be worth mentioning to the police.'

'Really?' Ruth frowned at Lizzie. 'You never told me.'

'Why should I?' said Lizzie, rather too sharply. 'Anyway I've only just remembered. And if it'll help the investigation then I'm glad I did.'

'Cathy thinks such a lot of you,' Mrs Cousins told Lizzie. 'She sees you as a sort of role model.'

'Don't we all,' said Ruth.

Lizzie caught the mockery in her tone and said, 'Somebody at the desk, Ruth. Would you mind…?'

While Ruth went to serve, Lizzie straightened up and wrapped an arm around the woman's trembling shoulders. 'Now you're not to worry. I'm sure there's a perfectly innocent explanation for all this. Cathy's more than capable of looking after herself. She's probably got herself tangled up with that photographer and lost all sense of time.'

'I hope you're right.' Mrs Cousins got to her feet. 'Rick, you said … the photographer.'

Lizzie nodded. 'Or Mick.'

Relief flooded over Lizzie as she watched the wretched woman drag herself through the library doors. That wasn't too bad. Could have been worse.

At the now empty desk Ruth said, 'Why didn't you tell her Cathy spent the night with Johnny Lee Rogers?'

'Because she didn't,' Lizzie said, glaring at her.

'But you said she did.'

'I did not.'

'You did.'

'Ruth,' said Lizzie, with the look of one trying to get through to a child, 'would a man like Johnny Lee want anything to do with Cathy Cousins? Oh come on.'

Ruth snorted. 'You gave the impression he was sex mad.'

'With the right woman, yes. With *me*, Ruth, but not with a girl like Cathy.'

'I think you should tell the police,' said Ruth, gathering up a pile of books that had just been returned. 'It's a known fact that the first few days in a missing person case are crucial. They'll want all the information they can get.'

She strode off to slot the books into their rightful places, unaware that Lizzie was silently admonishing herself for sharing details of Cathy's night-time tryst with Johnny Lee. How could she have been so stupid as to put her man into such a precarious position?

She'd better keep her mouth firmly shut from now on. And more importantly she'd better remember everything that had already been said. Good liars needed to have good memories.

And what about Ruth? Would she keep her mouth shut?

Lizzie's narrowed gaze followed her across to the Asian section and that knot of tension in her stomach suddenly unravelled. Lizzie smiled. Ruth Findlay had better watch her step. Nothing must be allowed to spoil her future plans with the wonderful Johnny Lee.

'He's gone? What do you mean, he's bloody gone?'

'He was given a caution and released at about eleven o'clock this morning, sir.'

Paul Wells hurled his car keys on to his desk with such force that they bounced off and slid towards the dusty corners of CID with all the grace of a pebble skimming the surface of a placid lake.

He'd arrived back at the office to find Nick and Mia huddled at their desks when they should have been downstairs wringing the truth out of Roy Barlow. And Nick was left to stutter out an explanation because Mia had suddenly found that her in-tray was stacked with papers needing her immediate attention.

Jack promptly retrieved the keys; then he poured Wells a coffee and scuttled back to his desk, glad for once that it stood in the furthest corner.

'Which stupid bastard let him go?' Wells spluttered.

'A new bloke,' said Nick. 'They've had a busy morning. You'd signed him in as drunk and disorderly and by the time they needed his cell Barlow was sober so this new bloke let him go. He was playing it by the book, sir.'

'I suppose,' said Wells, sinking into his chair with an irritable sigh. He'd slipped up there. He should have made it plain that Barlow was to be interrogated when the booze had worn off. God bless all new recruits – the tossers. 'So what have you two been doing to fill the time?'

Nick handed Wells a dog-eared buff folder. 'That's the file from when Rachel Mandley went missing, sir. And as we're now more or less sure the dead girl's Cathy Cousins we've been on to uniformed for all the info they got from her parents.'

Wells took a sip of coffee, his eyes fixed on Mia. 'You're quiet,' he said.

'Just clearing my tray, sir. Giving myself a clear run.'

'Pity you weren't so conscientious this morning. If you hadn't buggered about so long with Sheila Reeves you'd have been back well before Barlow went walkies.'

Mia was quick to relate that morning's events, embellishing the parts that highlighted her talents and playing down those that showed her in a bad light. And by the end she was trembling with suppressed rage. Why was she having to explain herself in such a way? She was a good detective; confident, too, as a rule. But Wells was making her feel like a rookie on her first day in the job.

'We would have been back sooner,' she said, refusing to be cowed, 'only when we heard the shout coming from the crime scene we thought you'd want us to get the gen.'

'True enough,' said Wells. 'And our dead girl is Cathy Cousins by the way.' He turned to Jack. 'Where's that report, mate?' Jack handed him a file and Wells spread its contents across his desk. 'John Lloyd reckons the knife that killed Cathy had a very sharp, thin blade, no shorter than six inches.'

'Not the sort of knife your average thug would carry about,' said Nick. 'Too bulky.'

'Exactly,' said Wells. 'What did you find out from uniformed?'

'There was a mock rehearsal at Stratton Manor on Saturday. Cathy went with one of her workmates, Elizabeth Thornton. The *Evening News* ran a competition, the prize being two tickets to the final concert and admission to the rehearsal. Miss Thornton won and took Cathy with her.'

Mia said, 'Uniformed are thinking she was killed outside the manor gates. They found blood spatters on the grass verge to the right of the gates and more traces leading to that break in the hedge.'

'We'll check the kitchens at the manor, see if they've got a knife missing.' Wells drained his coffee and returned to the report. 'It says here there were no signs of a struggle, no DNA under her fingernails, no defence wounds. What does that tell us? Cathy had sex some time prior to her death so, could the lover and the killer be the same man? Hopefully we'll get some clues from forensics when they've finished with the T-shirt.'

Mia said, 'That was the only significant find this morning, sir, up until we left anyway.'

'It'll do for a start, darling.'

'What was used to smash the face in?' asked Nick.

Wells shrugged. 'Lloyd found grit in the wounds, but there's nothing conclusive. I'd say the killer used a rock he found lying about. We'll get uniformed to widen the search.'

'What about time of death?' asked Mia.

'Sometime before she was found,' said Wells, with a wry look. 'You know these pathologists – don't like to make our job easier.' He pulled at the knot in his tie, unfastened the collar of his shirt. 'Stomach contents might give us a clue though. Coffee, toast, and scrambled egg. Only partly digested.'

Jack had wandered across and perched on the edge of Mia's desk. His own was too far from the action now that Wells's mood had lightened.

He said, 'A bit of nooky and a nice breakfast to finish it off.'

Wells fell back in his chair, hands behind his head. 'Now let's think … that lane leads to Stratton Heights and the motorway junction so it'd get a fair amount of traffic even on a Sunday, which means there'll be no significant tyre marks. But the murder must have taken place quite early on or the killer risked being seen by a passing car.' He paused for a moment. 'Those gates … are they electronically controlled?'

'Not sure,' said Mia. 'They were open when we went to see Bulmer. I'll check, sir.'

'Did you say Sir Nigel's abroad at the moment?'

'Yes. South of France.'

'Very nice. Who's in the house now?'

'Johnny Lee Rogers has a suite there.'

'On his own?'

'No, sir, he's got an entourage, but I don't know who they are.'

'An entourage … very rock and roll,' Wells sneered. 'What about the staff? Do they live in?'

'There're a number of cottages on the estate. They could be staff accommodation. I'll find out, sir.'

'That Bulmer bloke – where does he live?'

'Don't know,' said Mia. But she'd find out very soon, hopefully.

Wells's phone buzzed. 'DCI Wells.'

It was Jim Levers on the front desk. 'The lads have brought Scott Beddows in, Paul.'

'OK, stick him in one of the interview rooms with a coffee and we'll be down when we can.' He replaced the receiver and returned the pathologist's report to its folder. 'They've brought Scott Beddows in. Anybody got plans for tonight?'

The men gave non-committal shrugs but Mia said, 'Yes, sir, I have an appointment. I need to get away quite soon.'

'Matter of life or death is it, this appointment?'

'Well….' She didn't know what to say. She could hardly tell them she was meeting Andrew Bulmer. Wells would hit the roof. 'Suppose not, sir, no.'

'Then you won't mind cancelling it.'

'But, sir—'

Wells stopped her with a cool stare. 'There'll be no more nine-to-five 'til we've sorted these cases. Overtime'll buy a few extra romper suits, eh, Jack?'

Nick said, 'Who's going to break the news to Cathy's parents?'

'Me and Jack'll do that after we've had a go at Beddows.'

'What about us?' asked a dejected Mia.

Wells was stuffing the pathologist's report and Rachel Mandley's file into his briefcase. He glanced up. 'You'll be going to Stratton Manor for a word with that singer and his hangers-on.'

Mia's stomach gave a nauseous turn. At any other time she'd quite like to meet Johnny Lee Rogers. But not like this, having to avoid Andrew Bulmer at all costs. What if he innocently mentioned their date? Nick would have a field day.

'And corner that Bulmer bloke if you can,' Wells went on. 'Can't be much happening there he doesn't know about. Oh, and don't forget to check the knives.'

While a horrified Mia sat rigid in her chair Wells grabbed his briefcase and made for the door. Jack followed closely, wondering what the hell you did with a romper suit.

CHAPTER TWELVE

Christine Taylor's granny had a saying for everything, and most of them made no sense at all. But a certain one sprang to mind the minute Johnny Lee Rogers swept into the reception area at Larchborough's local radio station that afternoon. Oh yes, Christine now had a fairly good idea what mutton looked like when it was dressed as lamb.

The man wasn't lacking in charisma. No doubt about that. He'd entered ahead of his henchmen and made eye contact with Christine immediately. He'd used sweet talk, subjected her to his lazy smile, made her feel like she was the only girl of any worth in his world. And she'd sat behind the reception desk enthralled, soaking up the compliments as readily as a sponge in a bathtub.

But he was so old. An old man pretending to be a hip young thing. Christine thought it was so sad when a man couldn't admit he was past it.

He must have plenty of fans though. The switchboard was jammed solid throughout the phone-in. And the majority of those callers hadn't rung with a question; they'd simply wanted to declare their undying love for the man.

Christine had decided to ask for his autograph at the end of the show – she might get a fair price for it on eBay – but, as it turned out, she didn't get the chance.

When Johnny Lee came once more into reception he was a different man altogether. Now he was edgy, tight-lipped, striding through the double doors without even a goodbye.

The reason for his staggering change of mood was a text that Bob Briscoe had received from Sally Simms during the broadcast. It read: *Call me quick. Cops want to talk to Johnny.*

Briscoe had slunk out of the studio at the earliest opportunity and called Sally, who'd left him with little doubt that Johnny Lee's rapacious sexual appetite might finally have tripped him up.

In the car on the drive back to Stratton Manor, with the privacy screen raised so the driver and bodyguards would be none the wiser, Johnny Lee turned on his long-suffering manager.

'I'm gonna have to talk to the law, Bobby? What do I goddamn pay you for?'

'But, Johnny, the kid's dead. D-e-a-d – you hear me? And you're one of the last guys to see her alive. How d'you expect me to get round that? Tell me, please, 'cause I ain't got a clue, Johnny, not this time.'

'You tell them it ain't nothing to do with me. You tell them I ain't even met the kid.'

Briscoe was sweating profusely, despite the car's efficient air-conditioning system. 'No can do,' he muttered, mopping his face with a dark-blue handkerchief. 'Too many people saw you with her. And they ain't all our own. Jesus, Johnny, you got the media guys at the rehearsal, the kitchen staff, the friggin' manager…. How d'you expect me to keep them all quiet?'

'Do what you always do – pay them off. What the hell, I gotta do your thinking for you now?'

'But you ain't thinking straight.' Briscoe lifted a bottle of water from the car's refrigerated drinks cabinet and took a long pull. Wiping a fat hand across his mouth, he said, 'Best thing you can do is tell the truth. Tell the truth but keep it simple.'

'Hell, there ain't nothing complicated about it. The kid was hot and I screwed her. End of story.'

'Then that's what you tell the cops. Like I said, keep it simple.'

'Hey,' said Johnny Lee, swivelling round to face Briscoe, 'you don't think I had anything to do with the kid ending up dead?'

Briscoe tried a grin. 'Johnny ... baby ... did I say that?' He gave his boy a sideways glance. 'But we all know you can get a little ... carried away with the ladies.'

Johnny Lee stared at his manager, totally unbelieving. 'You think I killed her?'

'No,' said Briscoe, laughing.

There was silence for a moment while Briscoe finished the water, his thoughts in a tangle. Finally, hesitantly, he said, 'Did you use anything?'

'Drugs?' Johnny Lee was appalled. 'You know me better than that. You know my body's a goddamn temple.'

'Not drugs ... a condom. Did you use a condom?'

Johnny Lee ran agitated fingers through his glossy hair. 'No, the kid said she had it fixed.'

'Great. Well, ain't that just fine,' said Briscoe, angry now. 'I can pay off every goddamn clown in this shitty place, but your juice'll be all over her. How do I get round that? Tell me, Johnny – huh?'

But for once Johnny Lee's silky tongue was silent.

Silver Street Police Station was a relatively small building but the interview rooms were still a fair trek away from CID. Paul Wells walked briskly, eager to confront Scott Beddows, and Jack was having a job to match his strides.

'What do you reckon he'll be like, sir?'

Wells pulled a face. 'Cocky bleeder, I'll bet. And clever. He'll see this as a game. Best man wins. He'll be good looking and full of charm, but it'll be all talk and no substance. I've met plenty of the tossers – run rings round you if you're not careful.'

'He can't be that clever though, sir. He's done time.'

'That won't bother him. A spell in nick's just an enforced holiday to most professional villains, something to brag about.'

'Funny to think Sky went for him. With her looks and background – rich dad and all that – she could have had anybody.'

Wells shrugged. 'Maybe she fancied a bit of rough.'

Scott Beddows was in interview room number one. Wells entered, nodding to the uniformed officer guarding the door, and was pulled up sharp when his keen gaze fell on their man.

Beddows was hunched over the grimy table, an untouched mug of coffee before him. And if anyone could be the antithesis of Wells's thumbnail sketch then Beddows was that man. He was small-framed and wiry; his fine blond hair cut short, the fringe brushed forward to cover a fast-receding hairline. Small, gold-rimmed spectacles sat awry on his gaunt features, their thick lenses magnifying the apparent terror in his pale-blue eyes. Rather than appearing arrogant and self-assured, Beddows was unassuming and strangely timid, like a serial swot suddenly trapped by the school bullies with nowhere to run.

DCI Wells, struggling to cover his surprise, dropped his briefcase and pulled up a rickety chair. Jack settled beside him, eager expectancy bringing a flush to his fresh face.

Wells deliberately ignored the man, using the time instead to forage for pen and notebook in his briefcase. Then he sat back and regarded him with a stony stare.

'So you're Scott Beddows,' he said. 'You haven't touched your coffee.'

'It's got sugar in it, sir. I don't like it sweet.' His voice was high-pitched, the tone apologetic.

'Sorry about that, mate.' Wells swung round to face the uniformed officer. 'Get our friend another coffee. No sugar.'

While the officer left the room Wells considered Beddows for a long moment. 'You know why you're here?'

The man shook his head. 'I haven't been up to anything. I'm on the straight now, sir. I've got a job, a nice flat....'

Beddows uttered the words with an earnest conviction, his eyes behind the thick lenses completely without guile. Wells searched for the merest chink in his artless demeanour but found nothing. He let out a long breath. This was going to be harder than he'd anticipated.

'Your missus – Sky Beddows. Know where she is?'

'Up north, last time I saw her. Why, sir?'

'You didn't know she was here in Larchborough?'

'No, sir.'

Wells's gaze narrowed. 'You didn't know she was missing?'

Beddows frowned, searched the DCI's face as if struggling to understand the words. He swallowed, his eyes flitting between the two detectives. 'Where are the kids?'

'They're being taken care of,' said Jack.

The officer returned with the coffee. Beddows nodded his thanks.

Wells gave him an old-fashioned look. 'You didn't know?'

'How could I?'

'There're posters all over Larchborough. You'd have a job to miss them.'

'I live in Corby, sir.'

'But you've been working here. Installing chemical toilets at Stratton Manor.'

'Yes, but that was just a two-day job. I won't need to go back 'til the concerts are finished.'

Wells paused, tapped his pen on the table top. 'So the fact that your missus went AWOL around the time you were installing toilets has nothing to do with you?'

'No,' Beddows said, eyes on Wells, fingers toying with the handle of the coffee mug.

'Why did you leave your family?'

'No choice,' Beddows huffed. 'Sky found somebody else, froze me out.'

'That's not what we heard. We heard you just pissed off, couldn't handle the responsibility any more.'

'Then you'd better take their word for it.'

The man looked bereft, kept chewing on his bottom lip. He was wearing a black T-shirt with the words JESUS SAVES emblazoned across the chest in thick orange lettering.

'You a religious man?' asked Wells, motioning towards the T-shirt.

Beddows pulled at the faded material and shook his head. 'Bought it from a charity shop. Got to count the pennies.'

Wells smiled. 'Should have guessed really, given your list of previous.'

Those fervent eyes met Wells's again. 'I've done wrong, sir. I kept getting in with a bad crowd. It was a failing of mine.'

'But not now.'

'No, sir, I've had enough of gaol to last me a lifetime.'

Wells searched the man's face again for traces of deceit, the smallest hint of cunning. But again there was nothing to be found. The man seemed to be genuine. Wells was nonplussed. If Beddows was putting on an act then he was good.

Even so it was too much of a coincidence that he should be in the area when Sky went missing. And Wells didn't like coincidences; they muddied the water, made it hard to sift the truth from the fiction. His gut instinct told him that this geeky-looking bloke knew more than he was letting on. Wells simply needed to find a way of unlocking the information, discover the right buttons to press. Maybe he should start at the beginning.

'How did you meet your missus?'

'At the fair,' said Beddows, reaching for his coffee. 'I was working for Parton's Travelling Fairground at the time. We came to Larchborough for a couple of weeks, set up in that park by the Corn Exchange.' He took a tentative sip; satisfied the coffee had cooled sufficiently he drained the mug. 'I was in charge of the ghost train and Sky kept coming back for another ticket.' He grinned. 'I could tell it was me she liked and not the ride so I chatted her up and it went from there.'

'Get on well with the ladies, do you?' asked Jack. Beddows hardly looked capable of chatting up a fence post let alone a looker like Sky.

The man gave a good-natured grin. 'Not as a rule. But Sky was easy to talk to, made me feel good about myself. When I asked her out and she said yes I was like, thanks, God, I owe you one.'

'Why does she call herself Sky?' asked Wells.

Beddows shrugged. 'It's her name.'

'She told you her name was Sky?'

'Yes. Sky Samuels. Why?'

'Her real name's Rachel Mandley.'

'News to me,' said Beddows, shrugging again.

'Her father's Robert Mandley ... successful lawyer ... big name in these parts.'

'Christ,' said Beddows. 'News to me.'

Wells was perplexed. He folded his arms, regarded the man coolly. 'Did you and Sky go through a wedding ceremony?'

'Yes, sir.'

Wells raised a suspicious eyebrow. 'So you either knew her real name or she had a false birth certificate. Which is it?'

'We didn't have a proper service in a church,' he explained. 'We got hitched in a meadow – all very New Age. I gave her a posy of forget-me-nots for true love and bluebells for constancy. She liked that.'

The words tripped off his tongue with an effortless ease. Either Beddows was telling the truth or he was a bloody quick thinker. Wells chose to believe the former.

'Did Sky give you any idea of her background while you were chatting her up by the ghost train?'

The man shook his head. 'She said nothing about her dad being a big noise in the law. Said she'd ditched her folks ages ago and was dossing on a mate's floor. Said she was looking to move on.'

'With you?' said Wells, with a teasing smile.

'Why not?'

'Was Sky pregnant when you met her?'

Beddows exhaled sharply, gave a dejected nod. 'Only I didn't find out 'til we were already on the road. 'Course, I realized then why she'd been so keen to get me on board. It wasn't me she wanted, just some bloke to help with the kid.'

'How did you feel? Cheated? Angry that you'd been duped?'

'No,' he said, stretching the word out. 'It isn't every day a bloke like me gets somebody like Sky. I was grateful more than anything. And I like kids. I was looking forward to being its daddy.'

'Did she tell you who the father was?'

'No, and I didn't ask.'

'Couldn't have been easy, working at the fair with a baby in tow.'

'I got out before Nathan arrived. We bought a caravan, got in with a load of travellers, made a few bob selling hippy stuff. Still a big market for that if you know where to look.'

'You were doing all right then.'

'Good times,' said Beddows, nodding.

'And then you had Amy,' said Jack, appalled at the thought of bringing yet another child into such a haphazard environment.

Beddows grinned. 'She's great, isn't she?'

'They both are,' said Wells. 'And you just buggered off and left them.'

'I thought I'd explained,' he said, his gaze intense. 'I found myself surplus to requirements. What was I to do? Anyway, I knew the kids'd be OK. Sky's a great mum.' He sat back with a loud sigh, smoothed down his fringe, adjusted his glasses.

'This new bloke – who was he?'

Beddows started toying with the mug again, his gaze averted. 'Just some chancer we met on the road.'

'What was his name?'

'Can't remember.'

Wells let out a disbelieving snort. 'A bloke takes your family, you're thrown out on your arse, and you can't remember his name? Do me a favour.'

Beddows looked at Wells, his eyes pleading. 'I can't. Honest. I hated the bastard. I just wanted to forget.'

'So you just gave in and walked off.' Wells sat back, regarded the man with a cynical glare. 'Didn't you want to lash out? Didn't you want to hurt your missus?'

'No,' said Beddows, with a furious shake of the head. 'I'd never hurt Sky.'

'Oh but I think you did. I think you've been harbouring a grudge. I think you saw Sky at Stratton Manor and all that rage came flooding back. This was your chance. Payback time. You wanted her to suffer like you'd suffered.'

'No, sir, you've got it wrong. I don't want to hurt Sky or anybody. I'm trying to get myself together, make a better life.'

'Installing chemical toilets is a better life?'

'It's a start.'

'What do you do with the rest of your time? Can't be easy, living in a strange town, no mates ... How do you keep occupied?'

A gleam came to the man's eyes. They'd moved on, thank Christ. 'I've gone back to school. Evening classes. Learning how to be a plumber. It's good.'

'Well done, mate.'

Wells sighed inwardly. Without evidence to prove the man's involvement in Sky's disappearance they were simply pissing into the wind.

He closed his notebook. 'I think that's all for now. Thank you for your time, Mr Beddows. Don't take any holidays in the near future. We need to know where you are.'

'Who needs holidays with weather like this?'

'And Corby's so nice this time of year,' said Jack, smirking. 'Better than gaol ... a whole lot better.'

Out in the corridor Jack said, 'Bit of a surprise, wasn't he, sir?'

'Did you believe him though?'

'Hard to tell.' He tutted. 'It's the kids I feel sorry for.'

Wells laughed. 'Seeing things from a different angle now you've got your own on the way?'

'Suppose I am.'

'It gets you like that.' Wells sobered suddenly. 'Now we've got to tell Cathy's folks they'll never see their precious daughter again. Great life, ain't it, mate?'

CHAPTER THIRTEEN

'Why didn't you let me phone ahead, Nick, say we were coming?'

A sneer marred his handsome features. 'Because Bulmer's a smarmy bastard and I want to surprise him.'

'He's probably gone home by now,' said Mia, wishing to God she could be right. She was sweating profusely, her discomfort nothing at all to do with the cloying heat.

'Stop worrying, there'll be somebody to let us in.'

They were in Nick's car, negotiating the narrow lanes. As he pulled up outside the wrought-iron gates they saw that the gap in the hedge had been sealed, the field beyond empty now but still an active crime scene. Police tape also cordoned off the grass verge to the right of the gates but, surprisingly, the lane had been reopened to traffic.

Mia jumped out, searched around for means of entry. The gates wouldn't budge but there was a small black control panel to the left of them. On it was a silver button positioned beneath a grille. Mia pressed the button and waited.

A quick burst of static. 'DS Harvey to see Mr Bulmer.'

'You're early.' It was the man himself, his voice awfully loud in the quiet of their surroundings. And Nick's side window was wide open. Mia winced.

'Police business,' she said, swiftly. 'I have DI Ford with me. Would you let us in, please?'

A very surprised 'Oh' reverberated from the panel and seemed to hang in the still air. But then the gates swung slowly open and Mia returned to the car.

Nick gave her a quizzical glance. 'What did he mean, you're early?'

'How should I know?'

'You didn't phone, warn him to expect us?'

'When did I get the chance, Nick? You've kept me under heavy surveillance ever since Wells paired us up.'

'That's because you're a fucking liability. Don't think you'll get the chance to make me look bad.'

Mia snorted. 'You manage that pretty well on your own, sweetie. Now, just drive, will you?'

Nick continued to shoot her puzzled looks as he followed the meandering path to the big house. Mia was slumped in her seat, watching the passing trees with a glum expression.

Trouble was Nick Ford's eagle-eyes missed nothing. If she wasn't exceptionally careful he'd spot in a second that there was something between her and Bulmer and chances are he'd lose little time in telling the DCI. Nick had always been a blab. Then Wells could add 'unprofessional conduct' to his growing list of grievances against her.

Nick smirked. 'Hey, maybe Johnny Lee Rogers'll treat you to a quick knee jerk. He'll have anything apparently so you might be in with a chance.'

Mia was still struggling to come up with a suitable rejoinder when the car swerved into the forecourt, its circle of trees prematurely shedding their leaves, bringing a sense of disorder to the normally immaculate space. Bulmer stood beyond the circle, dwarfed by the monkey-puzzle tree. He'd changed out of his formal suit, was now casually dressed in cream slacks and a rather sexy denim shirt. Mia smiled despite the situation. At least he'd made an effort for their date.

The smile left her face, however, as she marched towards Bulmer, hoping for a few seconds alone with him. But it wasn't to be. Nick matched her strides, was first to shake the man's hand.

'Glad to find you in, sir. We'd like to ask a few questions if you wouldn't mind.'

Bulmer looked decidedly confused, and all the more so because Mia was behind Nick making wild gestures with her hands for him to say nothing about their arrangement.

He gave a rueful sigh. 'Not about the missing girl again?'

'Different case altogether,' said Nick. 'You've heard about the body found nearby?'

'Of course. A young girl, wasn't it? Terrible business.'

'Yes, sir, and she was last seen at the rehearsal you had here on Saturday.'

Bulmer's eyes widened. 'Good Lord.'

'So you can understand the importance of anything you and Mr Rogers's team might be able to tell us.'

'I'll help in any way I can,' said Bulmer, nodding briskly. 'As for our … *guests*' – he said the word with a slight sneer – 'you might have a job to get an appointment. They're rather inhospitable, I'm afraid.'

'Mr Rogers knows we're coming. I'm surprised he didn't mention it.'

Bulmer lowered his voice. 'I try to keep out of his way to be honest. He's not the easiest of men.'

Nick motioned towards the doorway. 'Shall we go to your office and do the necessaries? Then you can take us up to Mr Rogers's suite.'

The office was much as Mia remembered it; only now the lights were on, all discreetly embedded within the walls to create a subdued ambience. A silver tray on Bulmer's desk held a bottle of red wine and two crystal glasses. Very good wine, too, Mia noticed.

'Expecting somebody?' asked Nick, nodding towards the tray.

Bulmer shook his head. 'Not particularly.'

Nick gave Mia a knowing glance but her eyes were averted. She was busy positioning two straight-backed chairs in front of Bulmer's desk.

When they were all seated Nick handed the man a copy of Cathy Cousins's photograph. 'This is our dead girl, sir. Can you remember seeing her at the rehearsal on Saturday?'

Bulmer studied the photograph carefully. 'Can't say I do. But I was only there for a matter of minutes.'

'What happened after the rehearsal?' asked Mia.

'What do you mean?' said Bulmer, carefully aligning Cathy's photograph with the left side of his desk diary.

'Was there a party or did everybody go home?'

Bulmer stared into space, shook his head. 'Everybody went home as far as I know. There wasn't a party, I'm certain of that.'

Nick glanced around the room, thought it was all a bit shabby. 'Nice office you've got, Mr Bulmer.'

'It'll do,' he said, smiling.

Nick left his seat and crossed to the wall of books, hoping for some reaction from Bulmer. Sure enough the man followed, hovered at Nick's side, trying desperately to retain his air of nonchalance.

'Good collection,' Nick said, running a finger along the spines of a set of history volumes. 'These all yours?'

'No, they came with the office.'

Bulmer was decidedly edgy, kept pulling at his shirt collar. Nick was quick to hear the man's relieved breath when Mia got to her feet and grabbed her bag.

'Shall we go upstairs?' she said.

'We're not finished down here yet,' said Nick, still perusing the books, taking his time, noting with interest the return of Bulmer's anxiety. The man was hiding something, and Nick was certain the cellar played a part. But how could he convince Wells to apply for a warrant? Gut instinct didn't impress their implacable boss, unless it was his own. For now Nick retrieved Cathy's photograph from the desk and turned to the jittery Bulmer.

'Would you take us to the kitchen, please?'

Bulmer's eyes took on that confused look again. 'The kitchen? Why?'

'We need to check the knives, sir.'

They could almost hear his brain computing that juicy fact. 'She was stabbed? Good Lord.'

They followed him along windowless corridors that were both chilly and drab, their footsteps echoing eerily on the parquet flooring. Huge portraits bore down on them from both sides. Dust lingered everywhere. Mia wondered how anyone could live in so ghastly a place. It was like a mausoleum; hostile and unwelcoming.

The kitchen however was sleek and modern, its green appliances state-of-the-art. A man in chef's whites was seated on a stool at one of the worktops, hunched over a notepad, a look of fierce concentration on his pockmarked face.

'Still here, Eric?' said Bulmer, ushering the detectives through a narrow concertinaed door.

'Just going through tomorrow's menu for his lordship.'

Mia frowned. 'I thought Sir Nigel was abroad.'

'He means Mr Rogers,' said Bulmer with a laugh. 'Our guest is rather pernickety about his food.'

'It'd be easier to cook for the bloody Queen,' the chef huffed. He put down his pen. 'Anyway, what can I do for you?'

'Oh nothing, Eric, you carry on. These people are from Larchborough Police. They just need a quick look around the kitchen.'

Nick said to the chef, 'I'm glad you're here actually, sir. You might be able to help us.'

'OK,' he said, sliding from the stool. 'What do you want to know?'

'Have you lost any knives in the last few days?' Nick consulted his notebook. 'The knife in question has a thin, sharp blade, no shorter than six inches.'

The chef was already shaking his head. 'I haven't lost any. I'll show you.'

He crossed to a drawer in the large central island, pulling keys from his pocket as he did so. Unlocking the drawer, he retrieved a black-leather case. Inside was a set of bone-handled knives. Mia was hugely impressed. She had no idea so many different types existed. Not much of a cook herself, she made do with two: one smooth-bladed and the other serrated.

'These cost me a fortune,' said the chef. 'That's why I keep them locked away. I'd cry for a month if I lost one of these.'

'You've not got any more?' asked Nick.

'There're these.' He pulled open another drawer, showed them an assortment of good quality cutlery, solid silver according to the markings. There were several knives, but not of the sort to interest them.

'I've got some cheaper ones over here.' The chef led them to where he'd been working when they came in. There they saw a long wooden block designed to hold six knives; and all were safely in their slots.

The chef grabbed one of the black handles and pulled its blade from the block. 'I guess this is the sort you're looking for.'

Mia stared at the long thin shaft of steel and shuddered. It was one thing reading details in a report, but actually seeing a facsimile of the murder weapon ... it looked absolutely lethal. Poor Cathy Cousins; it wouldn't have been an easy way to die.

Nick said, 'Thank you, sir, you've been very helpful,' and then he turned to Bulmer. 'We'll go and see Mr Rogers now.'

'Fine, I'll just give him a quick bell.' He reached for the wall phone.

'I'd rather you didn't. Let's surprise him.'

Bulmer grimaced. 'He won't like it.'

'Not to worry,' said Nick.

Bulmer led the detectives up a wide sweeping staircase. This was more like it, thought Mia – very *Gone With The Wind*. And no dust anywhere. The cleaning staff obviously shared her mindset: concentrate on the bits that can be seen and sod the rest.

Johnny Lee Rogers was in the sitting-room at the end of a long, elegant landing. They stood outside the room's tall oak doors for a few moments, listening to an angry tirade issuing from the singer's mouth. No actual words were discernible, but they got the gist well enough. Nick glanced at Mia, brows raised, and she returned his look with a grimace.

Bulmer lifted his fist to the wood, stared questioningly at Nick. He nodded and Bulmer rapped sharply. 'Mr Rogers, the police are here to see you, sir.'

Complete silence greeted his words, and then the door was pulled open by a fractious Sally Simms. She was trying her utmost to appear relaxed and offered them an expansive smile, but her eyes were huge with panic.

'Hi, come in,' she said, pulling wide the door.

Bulmer, already edging back along the landing, said, 'Right, I'll leave you to it.'

Mia said, 'Thank you, sir. We'll be in touch … soon.' She hoped he'd get the message. Short of winking on the word 'soon' there was little more she could do.

They entered the room to find Johnny Lee lounging in an armchair, those famous legs stretched out. Two other men were sitting on a sofa to his right, both trying too hard to look casual.

Johnny Lee rose to his feet, a hand proffered towards Nick. 'Glad to see you,' he said.

Nick held out his warrant card. 'Good of you to give us your time, Mr Rogers. I'm Detective Inspector Nick Ford, and this is Detective Sergeant Mia Harvey.'

'Wow,' he said, shaking Mia's hand. 'No cops look this good where I come from … no, sir.'

Mia grinned, but inside she was struggling to control her disappointment. Up close she could see the tiredness in the singer's face, the way his skin was starting to sag at the chin, the deep crow's feet around his eyes. Whoever airbrushed his photographs deserved a medal.

She said, 'Pleased to meet you, Mr Rogers. And your friends are…?'

The shorter of the two men rushed to her side. 'I'm Bob Briscoe, ma'am – Johnny's manager. And if there's anything we can do to help with this terrible tragedy, you just let me know.' He nodded towards the sofa. 'That there's Lenny Price, Johnny's lead guitarist' – the man waved a hand, gave a lazy smile – 'and the little gal who let you in is Sally Simms, Johnny's PA.' Sally was slumped in a chair by the window, all pretence of geniality now gone.

They were offered comfortable recliners but the room was very large, the seating too spread out for the type of interrogation they had in mind, so Nick pulled two wooden chairs away from a small oval table and positioned them close to Johnny Lee.

They all sat down, but an overflow of nervous energy had the singer on his feet again almost immediately. 'How about a drink?' he said to the detectives. They were quick to decline and he returned to his chair, long legs sprawling, right boot-clad foot tapping along to a noiseless beat.

'You obviously know why we're here,' said Nick.

It was Briscoe who nodded. 'The dead kid. One of your pals told Sally on the phone.'

'You were at the rehearsal on Saturday, Mr Briscoe?'

'Yes, sir.'

Nick produced Cathy's photograph and handed it across. 'This is the girl in question. Cathy Cousins. Did you see her there?'

Before Briscoe could speak Johnny Lee had sprung forward, shirt gaping open to reveal those firm pectorals that had women drooling in their thousands. 'Yeah, we saw her,' he said.

'Johnny …' Briscoe warned.

'Hell, Bobby, I ain't got nothing to hide, and they'll find out anyway.'

Nick said, 'Find out what, sir?'

Johnny Lee was hunched forward, elbows on knees, his finely manicured fingers fiddling with his massive rings.

Presently he looked up. 'Me and the kid ... we spent Saturday night together.'

Over on the sofa Briscoe was mouthing the word 'shit' and punching its arm with his fist. Lenny Price made no movement, but his breathing increased and a sudden flush reddened his suntanned cheeks. And Sally Simms had turned her back to the room as though wanting no further part in proceedings.

Nick gawped at the singer. 'Are you saying you had sex with Cathy Cousins on Saturday night?'

'Yeah, that's what I'm saying.'

'Was Cathy a fan?' asked Mia.

The man sat back, gave her a frown. 'Sure. Why?'

Mia shrugged. 'Cathy was only twenty-three. I'd have thought she'd be a bit young for you, if you don't mind me saying.'

But he did mind; Johnny Lee visibly balked at the inference. 'The kid didn't need forcing, if that's what you mean.'

'Talk us through Saturday,' said Nick. 'Starting with the rehearsal.'

'OK.' The singer hauled himself from the chair. He started to pace, a hand on one hip, the other ruffling his hair.

Briscoe said, 'It wasn't a proper rehearsal, you understand. More of a photo-shoot ... publicity exercise ... a chance to get my boy in the papers.'

'And the kid was there with this old gal,' said Johnny Lee.

'Elizabeth Thornton,' said Mia, consulting her notebook.

'Yeah.' The singer gave a rueful shake of the head. 'Man, was she *ugly*....'

Briscoe let out a high-pitched laugh. 'The lady had to be physically restrained. She sure had the hots for Johnny.'

'Just my sweet luck,' said Johnny Lee, assuming a pained expression. 'But the kid ... hell, she was a goddamn dream. Said she was interested in a musical career. Couldn't wait for me to hear her sing.'

'You must have wannabe pop singers throwing themselves at you all the time,' said Mia.

'Yeah, and most of them can't sing a note. But I was hoping she could. That little gal had it all. She'd have the kids creaming their pants just looking at her, so I thought I'd give her a try.'

'In bed?' said Nick, taunting the man.

Briscoe bristled. 'Hey, Johnny's already said he had the kid. What's with the attitude?'

Nick held up a hand. 'Sorry. Carry on, Mr Rogers.'

Tired of pacing, Johnny Lee returned to his seat and cast a resigned look at the detectives. 'After the rehearsal we came back here.'

'Just you and Cathy?'

'All of us.'

'Did Elizabeth Thornton join you?' asked Mia.

'No way,' said Briscoe. 'I got one of the guys to see her to her car.' He let out a low whistle. 'That lady was trouble.'

'What time was that?' asked Nick.

Johnny Lee was squinting into space. 'About one-thirty. We had a bite to eat, talked awhile.'

'Nice of you to give Cathy your time,' said Mia. 'You must be a busy man.'

'We had a clear diary for the rest of the weekend,' said Briscoe. 'And Johnny's big on helping the fans when he can.'

Nick said, 'So you had lunch and you chatted. What happened then?' Briscoe was about to speak but Nick stopped him. 'I'd like Mr Rogers to answer.'

Johnny Lee motioned towards a grand piano positioned at the far end of the room. 'We had a jamming session – me on piano, Lenny on guitar. The kid wanted to sing and we wanted to listen.'

'Could she sing?' asked Mia.

'Hell, no,' said Johnny Lee.

'Never heard nothing like it,' said Briscoe, grinning. 'I tell you, today's technology can make *anybody* sound good. But that kid … she was way beyond help.'

'Did you tell her she was no good?'

'And smash her dream?' said Briscoe. 'No way.'

'So you strung her along,' said Nick.

'Goddamn right,' said Johnny Lee.

'To get her into bed.'

'Hell, no.'

'You gotta understand,' said Briscoe, with exaggerated slowness. 'My boy don't need subterfuge to get a pretty gal to do the business.'

The manager was laughing, fat belly wobbling on hefty thighs. They were favoured with Johnny Lee's famous grin too. Mia was almost trembling with disgust. How she would have loved to wipe away those self-satisfied expressions with one well-aimed retort. But now was not the time. They needed to keep the bastards sweet; string *them* along for a while.

She said, 'I bet you've got a long line of pretty girls just dying to jump into bed with you, Mr Rogers.' The man offered her a knowing smile, raised a neatly plucked eyebrow. 'And who can blame them. You're even more handsome in real life than in your pictures.'

'Why, thank you, ma'am,' he said, bowing slightly.

'Unfortunately,' said Nick, 'Cathy Cousins ended up murdered quite soon after she'd … done the business.' He shrugged. 'Gives a whole new meaning to the words "dying to jump into bed". Wouldn't you say?'

Briscoe was on his feet, waggling a fat finger in Nick's direction. 'There you go again with the attitude,' he said. 'We're trying to help here and all you can do is stick the friggin' knife in and twist it.'

Nick tut-tutted. 'Another unfortunate choice of words, sir. Cathy Cousins was stabbed to death. Or didn't you know that?'

He stared at Briscoe long and hard until the man flopped back on to the sofa with all the grace of a deflated balloon. 'No friggin' way. Shit.'

'Ever owned a knife, Mr Rogers?'

Johnny Lee pulled himself upright in the seat, his face indignant. 'Goddamn it, don't you try to stick this on me. I fucked the kid but that's all.'

The easy-going atmosphere had suddenly become a fraught tension. In order to allay it Mia said, 'Nobody's accusing you of anything, Mr Rogers. On the contrary, we're really grateful for your help.'

'OK,' he said, his challenging glare still on Nick as he settled back in the seat.

Keeping her tone light Mia said, 'Did you sing during the jamming session, Mr Rogers?'

'Yeah, I sang a few of my old hits.'

Nick hid a snigger behind his hand. '"Old" being the operative word,' he muttered.

'What's that?' said Johnny Lee, frowning.

Mia quickly cut in. 'It must have been magical. I wish I'd been here.' She lowered her eyes, assumed an awkward shyness. 'I'm a big fan, in case you hadn't noticed.'

Johnny Lee rewarded her with a sexy grin. 'Is that so?' he said, pulling open his shirt to uncover even more of his hairless chest.

Mia regarded his smug expression and inwardly gave a thankful sigh. The shallow narcissist was back; exactly what she'd been trying for. That oily bastard was so much easier to handle than the indignant Johnny Lee.

'What happened after you'd finished singing?'

The man thought back. 'It was getting late and I needed a break. The guys went off to do their thing and Sally took the kid downstairs to get some food.'

Mia glanced across at the girl, saw she was still rather taciturn. 'Is that correct, Miss Simms?'

She managed a nod. 'We ate in the kitchen. It made a change.'

'Was anyone else there?'

'No, we had the place to ourselves.'

'So neither of you spoke to anyone while you ate?'

The girl rolled her eyes. 'I already said … we had the place to ourselves.'

Mia felt her hackles rise in response to the girl's frosty attitude. She decided on a different line of questioning. 'How did you two get along?'

'What's that got to do with anything?'

'You're both around the same age. Did you have much in common?'

The girl's irritable sigh filled the air. 'I wasn't out to make a friend. I was just doing my job.'

'I get it,' said Nick. 'You were feeding her up ready for the slaughter.'

'Hey,' said Johnny Lee, about to remonstrate.

But before he could, Sally said, 'Johnny was tired. He needed some down time. I was keeping his guest entertained 'til he was ready.'

'Part of your job description, is it?' said Nick. 'Keeping his latest fuck out of the way 'til he feels the urge?'

Johnny Lee sprang to his feet. 'That's enough, goddamn it. The kid came on to me. I didn't stand a goddamn chance.'

'Oh right,' said Nick, not even trying to hide his smirk.

An angry flush distorted the singer's face as he made to pounce on the detective before thinking better of it. This was the real Johnny Lee Rogers; no posturing or preening for the cameras. And he suddenly looked his age; slightly ridiculous too with his jet-black hair and those absurd clothes.

For a fleeting moment Mia wondered how she could have found him at all appealing. But that was irrelevant; they were losing momentum again and they needed to get it back.

Resting a hand on Nick's arm she said to Johnny Lee, 'DI Ford can't possibly know the effect you have on women. And he's probably more than a little jealous….' She became aware of Nick's incensed inhalation of breath, could feel him attempt to wrench his arm from her grip but she held on fast. 'I can understand Cathy's reaction to you though. I'd have felt the same. God, it's every girl's dream, having you all to herself.'

From the corner of her eye Mia could see Nick studying her as one would a hideous specimen in a zoo. He probably thought she'd lost the plot. But she didn't care because the man was sitting back again, that cocksure grin reappearing. She was winning him over and it was all so easy. Men were such prats.

She heard Nick take in a breath to speak. No way was she going to let him ruin all her good work. Pulling her hand from his arm, she said, 'I assume you were alone with Cathy on Saturday night, Mr Rogers?' She grinned. 'You look like a tight-knit group, but some things are best done in private, aren't they?'

He laughed. 'Guess so.'

'What did the rest of you get up to?'

Briscoe said, 'We went to that little pub along the way. The Crown and Anchor, I think you call it. We just love your village pubs.'

She shifted her attention to the guitarist. 'You went as well, Mr Price?'

He gave a languid nod. 'Nothing else to do, seeing as the other broad was a freakin' witch.'

'Elizabeth Thornton?'

'Yeah.'

'Wasn't she your type?'

'Have you seen the bitch? Jesus, she's a freakin' nightmare.'

He made a scary face and half-rose from the sofa, arms sticking out from the shoulders, hands dangling. Briscoe and Johnny Lee fell about laughing. Even Sally Simms managed a smile. Mia wanted to pummel the guitarist to death but, being an officer of the law and needing to keep him talking, she laughed along with them instead.

'I see,' she said, wiping imaginary tears from her eyes. 'You were hoping the competition winners would be gorgeous lissom blondes and you could *both* have a good time on Saturday night.'

'That's about it, ma'am.' Still laughing, Price aimed a stern finger at Johnny Lee. 'And that guy there – my so-called best buddy – couldn't wait to point out my date for the night.'

'Poor you,' said Mia. 'There was Mr Rogers enjoying a whole night of passion and you had to sleep alone.'

Lenny Price hastily shook his head, couldn't wait to correct her mistake. 'No, ma'am, me and Johnny were in here composing all night. We like to write our songs in the early hours. It's quiet … less distractions.'

Mia's eyebrows rose in surprise as she glanced across at the singer. 'You didn't spend the whole night with Cathy?'

'Hell, no. We had our fun, yeah, but a guy's gotta work.'

'So Cathy was alone in your bed for most of the night.'

'Not mine – Sally's.'

Mia stared at the girl with genuine astonishment. Nick did too. After his initial disgust at Mia's seemingly unashamed adoration of the man, he'd cottoned on to her sneaky technique. And he had to admit – albeit grudgingly – that it was working a treat so he had no qualms about leaving her to it.

The recalcitrant Sally Simms was quick to take umbrage at their piercing stares. 'Don't get the wrong idea now. There's *two* beds in my room. Johnny used the spare while I was drinking with the guys. It just seemed easier to leave her in it when he'd finished.'

'You didn't even use your own bed?' said Mia, making no attempt to hide her disgust.

'I don't like sleeping on dirty sheets,' the singer said, smiling.

If only his legions of fans could hear this, Mia thought. Cathy Cousins had been nothing more than a sex toy to be heartlessly tossed aside once the fun was finished. She might have been all over the man. She might even have instigated the sex. But she hadn't deserved to be so blatantly disregarded. Her last night alive too. Johnny Lee Rogers sang of love and heartache and commitment, seemed to understand completely a woman's psyche, but in reality he was an absolute *sleazeball*.

Trying hard to maintain her friendly persona, Mia said to Johnny Lee, 'We know Cathy had breakfast on Sunday morning and I'm assuming she ate it here … How did she seem to you?'

'Dunno. I slept late. You'd better ask Sally.'

Once again Mia turned her impatient stare on the girl. 'Well, Miss Simms?'

'Well what? She ate breakfast and took off. What's left to say?'

'We'll need more than that. You were one of the last people to see Cathy alive.'

That waspish shrug again. 'She was OK, I guess. I got the idea she was hoping to see Johnny again, but she wasn't upset or nothing.' The girl sighed dramatically. 'She kept on and on about what she'd be wearing for Wednesday's dinner date. *So* boring….'

'Where did you eat your breakfast?'

'In the kitchen.'

'Who cooked it?'

'I did.'

'Was anybody else there?'

'Just us.'

'And what time did Cathy leave?'

'About seven-thirty.'

Mia made a face. 'You are an early riser. Don't you lie in on Sundays?'

Sally's eyes were ice cold as they held Mia's. 'I wanted her gone. She was taking up my space.'

'I see.' Mia spent a moment studying her notes. 'We believe Cathy was killed outside the manor gates, Miss Simms, which seems to imply she was waiting for a lift. Why didn't one of your drivers take her home?'

'No one was up. Like *you* implied earlier, folks like to sleep late on Sundays.'

'Did she phone for a taxi?'

'She phoned *somebody*, then asked how she got out. I told her I'd have the gates open and she left.'

Mia glanced at Nick. 'Anything you want to add?'

He turned to Bob Briscoe. 'This meal tomorrow night – where's it going to be?'

'There ain't gonna be no meal. No concerts either.' Briscoe spread his hands. 'You gotta understand, all this publicity ain't good for my boy's profile. So I've cancelled the whole shebang – it'll be in tomorrow's papers – and we'll be heading home as soon as we can get a flight.'

'And sod the Rainbow Hospice,' Nick snorted.

'They've got the money from the competition,' said Briscoe, puffing out his ample chest. 'And we'll be making a sizeable donation, of course. The kids'll be just fine.'

Nick huffed. 'The very fact they're in a hospice means they're anything but fine.' His eyes narrowed as they settled on Johnny Lee's lolling figure. 'Sorry to put a spoke in your publicity wheel, Mr Rogers, but you'll not be going anywhere for the foreseeable future.'

'What?' said Briscoe, quick to get to his feet for such a stout man. 'You mean we gotta stay in this friggin' dump?'

Johnny Lee was looking towards his manager like a child who'd lost his security blanket. 'Do something, Bobby. Goddamn it—'

Nick hid a smile. 'This is a murder investigation, in case you hadn't noticed. We'll need you to stay put, I'm afraid.'

'Jesus,' said Briscoe. 'How long?'

Nick lifted his shoulders. 'Depends on what comes to light. We may need you for the trial, we may not, but no one goes anywhere for now.'

'Trial,' said Briscoe, turning pale. '*Jesus.*'

*

'I enjoyed that,' said Nick, slipping his key into the ignition.

Mia gave a theatrical shudder. 'Talk about falling into a viper's nest.'

He cast her a sly glance. 'You did OK in there.'

'Thanks.'

'Pity you didn't get a shag though.'

She gave a repulsive gasp. 'I'd rather have yours, and that's saying something.'

For once Nick didn't take offence. He simply grinned and released the handbrake. 'You shouldn't meet your heroes, Mia. They *never* live up to the hype.'

CHAPTER FOURTEEN

'Tosser.'

That single word was the greeting Wells threw to his team as he burst into CID next morning. Mia and Nick said nothing, merely waited for him to elaborate while Jack fetched him a coffee.

'What's up, sir?' he asked, resting the mug on Wells's desk.

The DCI scowled. 'Bloody Shakespeare wants to bring another team in. He's thinking these cases are too much for us to handle.'

Nick made a face. 'Not like the super to throw money about.'

Wells emptied his briefcase, tossing the files on to his desk and nearly toppling the mug. 'He's giving us seven days to come up with a breakthrough. After that—' He drew a finger across his throat, his expression deadly. 'So now we drag this parochial little shithole out of the nineteenth century and get some bloody results.'

He started by recounting to his senior officers the non-event that was Scott Beddows's interview, then grabbed Rachel Mandley's file and opened it with some force. 'Don't know what I was hoping to find in here, but there's sod all anyway. Rachel was the perfect daughter apparently. Got ten GCSEs, all As. Set to take three A-levels. Had a place provisionally booked at St Andrews University. She was going into law like her dad.'

'*Something* must have gone wrong,' said Nick.

'What about her friends?' asked Mia. 'They must have been interviewed.'

'They were.' Wells skipped a few pages. 'When little Miss Perfect wasn't studying she was partial to a bit of dancing at the Adelphi. She had a couple of boyfriends – nothing serious, though, according to this.'

'She must have got serious with somebody,' said Jack. 'She couldn't get pregnant on her own.'

Nick said, 'Have we got names, sir? She might have tried to contact the father when she came back.'

'I thought that. We know she went to meet somebody. I've left the names downstairs. But with my bloody luck they'll all be in Australia by now.' Wells lunged for his mug as though it meant him harm and took a long drink. Superintendent Shakespeare had him seriously riled.

Jack handed him a thin buff folder. 'Here's the forensic report on Sky's car, sir. Came in this morning.'

Wells quickly scanned the pages. 'A few good prints,' he said, nodding. He glanced up at Nick and Mia. 'Did we fingerprint everybody at the caravan site?'

'Not yet,' said Nick, fiddling nervously with his cuff-links.

'Get it sorted then. Christ—'

Jack said, 'I've asked for a set of Scott Beddows's prints to be sent over, sir.'

'Thanks, mate.' Wells looked towards the whiteboard and said to Mia, 'You've listed what Sky was wearing at last. Well done, love.'

Mia squirmed in her seat. She couldn't tell whether he was being complimentary or just plain sarcastic.

He turned again to the whiteboard. 'Black T-shirt, blue denims, blue plastic flip-flops. And nothing's been found yet.'

'Doesn't look good,' said Mia, shaking her head.

Wells swivelled round to face her. 'You think she's dead?'

She gave a non-committal shrug. 'Probably.'

'Good, we can stop looking,' he said, his expression pure evil. 'Shakespeare's going to be pleased as hell.'

'Hold on,' said Mia, indignant now. 'You asked, sir, and I gave an honest answer. A week's a long time in a missing person case and statistics indicate—'

'Bollocks to statistics,' he yelled, spittle spraying the papers spread out in front of him. ''Til we know for sure we keep an open mind. That's the least we can do.'

Nick said, 'Are you discounting Scott Beddows, sir?'

Wells fell back in his seat. 'No way, mate. He turns up in Larchborough and his missus suddenly vanishes. That's too much of a coincidence in my book. Problem is we've got nothing to hold him on.' He tapped the forensic report. 'I'm just hoping his prints match one of these. Then we've got him.'

His phone buzzed. 'DCI Wells.'

It was PC Burton, the uniformed officer trailing Philip Hunt. Wells had to hide a smile. The voice on the other end of the line possessed all the earnest dedication of a new recruit; his language, only recently learned, archaic and long-winded. Wells imagined the youngster conversing with everyone in his daily life as though offering evidence in the witness box. He must really get on his family's tits.

'Not to worry,' Wells said, eventually. 'And thanks for your help. I appreciate it.' He replaced the receiver. 'We've lost our surveillance on Phil Hunt. He's been given other duties.'

'What did he find out?' asked Nick.

'Nothing. Cheered me up though.'

Thank God for that, thought Mia. 'Mr Hunt wasn't up to anything then?'

Wells sat back, rested his hands over his scrawny ribcage, his expression thoughtful. 'He's spent time round the corner in Rushall Street these past two days. Just hanging around, according to the lad.'

Nick frowned. 'Why Rushall Street? There's only the Law Courts and the staff entrance to the Town Hall.'

'Who knows?' said Wells, suddenly straightening up. 'We'll be having a word with Mr Hunt. We'll be doing all of them.' He scooped up the reports and returned them to their relevant files. 'OK, what else have we got? Come on, kiddies, the clock's ticking.'

Nick said, 'I reckon Andrew Bulmer's not being totally honest, sir. He was definitely shifty last night. Stuck to me like a leech as though he was worried I might see something I shouldn't. And he'd got some wine and glasses on a posh tray, but when I asked who he was expecting he said nobody.' He gave a cynical snort. 'Mia couldn't see anything wrong with him, though.'

Wells gave her a challenging glance. 'Fancy him, do you?'

'Not at all,' she said, keeping her tone light. 'I don't like making snap decisions, that's all, sir. They can be unreliable, especially at the start of an investigation when we're looking at everybody as possible suspects.'

'So you don't go much on first impressions?'

'I do, actually, and I found Mr Bulmer to be very helpful, his answers frank and to the point.'

'Might be worth keeping tabs on him, just in case.' Wells clapped his hands together smartly. 'Right, Cathy Cousins … what have we got so far?'

Nick related their interview with Johnny Lee Rogers and his dubious gang; Mia interjecting periodically with her own musings. She might be dead in the water as far as Wells was concerned, but she refused to putrefy without a fight. She was voicing her doubts concerning Sally Simms when Wells locked eyes with her.

'I thought you didn't like making snap decisions,' he said, his cold smile provoking. 'But here you are lambasting the hired help. Jealous, are you, 'cause she's working for your heartthrob?'

While Mia considered Wells's jowly face, the teasing look in his eyes, her patience snapped. She knew he was under pressure, knew too that his professional pride would take a beating if another team was brought in, but she refused to be his whipping post.

'Let's get one thing straight,' she said, anger bringing a flush to her cheeks. 'I might be pushing thirty with no husband in sight, but I don't lust after every man I talk to.' She pointed a warning finger at Wells. 'I don't fancy Andrew Bulmer, sir, and I *definitely do not* like Johnny Lee Rogers.'

Mia suddenly became aware of her finger, still aimed aggressively at her boss, and she brought it down to her lap while the flush on her cheeks deepened. She fully expected Wells to explode but he surprised them all by holding up his hands, his expression penitent.

'I'm sorry,' he said. 'I've overstepped the line, darling. It won't happen again.'

There was an uncomfortable silence, the only sounds coming from the bustling street below their windows. Mia acknowledged his apology with a slight nod, pulled at the front of her blouse. The outburst had brought on a sweat; she felt sticky and disconcerted.

'I was only passing on my observations, sir … *relevant* observations, given that Sally Simms was one of the last to see Cathy alive. You said yourself the clock's ticking.'

'Fair point,' he said, nodding. 'Carry on then.'

Warming to her subject now she was on safe ground, Mia eagerly continued. 'Sally made it clear she wasn't happy being stuck with Cathy on Saturday night. Couldn't wait to get rid of her, she said.'

'Any ideas why?'

Mia shrugged. 'Who knows? Maybe *she* was jealous. Maybe Sally fancies Johnny Lee Rogers and wants him for herself. And if that's the case it can't be easy having to nanny his conquests 'til he's ready to grace them with his presence.'

Wells was quiet for a moment, took to fiddling with his pen. 'What did you think of this Sally Simms, Nick?'

'Same as Mia, sir. Everybody else seemed happy to answer our questions, but she was surly and uncooperative.'

'And she said Cathy called somebody on her mobile just before leaving,' Mia went on. 'Why say that if not to lead us away from the scent? The call wasn't to her parents. They'd have said.'

'Could have been to a taxi firm.' Wells riffled through a pile of papers on his desk. Finding the appropriate one he quickly read its contents. 'The parents have given Cathy's mobile number and provider.' He turned to Jack. 'Ring downstairs, mate. Ask what's happening about her mobile.'

Mia said, 'Think about it, sir. Everybody else was in bed. Sally could easily have killed Cathy and nobody would be any the wiser.'

Wells turned to Nick. 'You did check the knives in the kitchen?'

'Yes, sir, the chef took us round. They were all there according to him.'

Mia leant forward, eagerness making her eyes sparkle. 'But Sally could have washed the knife and had it back in place before anyone knew it was missing.'

Wells frowned. 'What's the motive?'

'Jealousy, like we said.'

'Like *you* said,' Nick pointed out. 'Sally didn't have anything to be jealous about as far as I can see. Rogers had his fun and couldn't be bothered with Cathy afterwards.'

'Even so we'd better get forensics to check the knives,' said Wells. 'And we've still got their report on the T-shirt to come. Please God there'll be evidence on that.'

Over in the corner Jack was finishing his call. 'Sir, we'll be getting a list of numbers from Cathy's mobile any time now.'

'Good.' Wells was sorting through the jottings in his notebook. 'Ah, here it is,' he said, sitting back. 'Cathy met a photographer at the rehearsal, apparently. A young bloke called Rick or Mick. We'd better follow that up as well.'

The DCI took a sheet of paper from his briefcase and hurried across to the whiteboard. 'This is a mug shot of Scott Beddows,' he said, pinning the paper to the board. 'Commit these pleasing features to memory, kiddies, 'cause he ain't as angelic as he looks.' He returned to his desk. 'Nick, you and me had better start on the loonies at the caravan site. We'll have them all in. We can get their prints at the same time. Mia, you can talk to Elizabeth Thornton at the library. After that, bring Sally Simms back here. She might be more talkative with the shit scared out of her.'

'What about me?' asked Jack.

'I want you glued to your computer, mate. Find out anything you can about our travellers. See if Bulmer's been done for anything. If he's had so much as a parking ticket, I want to know about it. And see if you can find that photographer. We need a word with him as well. Oh, and get forensics to check the knives at Stratton Manor.' Wells waited while Jack made a list of all his jobs, grinning when the young DC pulled a face. 'You did say you're a computer wizard, mate. Now's your chance to prove it.'

Just then Wells's telephone buzzed. It was central control. Wells wrote vigorously in his notebook while he listened. Then he replaced the receiver and looked at his team, his grin euphoric.

'We've had a sighting of Sky Beddows in Larchborough,' he said.

*

Over at the caravan site Kelly Barlow was at last standing up to her husband. It would seem that, along with the new baby, a raw determination was beginning to blossom within her. She was no longer willing to be the down-trodden little woman, his convenient and silent scapegoat.

He'd taken the news of her pregnancy badly, but she'd expected nothing less. All but the first of her pregnancies had been met with a raging monologue about her rampant incompetence; her juvenile expectations of happy family life.

How ridiculous that was. He wouldn't know a happy family if one fell from the sky and smashed his brainless skull into a thousand pieces. And why did men always blame the women when unplanned babies came along, as though they'd had no part to play in the process?

They'd hardly spoken since she'd given him the news. And now he wanted to go off again to his secret place; to his well of creativity as he called it. But she wasn't having that. Why should his selfish art be bolstered when hers had died from lack of sustenance years ago?

Barlow was filling his small holdall with essentials: a sketch pad and pencils, a slab of cheese and a selection of crackers, a quarter bottle of whisky.

Kelly was slumped on the window seat, cradling her nauseous stomach. Her new pregnancy was certainly taking its toll.

'What are you doing?' she asked.

'I told you, I'm going out for a while. I shouldn't be long.'

She was off the seat in a heartbeat. 'And I told you I need you here.'

'Kelly—'

'You're going to see her. Am I right?'

He gave her a long-suffering look. 'Who, Kelly? Who am I going to see?'

'Sky Beddows, of course. Your muse, your lifeblood … your fucking *whore*.'

Barlow was fastening the bag, his back towards her. 'Your hormones are making you hysterical. I don't know where the girl is. Nobody does.'

'No?'

Kelly threw open the door to a thin upright cupboard, hauled out its contents until she came upon a small burgundy leather case lurking in a corner. Bringing the case to the dining table and flicking open its latches she turned on her husband.

'What are these?' she said, clutching a wad of papers. 'How did you manage these if you don't know where she is?'

Kelly shoved the case from the table and covered its surface with the papers. Page after page showed abstract images of a woman in a stark and lonely setting.

A beautiful woman with long shining hair and startling eyes.

Sky Beddows.

Barlow stared at the sketches, unchecked anger bringing a sudden harshness to his face. 'You've been looking through my fucking stuff. How dare you?'

'Oh I dare. Now I do,' said Kelly, her mercurial grin holding little joy. She turned towards the tiny kitchen window and pointed to their brood having fun in the dirt. 'This stops now, Roy. We've a family to bring up.'

'You want me to stop working?' He snorted. 'Now isn't that a good plan for the future.'

'Your obsession stops now. No more lusting over that tramp. Either that, or I go to the police.'

Barlow glared at her. 'And tell them what exactly?'

Kelly picked up one of the sketches, held it towards him. 'You need the girl's physical presence to produce work of this quality. I'll go to the police and tell them you know where she is. They'll follow you. They'll find her. Or better still, they'll lock you in a cell and she'll be lost to you for ever.' She bent forward, clutched at her stomach, a sudden wave of nausea making her swallow hard. And when her eyes found his face once more they were glistening with emotion. 'We need you here, Roy. You're needed here.'

Barlow, uttering tiny shushing sounds, pulled Kelly into his arms and squeezed her tight. 'I've been here, for days now. Isn't that the truth?' He held her at arm's length, his eyes pleading. 'But I need to get out. A man needs his space, or he'll shrivel up and die. Is that what you want?'

'I want you,' Kelly said, laying her face against his chest. 'I want us to be how we were.'

'And we will, my darling, but I need to get out today. Set me free this one last time and I'll make it up to you. I promise.'

Kelly stiffened in his arms. Pushing him away she returned to the window seat and studied him with a measured look. 'Go, then. But we won't be here when you get back. We'll be at the police station.'

'For fuck's sake—'

Exasperated, Barlow unfastened the bag and wrestled the whisky bottle from its belly. Then he sat on the caravan steps, taking long swigs while his children called for him to join them.

Kelly stared at his hunched back and smiled as a growing sense of empowerment chased away the nausea.

Round one to her.

CHAPTER FIFTEEN

Mia decided to walk to the library. It was quicker than taking the car – cut through Marks & Spencer and you were nearly there. Parking was a nightmare in town anyway. As she trudged through the ladieswear department, head down, only vaguely aware of the quiet hum of conversation emanating from the many women perusing the garments, Mia was mulling over her flare-up with the DCI when she should have been planning her chat with Lizzie.

She was glad she'd made a stand. It was long overdue. But Mia had never been the delicate feminine type, putting in a complaint every time a male colleague made a sexist remark. She simply gave as good as she got and left it at that.

However the spat with Wells had caused Mia to doubt herself. After all he was very nearly right. She *did* fancy Andrew Bulmer. And she had almost gone on a date with him too, even though she knew it would have been frowned upon.

As the automatic doors opened before her, the heat from outside seeming as solid as a wall after the coolness of the store, Mia resolved to cut all personal ties with Bulmer. From now on she would keep their relationship on a purely professional footing. It was best for all concerned.

The library loomed ahead. It was a beautiful building, austere yet welcoming. And it held a very distinctive smell. Each time Mia stepped through its doors she was transported back to her primary school hall at harvest festival. Good memories.

At the main desk Ruth Findlay was furnishing a teenaged boy with the necessary pin-number for Internet access. When the boy wandered off Mia approached, warrant card in hand.

'Hello, I'm looking for Elizabeth Thornton.'

'Oh,' said Ruth, becoming flustered as she studied the card. 'Lizzie's just gone out the back. She's rather distraught, I'm afraid.'

Mia gave the woman a sympathetic smile. 'Cathy's death must have affected you all.'

'It's not that.' Ruth leant towards Mia, lowered her voice. 'Lizzie was supposed to be having a meal with Johnny Lee Rogers tonight only he's on his way back to America. Look—'

Ruth turned her computer monitor towards Mia. On the screen was a page from the BBC News website with the words JOHNNY LEE ROGERS LEAVING ENGLAND AFTER BODY FOUND above an old picture of the singer and a number of paragraphs of text.

Mia said, 'Mr Rogers won't be going anywhere for a while,' and then regretted the disclosure immediately. Still, his temporary detainment would soon be all over the local newspapers so she wasn't actually divulging confidential information.

'Lizzie will be pleased,' Ruth gushed. 'I'll go and get her.'

While Ruth scuttled off towards the staff entrance Mia browsed through the titles on the 'Just Returned' trolley, making a mental note to read more. She used to devour scores of books when she was younger, but nowadays there simply wasn't the time. She was perusing the poster for a forthcoming book-signing when Lizzie Thornton came running towards her.

'Johnny Lee's still here?' she said, her round face red with delight.

Mia nodded and ushered the woman towards a quiet corner where two chairs stood side by side. 'I need a word, Miss Thornton. I'm investigating the murder of Cathy Cousins and I'm hoping you'll be able to help me.'

Mia sat down, dumped her shoulder bag on the floor while she studied the woman. Elizabeth Thornton wasn't at all the type Mia would have associated with the sleazy singer.

'You're a fan of Johnny Lee Rogers?' she said.

Lizzie beamed. 'I'm probably his *biggest* fan.'

'And you won the competition in the *Evening News* – is that right?'

She gave an enthusiastic nod. 'I'm having dinner with him tonight, at the Fox and Hounds.'

'You're not, I'm afraid. The meal's off.'

Lizzie gave the detective a pained look. 'But you said he wasn't going home. You said he was staying here.'

'He is, but the meal's off. So are the concerts,' said Mia, searching for notebook and pen within the depths of her bag.

Lizzie seemed to shrink into the seat, her plain features settling into a sorrowful pout.

Mia opened her notebook. 'Now, you gave Cathy Cousins your spare ticket to Saturday's rehearsal. Why? Were you close to Cathy?'

'Not particularly.' Lizzie pulled a lace handkerchief from the sleeve of her cardigan, bit on her lower lip as if to fight back imminent tears. 'I gave Cathy the ticket because Ruth didn't want to go.'

'OK, talk me through the rehearsal.'

Lizzie lifted a petulant shoulder. 'Nothing much to tell. I left before he'd even started to sing.'

'Why?' asked Mia, frowning. 'Wasn't that the best part?'

Lizzie's dour features suddenly became animated as she stared into space, imagining that afternoon as it should have been. 'When Johnny Lee saw me he became a man possessed,' she said, fanning her flushed cheeks with the handkerchief. 'He wouldn't leave me alone, kept pawing me, thrusting his bare chest into my face. Cathy was incensed, I could tell.' She lunged forward, laid a hand on Mia's arm. 'I did tell him to stop. I'm not that sort of woman. But he wouldn't listen. In the end I asked his bodyguards to escort me off the premises.'

Mia had to look away in case the cynicism in her eyes was too blatant. She made a show of searching her notes for Bob Briscoe's testimony. *She had to be physically restrained*, he'd said. *That lady was trouble.* Mia was torn between feelings of pity for the woman and a sense of irritation because she was wasting valuable police time.

'You told Cathy's mother she was attracted to one of the photographers. Could you enlarge on that?'

Lizzie shrugged. 'His name was Rick, I think. He liked Cathy and she liked him. What more can I say?'

'Which publication does he work for?'

'How should I know?'

'Didn't he have some kind of identification?'

Lizzie let out a heavy breath. 'Johnny Lee was about to arrive. It was a moment of great excitement. I can't be expected to remember every irrelevant detail.'

'How did you get to Stratton Manor, Miss Thornton?'

'In my car.'

'Wasn't Cathy worried about losing her lift?'

That petulant shrug again. 'Shouldn't think so. Cathy loved being centre of attention. She was lapping up the adulation like the little cat that she was.'

'What adulation?' asked Mia. 'You reckoned she was being ignored. You said you were the victim of Mr Rogers's attention and that's why you asked to leave.'

Lizzie was seriously ruffled. She took to patting her forehead with the handkerchief, her eyes darting all ways as she gathered her thoughts.

'She *was* being ignored by Johnny Lee. He only had eyes for me. But others were lusting after her. That photographer … the journalists….' Lizzie almost laughed out loud. 'Cathy was half-naked, for goodness' sake. She wanted to be noticed. As usual.'

Mia was surprised by Lizzie's irreverent attitude towards the dead girl. It was obvious that they'd have had little in common but even so; Cathy Cousins had been murdered in the most shocking of circumstances and this woman was showing not one shred of sympathy or disbelief. Could she really be so hard-hearted? Mia decided to delve a little deeper into Miss Thornton's psyche.

'We know that Cathy spent Saturday night with Mr Rogers. How do you feel about that?'

Lizzie's mouth became a bitter line. 'Men can't help themselves, can they? Johnny Lee couldn't have me, so he settled for second best.'

Mia regarded the woman with surprise. 'You knew that Cathy spent the night at Stratton Manor?'

'I half expected it.'

'Why? Because of the attention she was getting from Mr Rogers?'

'No, no, *no*, …!' The words came out like repeated gunfire as Lizzie banged her clenched fist on the arm of her chair. 'Cathy was asking for trouble. Her clothes. Her sluttish behaviour. It's no wonder she ended up stabbed to death with her face smashed in.'

Mia was puzzled. Elizabeth Thornton looked like everybody's favourite granny, and yet she acted like a sullen teenager who'd just lost her boyfriend to the school flirt. She was formulating her next question when a man's discordant voice cut into the quiet of their surroundings.

Lizzie tutted harshly. 'What's going on now?' she muttered, heading for the fracas before Mia could hold her back.

Mia found the woman in a small section cut off from the main body of the library by opaque glass walls. A long line of computers stood behind those walls, the majority unmanned, and Lizzie and Ruth were positioned beside a low desk at the centre of the space, their body language alerting Mia to the fact that the man was not responding to reason.

'What's the matter?' asked Mia, showing the man her warrant card.

'This gentleman is being unnecessarily obtuse,' said Ruth, glaring at him.

'I asked a simple question,' the man said, spreading his hands.

'And I gave a simple answer,' Ruth fired back. 'Only it wasn't the one he wanted, so he started getting uppity.'

Mia considered him, eyes narrowed. 'Is that true?'

He gave an impatient sigh. 'I want to get into my computer only I've forgotten the password and I thought this lady could help me.' He glanced towards the computer terminals. 'She's got enough. I thought she'd know.'

'And I told him' – said Ruth, rather enjoying this change to routine – 'that he should contact his service provider. We can't help.'

'You shouldn't have forgotten it in the first place,' Lizzie cut in. She could afford to be contrary with a police officer standing by.

'Doesn't your computer give a prompt?' asked Mia. 'Like "dog" if your password's the name of an old pet?'

'Yes, only I still can't remember.' He looked at Ruth, anger sharpening his features. 'You should know. You're here to help, for fuck's sake.'

Ruth flinched. 'Don't come here with your filthy language.'

'But I need that password.'

Mia was still holding on to her notebook. She opened it in front of the man; a deliberate threat. 'What's your name, sir?'

'Oh forget it,' he said, sidling towards the glass walls. In the doorway he threw back, 'Thanks for nothing,' and then disappeared from view.

'Try having a bath once in a while,' said Lizzie in a stage whisper.

Mia stared at the woman's surly features and decided she'd had enough of Elizabeth Thornton for one day. She'd encountered people from all corners of the social stratum during her years in the force, but never one so lacking in the skills of sensitivity and basic human kindness as that cow.

'I'd like your phone number, Miss Thornton, in case we need to talk again.'

Lizzie handed her a library flyer from the desk. 'Here it is.'

'Your home number as well, please.'

After a small huff of displeasure Lizzie added the number and, as Mia strode towards the door, she asked, 'The meal's definitely off?'

Mia turned and nodded, a vindictive smile tugging at her lips. 'And the concerts.'

'Doesn't matter,' said Lizzie, grinning at Ruth. 'He'll find me somehow.'

Mia was preoccupied as she weaved through the shoppers *en route* to the police station car park. A particular point in her conversation with Elizabeth Thornton was straining to be remembered, but try as she might Mia couldn't bring it to mind. She retrieved her car and was almost upon Stratton Manor for the purpose of bringing in Sally Simms when that eureka moment at last occurred. Pulling up outside the main gates Mia grabbed her mobile and dialled the office.

'Jack, I need a favour,' she said, holding the phone at arm's length while he ranted about his workload. 'Sorry, sweetie, but this is important. I want you to get me all we've published about Cathy's death, in print and online. Thank you, daddy.' And then she cut the call before he could get started again.

Mia remained in the car for a few moments, deciding on the best way to let Andrew Bulmer down gently. But when she pressed the button for entry to the estate a female voice responded. Sod's law, Mia thought; she'd psyched herself up for it as well. She gave her name, the reason for her visit, and waited while the gates swung apart.

All along the tree-lined approach Mia concentrated on the intractable Sally Simms. She'd phoned Bob Briscoe that morning, had spoken of the need for further discussion with Sally, only she'd intimated that the interview would take place within the suite. How would Miss Simms react to being hauled along to the police station? Not too well, Mia surmised.

She parked in a shaded corner, well away from the house. The car park was practically empty because the venue was still closed to the public and would remain so until all those within it were cleared of any connection with Cathy's murder.

Mia was reaching for her bag on the back seat when her attention was momentarily caught by sunlight glinting off a large metal object. From her position she had a good view of the west side of the building where the bronze statue of a naked man stood beside an open doorway. A tradesman's entrance, perhaps? A number of hefty boxes lay beside the statue, and they in turn were propping up two small portraits, their gilt frames also catching the sun.

Mia was about to step out of the car when a man appeared in the doorway, his stance familiar. It was Andrew Bulmer. He was wearing khaki overalls on top of his smart suit, and what looked like gardening gloves on his hands. Mia was surprised to see him in such a ragged condition. Surely the estate manager shouldn't need to get his hands dirty? He had plenty of staff to do that for him.

She was wondering whether now was a good time to inform him of her decision, when a large black van appeared from the back of the building and pulled up beside Bulmer. A man jumped down from the van. Mia leant nearer to the windscreen, eyes squinting for clearer vision. The man's face was familiar. Where had she seen him before?

He was helping Bulmer load the items into the vehicle, his wary glance darting about. And he seemed to be issuing staccato orders that Bulmer was quick to discharge.

Mia let out a huge gasp as she remembered where she'd seen the man. His mug shot was pinned to the whiteboard in the office. That man, whose body language spoke of deceit, was none other than Scott Beddows.

The Red Lion was Larchborough's oldest public house. It was situated in Stratton End, an area of shabby council properties and small industrial concerns, the majority of which lay derelict or on the verge of closure.

As DCI Wells negotiated the narrow rubbish-strewn streets he pondered that the council's money – wasted on poncy arts centres and grandiose building schemes – would have been better spent redeveloping this godforsaken place. It was no surprise to him that a large number of their clients originated from this dump. Wells pulled up outside the pub, eyeing the deserted patch with displeasure as he activated his car-locking system.

What the hell was Sky Beddows doing here?

The pub's interior was dingy and sauna-hot, its ripe stench of spilled beer and deprivation a sharp shock to Wells's nostrils, the walls and net curtains a lurid orange from nicotine. Clearly the landlord had seen no reason to redecorate since smoking became a major crime. A number of elderly men sat in small huddles, silently reflecting while striving to make their pints last the morning, all oblivious to the wall-mounted television showing horses and jockeys nearing their starting pens, the volume turned down.

Wells wandered across to the bar where a middle-aged man in a Kylie Minogue T-shirt was buffing up glasses with a grubby cloth, his eyes glued to the television set.

'Yes, mate, what's your poison?' the man asked, taking up one of the glasses as the well-dressed stranger approached.

'Just a tonic water,' Wells said, showing the man his warrant card. 'We had a call from Mr Peck.'

'That's me,' he said, handing over the drink.

Wells gave Peck a five-pound note and took a long swallow to sate his thirst. Then he put down the glass and took from his inside pocket the snapshot of Sky.

'This is definitely the girl you saw?'

Peck put Wells's change on the counter and took the photograph, scrutinized it carefully. 'Couldn't swear under oath,' he said, 'but it looks like her – same hair, same smile. We don't get her sort in here very often. That's why I remembered.' Peck gave a lewd whistle as he handed back the picture. 'Small tits, mind, but I wouldn't have said no.'

'When did you see her?'

Peck considered for a moment. 'She's been in a few afternoons. Not for a couple of days though.'

'Was she with anybody?'

'A bloke. Always the same bloke.'

Wells took out his notebook, scribbled a few words. 'Can you describe him for me?'

'I only served him once. The wife usually helps out only she's at the hospital – women's stuff.' The man scratched his head, distorting Kylie's face and showing a patch of sweat at his armpit. 'He was taller than me. Stank of scotch. And he'd got smooth hands, clean nails. He'd never worked down no coalmines – get my drift?'

'Was he dark? Fair?'

'Dark,' the man said, nodding. 'And he'd got an accent. He weren't from round here.'

'Did they seem close to you?'

'That's the funny thing,' said Peck, frowning. 'Like, he was all over her, but she didn't want to know … kept fidgeting, looking at her watch. The gal was bored rigid, if you ask me.'

'Can you remember what she was wearing?'

'Jeans and t-shirt.'

'And the man?'

Peck shook his head. 'Couldn't say.' Then he clicked his fingers. 'Hold on, he had a hat – a straw hat. He laid into the wife 'cause he'd put it in a puddle of beer, said we ought to clean the effin' place once in a while.' He grinned, showing Wells a line of brown uneven teeth. 'She gave him a mouthful.'

Wells pocketed his notebook and finished his drink, favoured the man with an easy smile. 'Thank you for your time, sir.'

'Have I helped?'

As Wells delved into his pocket for the car keys an image loomed large in his mind – an image of Roy Barlow tossing his straw hat into the dust as Jack held up the painting of Sky.

'Oh yes, Mr Peck. You've helped enormously.'

CHAPTER SIXTEEN

Philip Hunt truly believed he'd helped countless souls in his years as a spiritualist medium. All of whom shared the same desperate quest: to find evidence that those lost to them were safe, were healing and coping well in their terrifying new existence. He'd supplied that evidence, time and again, with messages that meant not a thing to him. And yet those messages had had the power to turn heartache into happiness, despair into hope.

Why, then, could he not perform that same miracle for himself?

The ginger-haired copper had asked why his spirit contacts couldn't tell them of Sky's whereabouts, and he'd trotted out his usual reply to enquiries of that sort. But deep within his own soul Phil was begging for some kind of clue, some small hint that Sky was still alive. So far she'd failed to make contact, and he was certain she would if the unthinkable had happened. Therefore his every prayer was centred around one gut-wrenching plea: *Don't let Sky be dead*.

His parents had over the past week spent hours in earnest meditation, yearning for that one small glint of inspiration that might lead them to the truth. For they bore daily witness to the searing melancholy that was eating away at their son, and both were fearful for his state of mind. He couldn't eat, could barely sleep; was continually overtaken by a fierce sense of foreboding. They needed to make progress for his sake as well as Sky's.

Phil worried too about Nathan and Amy. He loved those kids as if he'd been party to their creation. He longed to hold them, to offer them comfort. But the coppers couldn't divulge their whereabouts, and the newspapers had simply reported that they were at a secret address, being cared for by individuals beyond reproach. Phil could only send out loving thoughts and hope that somehow the kids would sense them.

Of course, Phil himself had always been beyond reproach. He was treading a spiritual path and battled continuously to keep his thoughts and deeds on a moral footing.

But all of that changed when they set up camp in Larchborough.

At the time Phil had believed that their actions were for the best, but he hadn't known then that Sky would simply disappear without a trace. In a way he still did believe they'd had no other option. But even so he was buggered because he needed to go to the police, and yet that was the one thing he couldn't do.

That morning's events, however, had started a shift in his way of thinking. He'd been to the library, had caused a scene with the good-natured assistant who hadn't for one moment deserved to be the focus of his fury. But it was said that the Lord worked in mysterious ways, and Phil could only agree. For hadn't the altercation brought to his attention the female copper?

Phil could no more bare his soul to DCI Wells than he could walk on water. But maybe that woman would listen. He'd sensed a high level of compassion within her, an empathetic aspect to her spirit that had reached out and touched him. Could she be the one to smash a hole in this crippling impasse?

Phil's stomach churned as he considered the possible implications of such a meeting. Was it the right thing to do? Or would he end up in a whole heap of trouble?

There was only one way to find out.

Mia followed the black van as it left the confines of the manor through a tradesman's entrance at Stratton End. Keeping a discreet distance in the smattering of afternoon traffic she wove around the tight lanes believing their destination to be an industrial estate two miles north of the manor. But, as they approached the turn-off, the van headed instead for the dual carriageway and Mia found herself following signs leading to Staples Brook.

She'd had few dealings with that part of town, but knew it to be crowded with reasonably priced new-builds: tiny starter homes and short terraces of mock-Georgian design, their miniscule open-plan gardens dotted with saplings, all of which were struggling in the interminable heat.

Staples Brook was purely residential. Why were they carting a vanload of artefacts – *valuable* artefacts – to a housing estate? Mia knew that Scott Beddows rented a bedsit in Corby. And Bulmer could easily afford better.

She was considering the ramifications of this puzzle when the van pulled into a side street which, even from her considerable distance, Mia could see was a dead-end. She parked behind a green Peugeot and hauled herself into the passenger seat where her view of the pair was unimpeded.

The road where they'd stopped was home to a number of lockup garages – five on either side of the badly laid cobbles. The garages were originally intended for use by the homeowners, but few could afford them on top of their mortgage payments and the construction company had therefore advertised them locally. Lack of space was a common feature in Larchborough's more expensive areas, and there were many who needed extra cover for their sailboats or motor homes or similar accoutrements.

175

The van was parked outside the furthest garage on the right-hand side. While Bulmer unlocked the brown up-and-over door Beddows scrambled into the back of the van and sorted through the stock. They worked speedily and methodically, tackling the boxes first of all.

Mia grabbed her mobile and dialled the number for Paul Wells but got Nick instead: all calls were diverted to him should the DCI be unavailable.

'Nick, I need back-up.'

'Why?'

Mia quickly related that afternoon's events. 'They've really been busy since Sir Nigel took off to France. There's a small fortune in the back of that van.'

She heard Nick's triumphant snort. 'I said Bulmer was up to no good.'

Mia made a face at the phone. 'OK, but the van's nearly empty. I need somebody here *now*.'

'I'll get central control to send the nearest car,' he said. 'And, for God's sake, don't do anything stupid.'

Nick was in the corridor outside interview room number two where he'd been rounding off his questioning of the travellers when his mobile buzzed. Roy Barlow and Philip Hunt - the main players in Sky's disappearance as far as he was concerned – were absent from the caravan site when he'd arrived unannounced in a police van. So he'd been left with the supporting cast.

Only Kelly Barlow had seemed willing to cooperate. But before Nick could extract even the smallest of facts the woman had doubled up in the chair, her face a deathly white, and the female officer standing in on the interviews had insisted that Nick terminate his interrogation and allow the woman to go home and rest. It had all been an abysmal waste of time. Short of grilling the snotty kids, there was little more he could do for the moment.

With a distinct lack of enthusiasm Nick made his way to where the travellers had all been fingerprinted and were now waiting to be transported back to the site – while their offspring systematically wrecked reception, no doubt.

He'd mention Mia's predicament when they were all off the premises. There was no rush.

Roy Barlow returned to his caravan that lunchtime to find a hastily scribbled note from Kelly declaring: *We've gone to the police station*. And straight away he thought the worst. He'd been painting just outside the camp, for fuck's sake. Kelly had helped him set up; more out of distrust than benevolence, he'd angrily assumed. But then, with quiet rage blossoming in his chest, Barlow noticed the stillness of the place, the distinct lack of people, and realized that they must all have gone to the station.

As intrigue replaced his fury, Barlow feasted on sweet blackberry pie – courtesy of Mrs Hunt – and took to wondering whether another visit to his delectable muse might be possible before Kelly's return. But he'd hardly had time to finish his lunch when a sharp rap came at the door and DCI Wells blustered into the cramped space. Wells hauled Barlow into his car with hardly a word of explanation and drove, grim-faced, back to Silver Street.

They were seated now – eyeballing each other across the rickety table – in one of the interview rooms, its open window inviting in more of the dry heat, a uniformed officer silently watching by the door.

'You're entitled to have a solicitor present,' Wells barked. 'You're gonna need one.'

'Am I?' Barlow's arrogance was shrivelling rapidly beneath the DCI's withering gaze, but his voice stayed strong, its tone defiant. 'Perhaps you could give me a clue to my crime and then I'll decide.'

Wells unbuttoned his jacket, opened it wide as he sat back in the chair, long legs crossed beneath the table. 'I've got a witness who's seen you with Sky Beddows since her disappearance. What have you got to say about that?'

'I'd say your witness is mistaken,' said Barlow, his insidious smile quick to form.

Wells studied his notebook. 'Sheila Reeves told my officers that you're always taking off for hours at a time. Where do you go?'

'Various places,' said Barlow, that smile still in place. 'I paint. You know I do. You ruined my session with your ridiculous notions – remember?'

'Ever been to the Red Lion, Mr Barlow?'

The man pursed his lips, a frown forming as he pondered. 'Can't say that I have. What is the Red Lion exactly?'

'It's a public house in Stratton End. The landlord told me you've been in a few times with a woman he's identified as Sky Beddows.' Wells folded his arms, favoured Barlow with a wry look. 'No use denying it.'

Barlow merely shrugged, but Wells detected a momentary lapse in the man's confidence and hope flourished. He was determined to get the bastard this time.

'You've been lucky so far,' said Wells, eyes narrowed.

'Have I?' said Barlow, matching the DCI's body language.

'If I'd been attending officer on that Tuesday night you'd be up for attempted rape by now.'

'And you'd be laughed out of court,' Barlow threw back. 'I could no more hurt Sky than cut my own throat.'

'I'm sure there's plenty'd do that for you,' said Wells, his glare taunting. 'But let's get back to Sky. It'd seem she's still uneasy in your company.'

The man rolled his eyes. 'What the fuck are you talking about now?'

'No, sorry, got that wrong,' said Wells, checking his notes. 'Not uneasy. Bored rigid. The landlord said Sky looked *bored rigid* in your company.'

For a fleeting moment Barlow glowered at the DCI, fists clenched, and Wells felt certain he'd cracked the man's defences. But then Barlow sank back in the seat, his quick rage a spent force as he pulled at the front of his shirt.

'Could I have a drop of water, do you think? It's awful close in here.'

Wells heard the uniformed officer pull at the door handle and held up a firm hand to stop him. 'No water for Mr Barlow. Not yet.'

'Thanks for your hospitality.'

'I'm not in this job to make friends.'

'Just as well,' Barlow muttered.

Wells let out a long breath. 'Why don't you come clean? We could settle this matter quite quickly with an identity parade.' He leant forward, his expression mocking. 'You ain't got nowhere to run, mate. Not this time.'

'Fuck off,' Barlow spat.

Wells riffled through his notebook, playing for time. He had no appetite for verbal ping-pong. It was too bloody hot. He needed to back the man into a corner, find his Achilles' heel.

While Barlow was being installed in the interview room Wells had been informed by the duty sergeant that he'd just missed the motley crowd from Heaven's Gate. Had to babysit the kids all morning, he'd complained. Needed to get the air freshener out to disguise the stink from the nappies. Bleedin' nightmare, it was. Wells had sympathized whilst trying to hide a grin. The usually jovial Jim Levers always looked comical when he was in a bad mood.

And now, as Wells recalled their conversation, he dared to hope that some clever manipulation of the facts might bring about his desired result.

'We've been talking to your missus,' he said, settling back in the chair.

'I know,' Barlow said, with the barest of flinches. 'She left me a note.'

'She was very forthright.'

Barlow moistened his lips, his gaze on the table top. 'What did she say?'

'What do you think she said?'

The man's heavy sigh was heartfelt. 'Look, Kelly's pregnant, Chief Inspector. Her body's in a state of flux. She gets overwrought. You shouldn't take any notice of her silly delusions.'

Adrenalin rushed through Wells's system as he dared to believe he was at last getting somewhere. Barlow was on the defensive, his brash posturing reduced now to an impassioned servility.

Wells remained calm, leant an arm on the back of his chair as he regarded the man with lightly veiled contempt. 'I've met your missus, don't forget. She didn't come across to me as silly – quite the opposite, in fact. 'Course, she did marry you, but we all make mistakes.'

'Are you married, Chief Inspector?' Wells nodded. 'Then you'll know what a stifling environment it is. Marriage continually grinds a man down until he ceases to exist, until he becomes … *nothing*.'

Wells considered Barlow's self-pitying expression with a wide grin on his lips. 'At a guess, Mr Barlow, I'd say you were nothing to start with.' He straightened up, pretended to search for a certain page in his notes. 'I can see now, though, why your missus was so willing to spill the beans. Life with you can't be much of a picnic.'

'But you mustn't believe her,' Barlow said, leaning over the table. 'She's upset. She's trying to get back at me.'

'And who can blame her?' Wells responded sharply. He gave Barlow a puzzled look, a frown slowly forming. 'If you're so against family life, why do you keep making the poor girl pregnant?'

Barlow shrugged. 'I was brought up a good Catholic, Chief Inspector. Children are given by God. It's wrong for man to interfere.'

'Oh right,' said Wells, humour showing in his eyes. 'Or maybe you can't manage the condom when you're pissed out of your skull.'

'Think what you like,' Barlow murmured, falling back in the chair.

Wells observed the man's cocksure expression and decided a few creative fabrications were called for. He took a moment to study closely the words in his notebook – words that happened to form a list of groceries he needed to purchase for his own wife – in the hope of undermining Barlow's confidence. Slamming the notebook shut Wells sat back, his own expression grim.

'Your missus certainly doesn't pull any punches,' he said. 'OK, on the strength of Mrs Barlow's testimony we have the right to detain you until such time as you tell us where and why you're holding Sky Beddows.'

Wells turned in his seat, started to call the uniformed officer across.

'Wait,' said Barlow, aghast, 'I'm not holding Sky anywhere.' Wells made a face. 'She wouldn't be away from her kids out of choice.'

'All right,' said Barlow, hands held high. 'I'll tell you the truth.'

'About bloody time.' Wells grabbed his notebook, got ready to write. 'Let's hear it then.'

The man took in a breath, pulled again at his shirt. 'I have been seeing a girl. Not Sky, but a girl like Sky. A girl with Sky's luminescence.'

'Pull the other one.'

'But it's the truth. I'll tell you where she is. I'll take you there.'

'What's her name?' asked Wells, his last vestige of hope about to disintegrate.

'Stacey Lewis. She's a prostitute. She works not far from the Red Lion. I met her soon after Sky disappeared. I was out walking. I needed to clear my head and there she was.'

Barlow stopped abruptly, his worried glance urging Wells to believe him. And, try as he might, the DCI couldn't disbelieve him. The words had come too quickly, too sincerely to be anything but the truth. Wells bit back a curse.

'Doesn't your missus let you have it when she's up the duff?'

'What do you mean?'

'The minute Sky vanishes you have to find another girl to screw.'

Barlow lunged forward, earnestly shaking his head. 'You don't understand. I've not had sex with Stacey or Sky. Dear God—' He sat back, attempted to control his emotions as he stared Wells in the eye. 'It's inspiration I'm after, Chief Inspector, because believe it or not I care about my art. It's what I live for. Sky inspires me. She allows my creativity to soar. With her I'm able to produce my finest work.'

Barlow's voice cracked and he lowered his gaze, swallowing loudly. When he next took in a breath to speak Wells was amazed to see tears glistening in his eyes.

'But without Sky I'm useless … less than useless. Even my charcoal sketches are second-rate.' He gave a helpless shrug. 'After Sky went off I was desolate, empty of all desire … until I met Stacey. She had that certain something, that special quality I found in Sky. I thought if I could use her as my model I'd maybe function until Sky came back.'

'You've been paying a prostitute to sit for you?'

'Yes.'

Wells scratched his head with the tip of his pen, face alive with amusement. 'So you just need these girls to massage your creative muscle, as opposed to one that's a bit more basic.'

'That's right.'

'Well, this all sounds very noble, Mr Barlow, but we've still got it on record that you attempted to rape Sky Beddows on the night of Tuesday the seventeenth of July … a matter of hours before she vanished into thin air.'

Barlow gave Wells a pained look, was about to offer a bitter retort. But instead he laid his hands on the table, rubbed at an old cigarette burn on its surface. 'All right, I admit I got a little overexcited—'

'A little?' Wells interrupted. 'The girl's clothes were ripped, according to the report. She was in a state of acute distress, according to the report.' Wells's voice had risen with each syllable and Barlow cowered before the sudden outburst. 'The report also states that during a fight between your good self and Philip Hunt you threatened to kill Sky Beddows. If you couldn't have her then nobody would – that's more or less what you said. Right?'

Barlow let out a long breath as he fell back in the seat. 'I was drunk. I can't remember.'

'You almost had me believing you,' said Wells, getting to his feet, the chair scraping loudly on the dusty floor tiles.

'Can I go?' asked Barlow, pushing back his own chair.

'No, you can't.'

The man's face became a mask of terror. 'Why, what's happening?'

'We're going to find your Stacey Lewis, Mr Barlow. My DS is on good terms with a number of the town's prostitutes so it shouldn't take long. You'd better just pray we do find her.' At the door Wells turned to the uniformed officer. 'Watch him. And if he even breathes too loud you have my permission to sling him in a cell.'

CHAPTER SEVENTEEN

'Rabbit's blood?'

'Yes, sir.'

'Actually on the T-shirt?'

'Yes, sir.'

Wells stared at Jack as though he'd grown an extra head. 'Let's have a look at the report,' he said.

Jack handed across a black plastic folder containing the findings of forensic tests carried out on Cathy Cousins's T-shirt. Wells perched on the edge of his desk, scratched the nape of his neck as he devoured the words. The report told him that antiserum tests performed on bloodstains within the fabric had produced two results: 1 – that the majority of the blood was type B positive, a match for Cathy's. And 2 – that a small stain found near the hem of the T-shirt was, in fact, blood from a rabbit.

'Weird,' said Wells. 'Did you ask forensics to test the knives at the manor?'

'Yes, they're making it a priority, sir.'

'Good.' Wells returned his attention to the report. 'It says here they found pollen from Trifolium Pratense – what's that when it's at home?'

'Red clover,' said Jack. 'Small pink flowers found in grassy places. I looked it up on the Web. I've printed it off actually, sir, thought we might need it.'

'You're a little treasure, mate.' Wells tossed the folder on to his desk and sat facing Jack, arms folded. 'Find out about the manor's gardening staff, will you? In the meantime I'm on the lookout for a prostitute.'

'Sir?'

Wells filled him in on Roy Barlow's interview. 'Stacey Lewis. Know her?' Jack thought for a moment then shook his head. 'Me neither. But Mia seems to spend an inordinate amount of time trying to keep them safe so I'm hoping she will.'

He was reaching for the phone when a fractious rumbling began in the corridor. As the noise grew louder the door to the office was flung open by Mia, indignation making her every movement brittle. Nick followed behind, a gloating expression spoiling his handsome face.

'What's up now?' Wells sighed.

Mia tossed her bag behind her desk and told him about Scott Beddows and Andrew Bulmer. 'Nick was supposed to be sending back-up, only it never arrived so I had to call it in myself.' She glared at Nick and tutted. 'It's not on, sir. The van was about to pull off when uniformed eventually got there.'

'I wasn't exactly twiddling my thumbs when you phoned,' Nick blustered. 'I'd got most of the travellers causing a riot in reception.'

'That's enough,' said Wells. 'Where are they now?'

'Downstairs,' said Mia. 'Trying to explain why they've got thousands of pounds worth of Sir Nigel's stuff in a lock-up in Staples Brook.'

'Well done. Now I need you to find a prostitute called Stacey Lewis. Roy Barlow reckons she's been sitting for him.'

'As in sitting for a portrait?' Mia snorted as she made her way to the coffee percolator. 'I've never heard it called that before.'

'Barlow's still in the interview room, darling, so you need to be quick.'

'No problem, sir, I'll get on to one of my girls.' She sniffed the milk carton and grimaced. 'Milk's gone off. Who wants black?'

They all did. Mia placed Wells's mug on his desk. 'I've got Sally Simms waiting downstairs, sir. Shall I leave her there while I find Stacey?'

'Yes, let's make her sweat.'

Mia handed out the rest of the coffees and slumped into her chair. 'Sally didn't like being hauled in. Gave me an earful all the way here.' She took a sip of her drink. 'That guitarist's a funny bloke.'

'Lenny Price?' said Nick.

Mia nodded. 'He came down to the car with us, having a go at me, threatening to do us for harassment. He looked like a reject from the Rambo films – army jacket, bandanna round his head, the lot.'

'Did you see Johnny Lee?' asked Jack.

'No, he was having a lie-down. It's all getting a bit much for him, apparently.'

Wells said, 'Did Elizabeth Thornton give us anything to go on?'

'Not much.' Mia recounted all she'd gleaned. 'That woman's obsessed with Johnny Lee Rogers. It's really sad.'

'By the way, Mia,' said Jack, leaving his seat, 'here's everything that's been published about Cathy's murder, like you asked for.' He dumped the papers on her desk.

'And what's this?' she asked, picking up the top page. 'All the calls from Cathy's mobile?'

Jack peered across. 'Oh, yeah.'

Wells said, 'Any luck with that photographer, Jack?'

'Yes and no, sir. His name's Richard Smith and he works for the *Echo*. The editor told me Saturday's rehearsal was his last assignment before a two-week holiday. Smith was on a flight to Ibiza when Cathy was being stabbed.'

'Pity.' Wells glanced at Nick. 'And I don't suppose your morning came to anything, mate, or you'd have said by now.'

Nick shook his head. 'Those interviews were a waste of time, sir. It's hardly worth typing them up.'

'We've got their prints though?'

'Yes, sir. And I've still got to do Philip Hunt. He wasn't there when I hauled them in.'

Jack said to Wells, 'I put their names in the system, sir, and they're all clean, apart from Sheila Reeves. She's been done twice for fiddling benefits, years back. I got on to the tax office, actually, because I found discrepancies in her details. Somebody's cocked up, but I don't know whether it's us or them. Anyway, they're looking into it and getting back to us.'

'OK.' Wells drained his coffee and banged the mug on his desk in a decisive fashion. 'Right, kiddies, we might have drawn a few blanks today but I'm happy about that. It narrows the field, gets us focusing on what's left.' He held up the forensic report and said to Nick, 'They found rabbit blood and clover pollen on Cathy's T-shirt. What does that suggest to you?'

Nick lifted a shoulder. 'Not sure, sir – she disturbed some poachers?'

A deflated Wells let the report drop. 'I was leaning more towards the gardening staff.' He heaved a heartfelt sigh. 'Christ, if the killer's some random poacher, how the hell are we gonna find him?'

'I think we already have,' said Mia. 'Only it's a *she* not a *he*.'

Silence fell and all eyes turned her way.

'When I spoke to Elizabeth Thornton this morning she mentioned Cathy's battered face. But the newspapers and online news sites only detailed her stab wounds.' She motioned towards the papers given to her by Jack. 'Nobody made any reference to her face.'

'Really?' said Wells, a sturdy grin stretching across *his* well-worn features.

'And that phone call Cathy made on Sunday morning,' Mia went on.

'It was to Miss Thornton?'

'The very same, sir.'

It took Mia a speedy thirty minutes to find Stacey Lewis. She'd built up a solid rapport with Larchborough's working girls over the years. Times were hard, the town's streets dangerous after dark, and Mia could always count on their unerring support when tracking down any threat to their safety.

One phone call and a short car ride found Mia in Adelaide Street where Stacey Lewis was busy pulling on a cigarette and tottering unsteadily on six inch heels, her large blue eyes gazing hopefully at every passing vehicle.

The unrelenting sun was for the moment concealed behind a cloak of diaphanous cloud, but the early evening was still in thrall to a savage heat which sucked energy from all that moved. Having already been alerted to Mia's hopes for a chat, the lethargic Stacey was happy to answer any questions relating to the bizarre specimen that was Roy Barlow. And in no time at all Mia was back in the car, mobile phone glued to her ear.

'Sir, it seems Barlow's kosher.'

Wells's agitated breath travelled along the airwaves. 'What did she say?'

'That Barlow's been paying her twenty pounds an hour to sit still while he sketches. No sex, not much chat….'

'Any mention of Sky?'

'She said not. They go to her place where he draws for a bit. He buys her a couple of drinks at the Red Lion, then hands over the money and disappears.'

'And you believe her?'

'No reason not to, sir. She said he's tedious as hell but harmless. Easy money, she said.'

'Does she look like Sky?'

'Not a dead ringer, no. Pretty, though – long blonde hair, same big eyes. I can see why she reminds him of Sky.'

Wells's disappointment was almost palpable. 'OK, I'd better let him go. You can call it a day as well.'

'What about Sally Simms, sir?'

'Nick's dropping her off on his way home. I'm still waiting for Elizabeth Thornton to be brought in.'

'You're seeing her on your own?'

'Yes.'

'I'll sit in, if you like.'

Wells snorted. 'You're keen.'

Mia only had an M & S Pasta Bake and the rerun of *Friends* to go home to and was eager to put off the dubious excitement for as long as possible, but she couldn't tell Wells that.

'I'd like to know what she's got to say, sir.'

'I'll tell you in the morning. Now get off, darling, before I change my mind.'

Mia couldn't actually go straight home. She'd left her flat keys in her desk at work – rather that than risk losing them during the day. She'd done it twice already.

Jack was still in the office when she got back. He was tidying his desk, a look of deadly annoyance bringing that familiar flush to his freckled features.

'Still here?' she said.

'No, I left ages ago,' he muttered, without looking up.

'Oh dear, somebody's in a mood,' she said, plucking her keys from the desk drawer.

Jack gave up on his erratic filing system and sank into his chair, pouting. 'Michelle's off out with the girls … *again*.'

'So?'

'So, she's supposed to be taking it easy. I've got a DVD for tonight. *Hancock*. She likes Will Smith.'

Mia gave him a maternal look. 'Listen, sweetie, she'll have plenty of time to watch DVDs when she's as big as a house. Let her have a good time while she can, as long as she doesn't drink.'

'She won't. She's got the car,' he said, his annoyance rumbling into life again. 'She was *supposed* to be picking me up.'

Mia retrieved her bag and turned off the coffee percolator, all the while displaying a benevolent smile. 'I'll give you a lift, sweetie. Let's go.'

The empty reception area at that time of day always reminded Mia of a cinema foyer after everybody's gone in to watch the film. It possessed a strange air of passive stillness while all the exciting stuff was being carried out behind closed doors.

After a few teasing words to the bored-looking duty sergeant they stepped into a slight but welcoming breeze that was trying its utmost to agitate the close evening air. And they were almost at Mia's car when a solitary figure stepped from the lengthening shadows into the sodium glare of a nearby streetlamp.

Mia gasped out loud, dropping her car keys in surprise. Stooping to pick them up she heard Jack say, 'What do you want, mate?' and a man's voice replying, 'It's the lady I've come to see.'

'Why?' asked Mia, the word heavy with suspicion.

'I need to talk to you.'

Mia peered across at him in the half gloom. He was of average build with nondescript features, but all the same he seemed strangely familiar. 'Hold on,' she said. 'Were you causing a fuss in the library earlier today?'

The man nodded. 'Can you help me?'

It was then that Mia noticed the laptop under his arm. 'For God's sake,' she said, sighing. 'Get on to your service provider.'

Mia was aiming her unlocking device at the car while Jack skirted round to the passenger side when the man said, 'I'm trying to find Sky Beddows. Please help me.'

Mia had the driver's door half open. She closed it again, frowning. 'Who are you?'

'Philip Hunt.' Mia watched as the man's face puckered and a torrent of tears tumbled down his cheeks. 'I don't want her to be dead. Please help me find her.'

'We're doing our best,' she said, her hand on his shoulder.

'But this might help find her quicker,' said Phil, thrusting the laptop at Mia.

'Why? What's on it?'

'I don't know yet,' he said, wiping the tears from his face. 'I can't get into the bloody thing.'

Mia stared at him, eyes clouded with puzzlement. 'It's not yours?'

He shook his head. Then, hesitating briefly as if afraid to release the words, he said, 'It belongs to Robert Mandley.'

Mia was taken aback. 'What?'

'I stole it from his car. I didn't want to, but Sky begged me. She had an idea we'd find evidence she needed on it.'

'Evidence of what?' asked Jack, stepping up behind him.

'I don't know. She wouldn't tell me. I know Mandley's her father and that she hates him. She said there're things from his past – *terrible* things – that he wouldn't want people to know about, but she wouldn't say what they were. She didn't want to come to Larchborough – she *hates* the place – but once we got here she said maybe fate had brought her back to finally make him pay.'

The words had come out in a rush, almost on one breath, and Phil slumped against the car, exhausted. The detectives exchanged a quick glance.

Jack said, 'I *knew* you weren't telling us everything when we questioned you before. *Do* you know where Sky was going on the day she disappeared?'

Phil shook his head. 'She said the least I knew the better. All I had to do was get into the laptop and she'd see to the rest.'

'Do you love her?' asked Mia.

He nodded. 'And the kids … more than anything.'

Mia's thoughts were oscillating wildly. There she was, interacting with a man who'd stolen property from the town's most prominent citizen – causing criminal damage to the man's car as he did so – and she was even now considering ways of entering said property. Wells would have a purple fit if he knew. And rightly so this time.

But then she imagined Sky Beddows. Missing for a whole week. Kept apart from children she clearly adored. Mia cast a surreptitious glance at Phil Hunt and made up her mind that he was telling them the truth. Not even the finest actor could fake such a harrowing display of emotions. He had to be for real.

Oh well, in for a penny....

'Do you like frozen ready meals, Phil?'

The man gave her a curious look, as though she'd spoken the words in ancient Latin. 'Sorry?'

'They're all that's on offer at my flat.'

And then clarity dawned. 'You mean you're willing to help?'

'If my partner's in as well,' she said, aiming a questioning look at Jack.

His responding nod was heavy with resignation. 'Go on, then. Who needs a monthly salary anyway?'

Mia's triumphant grin lit up the surrounding gloom. 'Philip Hunt,' she said, 'meet Jack Turnbull, Larchborough's finest technical wizard.'

Paul Wells's first sighting of Lizzie Thornton – being forcibly led across reception due to the fact that she was screaming blue murder – had made his jaw drop almost to his chest. He'd expected a more mature woman on account of Mia's rather brutal 'she'll never see forty again – and fifty's probably a faint memory by now'. But he'd expected one of those classic beauties, with luminous skin which refused to acknowledge gravity and a youthful spirit glowing from eyes that time had forgotten to age. Instead, he found she was a horse-toothed harridan whose ghastly hair and even ghastlier attitude would befit any one of the witches in *Macbeth*. Little wonder that singer had given her a miss.

By the time she was installed in the interview room Lizzie had ceased her ranting and was sitting tight-lipped; the uniformed officer who'd almost dragged her there massaging his strained biceps as he positioned himself at the door. And, as she held Wells's gaze with small piggy eyes lurking beneath brows that resembled a pair of antagonistic black caterpillars, the DCI was wishing he'd taken up Mia's offer to sit in. He was becoming quite uncomfortable under her steady glare. Could he be hexed in such a routine setting? *Was* she a witch?

'You don't have to say anything, Miss Thornton. If you prefer I could caution you and put this interview on a more formal footing.' Wells took out his notebook. 'Care to give me the name of your solicitor?'

Those words, that notion, had the desired effect, and Lizzie was lifted almost immediately from her rather disturbing trance.

'I'm frightened you'll put words in my mouth,' she said, the sentence hardly audible.

Wells had no intention of getting anywhere near that mouth, those hideous teeth. He nodded towards the uniformed officer. 'If I tried that, love, our friend here'd soon start blabbing to my boss.'

'Oh … good,' said Lizzie, unbuttoning her cardigan and shifting her position in the chair. 'Although I did tell your female colleague everything this morning. What else can I say?'

Wells fixed her with a determined look. 'You could start by explaining how you knew Cathy had injuries to her face.'

'I beg your pardon?'

'You heard.'

Lizzie frowned, causing those brows to collide spectacularly. 'It's been in all the papers, on the news. Everybody knows.'

Wells shook his head. 'The press only reported that Cathy had been stabbed. No mention was made anywhere about her other injuries.'

'Sorry, but you're wrong. I read it in the paper. *The Evening News*, most probably. That's the one I normally take.'

Wells retrieved his briefcase from the floor and proceeded to unbuckle its leather straps. 'Thing is, Miss Thornton, I've got every report from the papers, TV *and* the Internet in here.

Now, we could waste time going through them, or you could tell me the truth.'

Lizzie tutted crossly, took to patting her hair and tucking stray strands behind her ears. But she said nothing.

Wells slammed shut his briefcase and let out an exasperated breath. 'You like Johnny Lee Rogers, I hear.'

'I do,' she said, still attending to her hair.

'You must have been pretty mad when he made a play for Cathy.'

'It wasn't at all like that,' said Lizzie, rolling her eyes.

'I think it was. And who can blame him for fancying her? Cathy was a very pretty young woman.'

'She wasn't his type – much too shallow and stupid.'

Wells snorted. 'They ended up shagging all night. It wasn't her intellect he was after.'

'Oh, please …' she said.

Wells rested his pen on top of the notebook and sat back, arms folded. 'Do you reckon Mr Rogers could have killed Cathy?'

'No,' said Lizzie, panic suddenly flaring in those piercing eyes. 'Johnny Lee's a sensitive man. He couldn't do such a thing.'

'I've been thinking about it,' Wells said, gazing into the distance as though considering the possibility. 'Let's say he had his wicked way with Cathy and then wanted rid of her come the morning. Only she wouldn't go, flatly refused, threatened to shout "rape". Rogers panicked. A charge like that could ruin his career, such as it is. He needed to shut her up, once and for all.'

'No,' she said, pulling at the handkerchief she'd plucked from her sleeve. 'That's absurd.'

'Nevertheless, it's a line of inquiry we're eager to pursue.'

Lizzie had started to tremble. This was a shocking state of affairs. She couldn't allow that awful man to incriminate Johnny Lee. How would their destiny ever be achieved if her lover was incarcerated in a prison cell?

'Did you help Mr Rogers kill Cathy, Miss Thornton?'

'What?'

'You must have been there. How else could you know about the poor girl's face?' Wells leant forward, fixed her with his hostile glare. 'Did you hold her down while Rogers shoved the knife in? Did you enjoy it?'

Lizzie's face took on a haunted look, eyes darting to the uniformed officer. 'Do something. *Please ...*' she begged. But the young man merely shrugged.

Wells continued his relentless attack. 'Why did the bastard destroy her face?'

'But, he didn't,' said Lizzie, crying now.

'Oh, I see, you did it. You were jealous because she'd managed to pull your bloke. You'd spent the whole night imagining Cathy in bed with him.' Wells let out a low whistle. 'You must have been mad as hell when you went back that Sunday morning.'

'No....' Lizzie was dabbing at her face with the handkerchief, trying desperately to regain her composure. 'I had no further contact with Cathy after I left the rehearsal.'

Wells's staccato laugh was entirely without humour. 'Come on, love, we both know that's a lie.' He opened his briefcase again, pulled out the list of calls from Cathy's mobile phone and held it up for Lizzie to see. 'Cathy called you that Sunday morning. It says so here.'

Lizzie reared up in the seat. 'I knew you'd try to incriminate me.' She shot a terrified glance towards the uniformed officer. 'Why aren't you doing something about this?'

Wells tapped the computer sheet. 'Sorry, love, but we can't ignore the evidence.'

Lizzie's eyes remained fixed to the paper as Wells laid it on the table. 'Maybe she did phone, maybe she phoned a hundred times, but I didn't answer. I swear.'

'Somebody did. The call lasted for almost a minute and a half.'

Lizzie shrugged. 'It wasn't me.'

'Do you live alone, Miss Thornton?'

'No, I share a house with my aunt.'

'Could your aunt have picked up the call?'

Lizzie gave a derisory snort. 'I shouldn't think so. Not at that time on a Sunday morning.'

Wells had to hide a smile. 'What time would that be, Miss Thornton?'

'Sorry?' said Lizzie, looking horrified.

They were on the home run now. God, he loved his job at times. 'Your aunt likes a lie-in on a Sunday then?'

Those eyes did another exaggerated roll. 'When doesn't she?'

'You must look forward to sleeping late yourself on a weekend.'

'Too true,' said Lizzie, nodding vigorously.

'So you must have been miffed when Cathy called.'

For a mere second Lizzie looked set to nod. Then she quickly brought the handkerchief to her face, but not before Wells caught the terror residing there.

'What time was she supposed to have called?' asked Lizzie, attempting indifference. 'You didn't actually say.'

'You can stop digging now,' said Wells, grinning. 'The hole's big enough for both of us.'

'I want to go home,' said Lizzie, eyes brimming again.

'So do I,' Wells huffed. 'I'm hungry and I need a shower.'

Lizzie tossed him a hopeful look. 'Then, let's go. I'm really late getting dinner on.'

'Sorry, love, your aunt might have to feed herself tonight.'

'But she can't—'

'She'll bloody well have to unless you start talking,' said Wells, his voice rising rapidly. 'We know you spoke to Cathy on Sunday morning, and we know you saw her dead body. Those are pretty incriminating facts, Miss Thornton. You could be remanded overnight on that evidence alone. Is that what you want?'

Lizzie shook her head, dislodging another batch of tears. 'I want to go home.'

'Then tell me what happened.'

But Lizzie was saying nothing.

'*Did* Rogers kill Cathy? Are you keeping shtum to protect him?'

A slight shake of her head.

'If he's guilty we're gonna get him, love. In fact, with today's forensic technology, there's no way we *can't* get him.'

Wells had leant in towards her, was placing emphasis on every word so that Lizzie would be in no doubt as to the strength of his resolve. She was staring at the table top, hands over her ears, trying to disengage herself from a reality that was growing increasingly more shocking with each beat of her troubled heart.

'You see, his semen and saliva were all over her. There were love bites we can match with his dental records.'

That last disclosure was pure fiction – in fact Wells wasn't entirely sure the forensic boffins could find anything from such a bite – but he needed her to imagine the singer in a sexual frenzy. And his ploy seemed to be working because a disgusted shudder thundered through Lizzie as she clasped her hands ever tighter over her ears.

'It must have been one hell of a night,' Wells continued blithely. 'Your bloke's skin cells were under Cathy's nails where she'd clawed at his back while he shagged her senseless. A pubic hair was found between her teeth from when she'd … well, best leave that to the imagination, eh?' He paused to clear his throat, allowed time for that little gem to sink in. 'Oh yes, Miss Thornton, your friend didn't leave him disappointed, I'll bet.'

'My friend?' Lizzie shouted, getting to her feet. 'Cathy was no *friend*. I couldn't stand the slut. Johnny Lee was *mine*. He's *still* mine, you'll see. Fate has brought him here for *me*. But Cathy had to be centre of attention, had to have all eyes of her. Standing there in next to nothing, face caked in make-up. Disgusting little whore….'

'Is that why you killed her?'

'The tart thought she could steal him, thought he'd want her instead of me.' She gave a loud hysterical laugh. 'What a joke?'

'Answer my question, Miss Thornton.'

'As if he'd want her for anything other than the carnal pleasures ... Cathy had no conversation, only trivial self-centred drivel. No opinions. No capacity for structured thought.'

'So you killed her.'

Lizzie stared down at the DCI, her round features drawn into a hideous scowl. 'I wanted to. Oh God, I did. And if he hadn't done it first I would have.'

If he hadn't done it first ...

Wells sank back in silence. Shock had stolen his voice for he was truly astounded. He hadn't expected that. He'd assumed that Lizzie had arrived at the manor that morning fully intending to do away with Cathy. Wells had come across many women – and men, for that matter – whose lives were overwhelmed by one crazy obsession or another. Elizabeth Thornton was clearly in the grips of a strong infatuation for the ageing singer, an infatuation that had spiralled out of control. And Cathy Cousins – probably unaware that such feelings could exist in one so dreadfully plain – had grabbed the chance of a night with somebody famous. A night she could boast about in the pub with her friends, not imagining for a second that such a move would totally devastate her workmate.

Wells stared up at Lizzie's horrified features, felt his quickening pulse pound away in his ears.

'Sit down, Miss Thornton, we're very nearly finished.'

He motioned for the uniformed officer to switch on the overhead fluorescent strip. The evening was growing dark and he hadn't even noticed. And as a now sobbing Lizzie Thornton resumed her seat Wells took up his notebook and pen.

Over at Mia's flat Phil Hunt had said a polite no thank you to everything except a cool glass of squash. But Jack couldn't wait to try the ready meal – Michelle was a health food fanatic; anything containing even the hint of an additive was banished from their shopping trolley – and he'd asked Mia to leave the tuna and pasta in its plastic dish in order to enhance the experience.

Now, with the tedious business of eating out of the way, they were kneeling before Mia's glass-topped coffee table, waiting for the laptop to boot up.

Jack had asked for a pair of latex gloves before he'd even think of touching it – breaking into the eminent lawyer's files was one thing, but leaving his fingerprints all over the show was a step too far – and she'd informed him, with heavy sarcasm, that as she wasn't in the habit of performing surgical operations in her spare time, there was none to be had. So Jack was now tapping at the keys, in the clumsy manner of an inquisitive chimpanzee, wearing a pair of pink Marigolds.

Jack's first attempt at entering a password – SHYSTER, because Mandley had successfully represented some pretty dodgy clients – resulted in "password hint: NAME" appearing on the screen.

'See, I told you,' said Phil. 'I've put in every name I could think of, but nothing works.'

'OK, folks, talk amongst yourselves,' said Jack. 'This could take some time.'

'Fancy some more squash?' Mia asked Phil.

He nodded and followed her into the kitchen.

She swilled his glass at the sink, her back towards him. 'Were you waiting outside the law courts to confront Mandley, Phil?'

He gave her a frown. 'How do you know I was there?'

She hesitated, busied herself with the tea towel to cover the awkward pause. 'We had you followed for a while,' she said, unwilling to meet his eyes. 'We thought you might have had something to do with Sky's disappearance.'

'Bloody hell, you don't still think—'

She turned to him then. 'No, I don't. Not anymore.'

'I just wanted to talk to him, hear what he had to say.'

'Good job you didn't get the chance,' she said, pulling a face. 'He's not the easiest of men according to my boss.'

Phil gave a sigh, wiped the sweat from his brow with the hem of his T-shirt. 'I was desperate to report her missing that Wednesday, only I was scared you'd find out about the laptop if I did. I couldn't risk getting arrested because of my folks. They need me.' He watched as Mia refilled his glass. 'You think Sky's dead, don't you?'

She didn't reply immediately. What could she say? Phil was a nice bloke; it would be too cruel to destroy his hopes with the truth.

Moving to switch on the kettle, she said, 'Do you?'

He gave a despondent shrug and leant against the sink, hands in his jeans pockets. 'What usually happens when somebody goes missing? Do you ever find them alive?'

'Oh yes,' she said, rather too heartily. 'More often than not, actually.'

The kettle was coming to the boil and Mia was glad for the chance to turn away from him. That look of helplessness in his eyes was almost too much to bear at times. She made coffee for herself and Jack and they returned to the living room.

'Any luck, sweetie?' she asked, setting Jack's mug beside the laptop.

'Not yet,' he said. 'But ve have vays of making zese things talk.'

'Nice accent,' she said, joining Phil on the sofa. 'Scottish, was it?'

'German, you plank.'

'In that case, don't give up the day job.'

Jack made a face. 'I might be forced to if we're found out.'

'Just get on with your criminal activities, there's a good chap.'

Phil put a hand on Mia's arm. 'I'm really grateful for this. You know that, don't you?'

She gave him a smile, took a sip of her coffee. 'I know.'

He toyed with his glass for a moment, followed the beads of condensation with his finger. 'Nathan and Amy,' he said, at last. 'They are all right?'

'Absolutely,' said Mia.

'Only the papers aren't giving anything away.'

'Trust me,' she said, resting a reassuring hand on *his* arm. 'I'm not allowed to tell you who's got them but, well, let's just say they're where they ought to be.'

He fell silent again, took to watching Jack's battle with the laptop.

'Phil,' said Mia, her tone rather hesitant, 'when you make contact … you know … with the spirits … can you call up a specific person? I mean, say Mrs Smith wants a chat with her hubby … do you sort of draw him to you?'

'Wish I could. It'd make my work a lot easier. I just get whoever wants to communicate at that particular time.' Phil gave her a sideways glance. 'Why? Who would you like a chat with?'

'My dad,' she said, feeling slightly silly.

'Was he a policeman?'

'Chief Superintendent, here in Larchborough.' She grimaced. 'God, he was so by the book. If he's watching us now he'll be going ballistic.'

'No, he won't. You're doing this for the right reasons. He'll be proud of you.'

Mia was suddenly horrified to feel tears forming in her eyes. She brought the mug to her lips, but could only pretend to drink because the lump forming in her throat would prevent anything going down.

Phil, sensitive to her feelings and wanting to give her space, wandered across to where a number of shelves held all the books that Mia had no time to read. And he found that her tastes were varied: horror, family sagas and true crime jostled for space with fantasy and romantic novels.

'Didn't have you down as the spiritual type,' he said, plucking a book from the top row.

'Which one's that?'

'*A Symphony Of Angels*,' he said, holding it towards her. 'Gabriel Walsh.'

She cringed. 'A birthday present from one of my more enlightened colleagues. I did skim through it, actually. Now, every time I see a white feather I think of our celestial friends.'

Phil was about to return the book, but stopped midway and looked again at the cover. 'Jack,' he said, hurriedly, 'try Gabriel.'

But Jack was having trouble with the cumbersome Marigolds. 'Hang on a minute, mate.'

Phil turned to Mia, caught the curiosity in her expression. 'Me and Sky were discussing kids' names once – thoughts of the future and all that – and I said I'd like Gabriel for a boy. But she said no way. She said that was her dad's middle name. He used to boast about it, said it was fitting because it meant "strength of God" and that's what he had in the courtroom.'

'How do you spell it,' asked Jack. 'G-A-B-R-I-E-L?'

Phil nodded and they both held their breath while he typed it in. Then the blue from the screen reflecting on Jack's face turned to violet as he said, 'Here we go. We're in business, folks.'

There were seventy-five files in all. And for the next thirty minutes they trawled through letters to clients, witnesses, police authorities, and Sir Nigel Stratton – who was a close friend as well as a paying punter according to the language used in his communications. Mandley had the previous year's tax return on there; financial spreadsheets; articles he was currently working on for legal publications; even the first sixty-one pages of a novel.

They were almost at the end of the list and had so far found nothing untoward; not one thing to justify Sky's apparent hopes of clues to crimes for which she thought him guilty. There were two files left to check. One entitled: NEW LEGISLATION; the other: MISCELLANEOUS.

'Try "miscellaneous",' said Mia.

So Jack did. And they found themselves staring at the horrific picture of a small girl being brutally raped by a grossly overweight middle-aged man. The man's face was out of camera shot, but the girl's showed all too graphically the excruciating pain and unholy terror caused by that thoroughly inhuman act.

A small box in the top left-hand corner of the screen indicated that the image was the first of two thousand, seven hundred and forty nine.

All three were silent, hardly daring to breathe, the only sound a faint drone of traffic filtering in from afar.

Jack scrolled through a few more pictures – each one showing the awful depths of Mandley's depravity – and then closed the file as quickly as the Marigolds would allow.

'Now we know,' he said, angrily pulling off the gloves.

Mia was clutching at her stomach, her fearful gaze upon him.

'God, Jack, and we let him have the kids,' she said.

CHAPTER EIGHTEEN

It was 8.15 on Friday morning. Mia was at her desk, heart pounding from too much coffee and the realization that immediate suspension was a strong possibility once DCI Wells arrived. She'd spent a sleepless night, the hours dragging interminably as she focused on that imminent bollocking with all the intensity of a wild animal gnawing at an injured limb, and she felt like death.

But those images on the lawyer's laptop couldn't be ignored. She'd seen enough filth during her years on the force to know that they were hardcore. Knew too that pictures could only satisfy sick bastards like Mandley for so long; sooner or later they'd start lusting after the real thing. And now he'd got Nathan and Amy. No wonder he'd been so keen to take on the parental role.

Wells would want Mandley out of circulation as quickly as possible, would probably be first in the queue to castrate him with a very blunt knife before leaving him to endure an arduous lingering death. Indeed, in different circumstances Mia would most likely be hailed as a strong contender for a commendation. But they'd come upon the information by criminal means, and Wells was from the same mould as her father. He'd never condone what they'd done.

Mia had urged Jack to deny all knowledge of the laptop, arguing that with a baby on the way he needed to keep his job. But his refusal had been loud and heartfelt, even though the panic in his eyes had told an entirely different story. She'd given him a lift in that morning, the journey conducted in a heavy silence that ended only when Jim Levers threw them a boisterous good morning from the reception desk.

Jack was presently in the loo, had been there for some time. His system was upset, he said, by the synthetic muck in that ready meal. But Mia guessed it was the genuine muck on the laptop that he couldn't stomach.

She was making a half-hearted attempt to sort through her in-tray, the laptop on the floor with her bag, when Paul Wells came breezing into the office with a white-faced Jack trudging closely behind.

Without a word, without even a nod of acknowledgement, Wells stomped to his desk and hurled his briefcase to the floor. He knows, thought Mia. She gave Jack a questioning look, was about to start on her grovelling confession when Jack put a finger to his mouth and stopped her.

The DCI shrugged off his jacket, revealing armpits already ringed with sweat. 'God save me from lovelorn bloody spinsters,' he muttered, draping the jacket over the back of his chair. 'Get me a coffee, darling, will you?'

Mia was quick to respond. After years of mentally berating the DCI for his politically incorrect 'darlings' and 'loves' she was glad to hear the affectionate term now. It wouldn't happen many more times, not once he'd heard what they'd been up to.

'What's wrong, sir?' she asked, handing him the coffee.

'Elizabeth bloody Thornton, that's what's wrong.'

'Last night's chat didn't go well then?'

'In a word, no,' he growled.

That was a huge pity. Mia had hoped some progress in the Cathy Cousins investigation, prompted by her own findings, might have brought him to the office in a mellow mood. No such luck, obviously.

Wells gave them a succinct and loudly uttered account of the interview whilst taking from his briefcase pens, papers, notebooks and files, all of which he tossed on to his desk with alacrity and aggression.

Mia was imagining those twitchy fingers grasping her neck and squeezing hard when an astonished Jack said, 'Johnny Lee Rogers killed Cathy then, sir.'

'If only it were that simple, mate.' Wells took a long drink of his coffee then picked up his notebook. 'Miss Thornton did eventually admit that Cathy phoned her on Sunday morning. She was after a lift and didn't want to bother her folks that early. Anyway Godzilla arrived and Cathy was nowhere in sight so she got out of the car and buzzed through to the manor. She dithered about for a bit, getting mad 'cause she was itching for a showdown with "that common tart" – her words, not mine. When nobody answered from inside, she decided to go home and Cathy could get stuffed. She was opening the car door when she saw blood on the grass verge and a trail of drops on the road leading to that break in the hedge. She looked into the field, saw Cathy, then panicked and drove off.'

'Hold on,' said Jack, frowning. 'What about the bloke who's supposed to have got to Cathy before she did?'

Wells shrugged. 'She wouldn't admit to seeing anybody.'

'Do you believe her, sir?'

'No, I don't,' he said, flinging his notebook on to the desk. 'She's either lying to save her own skin, or Rogers did it and she's saying nothing to protect him.' Wells let out a humourless snort. 'Our Miss Thornton's got this crazy idea that fate brought Rogers to Larchborough just for her and they're gonna spend the rest of eternity in each other's arms like Romeo and bloody Juliet.'

'Weird,' said Jack. 'And she'd help him get away with murder?'

'I reckon she would, if he did actually do it.' Wells crossed to open the window. 'My money's on Godzilla though. She prattled on about that rehearsal being her moment of destiny, the time when their love would finally ignite – I tell you, she's bloody mental. But beautiful Cathy got him instead, didn't she? Godzilla must have been seriously pissed off. She didn't know Saturday night's shag was a one-off. She probably thought she'd lost Romeo for ever. So, Cathy had to go – but how? Then the girl phoned for a lift and Godzilla had the perfect opportunity – early morning, nobody around. She turned up with a knife and gave it to Cathy good and proper, smashing her face in for good measure.'

'But what about the rabbit blood?' asked Jack.

'You tell me, mate. That's the only bit I can't get to fit.'

'Where's Miss Thornton now, sir?'

'I had to let her go. No reason to keep her.'

All throughout Wells's account Mia had remained silent, following their verbal exchanges like a spectator at a tennis match. Hands in his pockets, back towards the window, Wells glanced at her now, his expression showing faint surprise.

'Not like you to keep your opinions to yourself,' he said. 'What's up?'

Mia took to fiddling with her computer mouse, eyes reluctant to meet his. 'I need a word about the Sky Beddows case, sir.'

'You can have half a dozen, darling.'

But before she could elaborate Nick burst into the office, wielding a black plastic folder. 'Sorry I'm late, sir, only Jim Levers stopped me on the way in. Uniformed are well into the Bulmer and Beddows theft case and wanted to know whether we were planning to charge them on anything linked with Sky's disappearance.'

'Not unless they've confessed to actually abducting her.'

'No such luck, sir. Bulmer did come clean about meeting Sky. Beddows saw them talking on the Monday apparently and put the frighteners on, made Bulmer agree to the heist. Beddows says the opposite, of course. Anyway, they've both got solid alibis for the time Sky went missing. Bulmer was with Sir Nigel all day, and Beddows was doing a job in Warwickshire. Uniformed have checked.'

'Pity,' said Wells. He nodded towards the folder in Nick's hand. 'What you got there?'

'The forensic report on the knives at Stratton Manor,' he said, handing it across.

'Great,' said Wells, heading for his desk.

Settling into his chair, legs outstretched, Wells quickly read the four pages. Then, with all eyes upon him, he tossed the folder on to the desk and let out a disgruntled sigh.

'Nothing … sod all … bloody *nada*,' he growled, rubbing at his jowls with heavy-handed annoyance. 'Christ, that rabbit blood'll be the death of me.'

'Fits in with Elizabeth Thornton doing it,' said Jack.

'True. But how did she get it on Cathy's T-shirt?'

No one could give an answer. While Nick offered to be mother at the coffee machine – getting an affirmative from Wells alone – Mia once more gathered her courage.

'Sir, I've got something you need to see.'

She retrieved the laptop and proceeded to access the Web with fingers that trembled horribly. Wells accepted his coffee from Nick in silence, Mia's reluctant body language telling him loudly that he wouldn't like what was coming next. After opening up the MISCELLANEOUS file, Mia deposited the laptop on Wells's desk and took a step back while he stared at the picture on the screen with teeth bared.

'What the hell's this?'

'It's the first of over two thousand similar images,' she said, hesitantly.

'And why the fuck am I having to look at it?'

'Because it's Robert Mandley's laptop, sir, and I'm worried sick about Nathan and Amy.'

Wells was breathing heavily, trying to contain an anger that was fast taking control. But before he could verbalize that anger Mia brought him up to date with the previous night's events.

'I was there as well,' said Jack. 'It was me that got into the files, actually.'

'What are you after,' Wells bawled, 'a bloody *medal*?'

'No, sir,' said Jack, his already pallid complexion turning a sickly grey. 'But I'm as much to blame as Mia. Just wanted you to know.'

'Very noble, mate.' Wells waved an irritable hand at Mia and Nick, both of whom were hovering at the DCI's shoulder. 'Sit down, the pair of you, for God's sake.'

While they sidled away Wells scrolled through a number of the images, utter disgust distorting his already ungainly features. With a scornful huff he exited the file and slammed the laptop shut.

'Tampering with stolen property. Bloody hell. And not just anybody's – ball-breaker Mandley's,' he said, staring incredulously at Mia. 'What possessed you?'

Mia straightened up, head held high. If this was to be her final plea for mitigation then she'd better make it good.

'Philip Hunt was in pieces when he stopped us in the car-park, sir. He'd been waiting for ages. In that blistering heat, as well. He genuinely loves Sky. And her kids. After listening to his story I couldn't just turn him away.'

'That bloody Mother Teresa complex again,' Wells huffed. 'Will you ever learn?'

'Probably not, sir. I hope not anyway,' she said, feeling stronger now as she held his gaze. 'I've always believed that empathy's a strong attribute for a police officer to have, sir, and I hope I never lose it.'

'Christ …' Wells said, eyes rolling.

'Sky had something on her dad, sir – something she couldn't share with Phil – and she was certain the laptop would give her the proof she needed. I don't know whether those pictures have anything to do with it, but I'm thankful we found them. For that reason alone I'm glad we decided to break the law. Mandley might get his thrills just looking at the pictures, but what if he takes his sick fantasies further? Nathan and Amy could be at risk, sir. We've got to do something.'

Wells thought for a moment, brows knitted. 'What else was in the files?'

Mia shrugged. 'Letters, articles, financial stuff …'

'Nothing, apart from the pictures, that could suggest illegal dealings?'

She shook her head. 'And if I could just say one more thing, sir. Jack's innocent in all this. I steamrolled him into helping me. He didn't really have a choice. And with Michelle pregnant he can't afford to lose his job, so—'

'Who said anything about him losing his job?'

'Well,' Mia stuttered, suddenly taken off guard, 'we've … I mean *I've* committed an offence, sir. Such an act requires instant suspension. Doesn't it?'

'Do you like your job, darling?'

'Of course, sir, I love it.'

Wells rubbed at his weary eyes, peered into his mug and saw that it was empty. 'Fill this up, will you, mate?' he said, thrusting the mug towards Nick. He looked at Mia, elbows on his desk, shoulders slumped. 'If you think I'm gonna sacrifice good officers for a tosser like Mandley, you can think again. He got up my nose from day one. And now this,' he said, nodding towards the laptop. 'We'll just have to come up with another way of getting him. If he finds out we've looked into his files we'll *all* lose our jobs.'

'We could print off some of the pictures,' said Nick, handing Wells the coffee. 'Make out we got them from an anonymous source.'

'That's possible.' Wells suddenly sank back in the chair, let out a long breath. 'God, as if this job ain't hard enough,' he said, glowering at Mia.

'What are we going to do about Nathan and Amy?' she asked.

Wells held up a hand for hush, selected a form from the pile on his desk, then picked up his telephone receiver and tapped out a number.

'Mrs Mandley?' he said, running his fingers along the edge of the laptop. 'Chief Inspector Paul Wells here, Larchborough CID. Is your husband about?'

There was a short pause, a sharp intake of breath. 'No, Robert's out, Chief Inspector. Important business for a client. You know how it is.'

'I do indeed, Mrs Mandley. Not to worry, I was calling to see how the nippers are doing. All right, are they?'

Another hesitation; this one so ripe with concern Wells could almost smell it. 'Of course. Shouldn't they be?'

'Well, it's been a strange time for them, hasn't it? Losing their mum. Finding family they didn't know they had. It's a lot for little 'uns to take in. Don't you think?'

'Oh, I see what you mean,' said the woman, her tone still on the defensive. 'They're fine. Absolutely. A pleasure to have in the house.'

'Good,' said Wells, frowning at Mia. 'Just needed to know they're safe.'

'They'll come to no harm, Chief Inspector. I can promise you that.'

'I'll rest easy then. Thank you, Mrs Mandley. Goodbye.' He replaced the receiver, his frown still aimed at Mia. 'She sounded frightened to death.'

'Mandley can't be an easy man to live with,' said Mia. 'Maybe he's ground her down over the years. We've all seen what intimidation and mental cruelty can do to a woman.'

'Or maybe she thinks we're on to him,' said Nick.

Mia shot him a horrified look. 'She wouldn't stand by and let him abuse kids, surely?'

Nick shrugged. 'She might, if she's frightened to death of him.'

'Oh God, what are we going to do?' she said, turning her fretful gaze on Wells.

The DCI said nothing for a while, sat rubbing at the deep lines on his forehead with long edgy fingers. Eventually, he turned to Jack. 'Did you mention any of this to your missus?'

'No, sir, she'd had a good night out and' – Jack lowered his gaze, embarrassment turning his cheeks a shocking shade of pink – 'to be honest, I knew she'd go off on one and I chickened out.'

'Good. We don't say anything to anybody. If Shakespeare gets to find out….' Wells's face fell into a sickening grimace at the very thought. 'Where's Phil Hunt now?'

'At the caravan-site,' said Mia. 'He should be anyway.'

'Is he likely to blab?'

'He was a bit of a mess when I left him there last night, knowing Mandley had got the kids and everything. But, no, sir, he won't say a word. He trusts us.'

'Get on to him, just in case.' Wells pointed a warning finger. 'If this does get out, darling, you're on your own. I can't afford to sacrifice my pension.'

'I understand, sir. I'll make it my first job.'

'OK, we all keep shtum. Agreed?'

As each one nodded briskly Wells transferred the laptop to Jack's desk. 'Print off some of the pictures, mate. Twenty or thirty should do it. And copy the file on to a separate disc. We might need it.'

'Why?' asked Jack. 'What's the plan?'

'I'm gonna make Mandley's day,' said Wells, returning to his seat. 'I'm gonna give him his laptop back.'

Mia was pondering on the wisdom of that strategy when the telephone on her desk buzzed. 'DS Harvey … yes, he's here, hold on.' She offered the receiver to Wells. 'The forensic laboratory for you, sir.'

The DCI perched on the edge of her desk. 'Wells.' He listened. 'Yes, it's just arrived.' He was picking at a pulled thread in his trousers when his face suddenly broke out into a wide smile. 'You don't say. Thanks, mate, thanks very much. I owe you one.'

'Good news?' asked Mia.

'Oh yes,' he said, replacing the receiver. 'That was one of the blokes who checked the knives at the manor. He knew we were interested in rabbit blood. And although there was none to be found on any of the knives he thought I might be interested to know there were two dead rabbits hanging up in the kitchen while they were there.' Wells grinned as he pulled on his jacket. 'OK … Jack, you work your magic with the laptop. Mia, get on to Hunt.' He motioned to Nick. 'We're on the hunt as well, mate … for the poachers at Stratton Manor. Come on.'

Wells brought his car to a grinding halt beside the circle of trees in the manor's forecourt.

'What's going on now?' he muttered.

A line of police vehicles – three area cars and one large van, its rear doors gaping open – was parked a short distance from the public entrance. As the detectives left the car, officers were emerging from the building with a variety of antiques and depositing them into the back of the van.

Nick led Wells to Bulmer's office, from where a cacophony of echoing voices could be heard. And there they found the man himself, subdued and contrite, as items being brought up from the cellar were added to an already substantial list.

'No wonder you didn't want us looking down there,' Nick said to Bulmer.

The man remained silent, his expression saying it all.

Nick gave him a mocking grin. 'Let's hope they don't scare the cat. Wouldn't want anybody to get scratched.'

Wells approached the officer with the list. 'Who's in charge now our friend here's been nicked?'

The officer pointed into the bowels of the cellar. 'That chap there, sir.'

Wells peered down to where Robert Mandley was directing the operation with a fair amount of arm waving and staccato demands.

'Is he now?' said Wells, smiling harshly. 'Mr Mandley? Sir? Could I have a quick word, please?'

Mandley favoured the DCI with a distasteful look then, issuing an abrupt order to the officer in charge, he made for the stairs.

'Chief Inspector,' he said. 'Know anybody who wants a kitten? That cellar's crawling with the little buggers.'

Bulmer caught Nick's eye, gave him a look which said, *'Told you!'*

'How did you know I'd be here?' asked Mandley, brushing dust from his immaculate suit.

'I didn't,' said Wells. 'I've come on a separate matter.'

'I've been in phone contact with Sir Nigel,' Mandley continued airily, 'who, I must say, is bearing up quite well considering his home is the focus of a murder enquiry and now an antique heist. As his attorney I've advised him to stay away and I'll be taking charge for the foreseeable future.'

'Lucky you are here, sir. I bring good news.'

'Oh yes?'

'We've found your laptop.'

'Why, that's wonderful, Chief Inspector. And so quickly too.'

Wells thrust his hands in his trouser pockets and shrugged. 'The public might think we're wankers, sir, but we do have our moments.'

'Indeed,' said the man, his face alive with expectation. 'So, where is it?'

'Oh, it's back at the station – quite safe, don't worry. You can either collect it, or I'll bring it to you. I'd quite like to see those kiddies again.'

'No, I'll collect it. I've put you to enough trouble.' Mandley let out a relieved breath. 'I'll be glad to get it back. All that confidential material … wouldn't do my career any good if it got into the wrong hands.'

'I can imagine,' said Wells, holding the man's gaze. 'Anyway, I'm continuing the investigation into our murder and we need to see the kitchen. All right if we just go along?'

'Of course. I'll show you where it is.'

'No need, sir, my colleague knows the way.'

The kitchen was a hive of frantic activity. One man chopped vegetables at an incredible speed while another knelt before a smoking oven, swearing richly. A third – whom Nick recognized from his previous visit – was supervising a number of copper pans on the hob, stirring and tasting the contents of each with the same wooden spoon, an activity which Wells thought highly questionable.

The atmosphere was steamy, the air barely breathable, and Wells tugged repeatedly at his collar as he looked around, hoping for a glimpse of their furry prey. But there was none to be had.

'Excuse me, sir,' said Nick, crossing to the man at the hob. 'I'm DI Ford. We've spoken before. Remember?'

'Oh yeah,' he said, wiping his free hand on his apron before offering it to Nick. 'Eric Shaw ... head chef.'

'Good to see you, sir,' said Nick, shaking the man's hand. 'And this is my boss, Chief Inspector Wells.'

'Chief Inspector,' said Shaw, nodding. 'What can I do for you?'

'You can tell us what's happened to the rabbits you've had hanging up.'

'They're in here,' said Shaw, dipping his spoon into the largest of the pans. 'Fancy a taste?'

'No thanks,' said Wells, nose wrinkling. 'Funny sort of menu for a posh place like this.'

Shaw made a face in agreement. 'Our guest has pretty basic tastes when it comes to grub, Chief Inspector. He didn't like our usual range of dishes, kept sending them back.'

'Mr Rogers?'

Shaw nodded.

'Where does he catch these delicacies, sir?'

'Oh, he don't catch them. He don't do sod all from what I can see. No, he gets his mate to do it for him.'

'Which mate?' asked Wells.

'That guitarist.'

'Lenny Price?' said Nick.

'Him, yeah.' Shaw took to stirring again, lowering the gas as he did so. 'He's out there now, lining up a few more poor sods for the pot.'

'How does he kill them?' asked Wells.

'Slits their throats. Fancies himself as a bit of a Bear Grylls – know what I mean?'

'Does he use his own knife?'

'Must do.'

'Where can we find him?'

Shaw pursed his lips. 'On the estate, definitely, but it's a big place. Try the pasture behind the house, near the River Stratton. Overrun with rabbits that was. His lordship had a big cull down there a couple of years back, but they breed like, well, *rabbits* - know what I mean?'

While Shaw laughed uproariously at his own joke Nick followed Wells out of the kitchen.

At the back of the house, standing on a low wall and shielding his eyes from the sun, Wells peered into the distance. The pastureland – just visible beyond the now abandoned stage and audience seating area – was a vast expanse of brown swaying grass. Beyond it, the depleted river appeared as a thin slash of sparkling silver.

'Sod this,' said Wells, jumping from the wall. 'It'll take all day to find him down there. We'll switch to plan B, Nick. Follow me.'

They returned to Robert Mandley, asked him to ensure that Rogers and his group remained on the premises for the rest of that day, and then beat a hasty retreat to the car.

Before starting it up Wells phoned Mia. 'Did you manage to speak to Hunt?'

'Yes, sir, he won't breathe a word.'

'Good.' Wells brought her up to date with unfolding events at the manor. 'Me and Nick are off to get a warrant to search upstairs. I want you to fetch Elizabeth Thornton and bring her here, quick as you can.'

'Why, sir?'

'I've a feeling she did catch a glimpse of somebody that Sunday morning, only she wouldn't say in case it turned out to be Romeo. She might be more forthcoming when she finds out we're after Price.'

'Will do, sir.'

'And if you arrive here first, wait in the car. I don't want Price spooked before we've got the warrant.'

It was well past lunchtime and Mia was checking her watch for the umpteenth time. She'd parked next to the area cars and was having to endure a detailed analysis of Johnny Lee's career from a starry-eyed Lizzie Thornton. Mia had clearly outlined the reason for their visit and was astonished by the woman's obvious excitement.

'You do understand why we want you here?' she said, as Lizzie stopped to draw breath.

'Of course.' Lizzie grasped Mia's arm and looked towards the upper windows of the house. 'Is Johnny Lee actually in there?'

'He'd better be,' said Mia, shrugging her off. 'They've all been ordered to stay put.'

'Unbelievable,' she said, hands cupping her face. 'I'd started to have doubts about us ever meeting again, I don't mind telling you, especially after the meal was cancelled.' She took to preening her hair and staring at herself in the wing mirror. 'I should have realized the universe would find a way.'

Mia turned towards her open side window to hide a look of disgust. The woman was seriously unhinged. A young girl had been violently struck down – Miss Thornton had actually seen the body – and yet she was more concerned about meeting that sex-mad bloody singer than apprehending Cathy's killer. She had to get away from her meaningless waffle, if only for a moment.

'Stay here,' she said, stepping out of the car. 'I won't be long.'

Mia wandered towards the circle of trees, frantically wishing Wells's car would appear. The asphalt was sticky underfoot, the hot air so dry it burnt the throat, but at least that crazy woman was out of earshot.

Why had she developed such a strong dislike for Elizabeth Thornton? She was to be pitied not castigated. Just then a subdued Andrew Bulmer appeared at the public entrance, sandwiched between two uniformed officers, and Mia had her answer. His unexpected presence produced an involuntary frisson of desire, a momentary sense of longing, and Mia realized she craved passion every bit as much as that woman in the car. In years to come, if she failed to find a man, Mia could *be* Elizabeth Thornton. That's why she'd taken against her – because every time she looked into that plain unfulfilled face Mia saw a possible future self and the prospect filled her with horror.

As Bulmer was led to the nearest police vehicle their eyes met and Mia could see nothing but contempt. She assumed indifference, her nose in the air, and turned once more to face the driveway where – thank you, Lord – Wells's car was hurtling towards the house.

He parked haphazardly and hurried to meet her, Nick hot on his heels. 'Bloody magistrates … think they're God's bloody gift,' he muttered, wiping the sweat from his forehead. 'Where's Godzilla?'

'In the car, sir.'

'Are you sure?' he barked.

Mia turned to follow his accusing glare and saw that her car was empty. 'But … oh shit.'

'If she balles this up you'd better make yourself bloody scarce,' he said, jabbing a finger at Mia.

They followed him into the gloomy hall where three uniformed officers were listening to a haughty lecture from Robert Mandley.

'You three, I want you upstairs … *now*,' shouted Wells.

'But I haven't finished,' said the lawyer, highly aggrieved.

'Tough,' said the DCI.

Wells instructed Nick to lead the way and just when all six had reached the upstairs landing a high-pitched scream rang out from a room to their left. It was followed by sounds of a tussle and a torrent of yelled expletives in a rich American accent.

'Looks like we've found our witness,' said Wells, glowering at Mia as he pushed open the door.

He was about to rush in, warrant card at the ready, but pure astonishment kept him glued to the threshold.

Johnny Lee Rogers was pinned within the depths of the four-poster bed by a half-naked lusting Lizzie Thornton, her frizzy hair tossing with abandon. She was writhing on top of him, cooing words of love and clawing at his black shirt with a fury that sent a shower of rhinestones flying all ways.

'Help me,' the singer pleaded, his petrified face just visible above Lizzie's left shoulder. 'Help me, goddamn it—'

And then Nick was shouting, 'Hey, where do you think you're going?'

Mia spun round to see Lenny Price bolting towards the stairs. But Nick was on the ball. He threw himself after the guitarist and, executing a perfect lunge, wrestled him off his feet.

While Nick pinned Price to the ground – his position almost identical to Lizzie's – Wells grabbed Mia's shoulders and propelled her into the bedroom.

'Get her clothes back on,' he ordered, sharply. 'We haven't got time to piss about.'

Wells hurried to where Nick was slipping handcuffs on to a cursing Lenny Price and thrust the search warrant into the man's face.

'Care to show us your room, sir?'

They had found three knives in all, each one ebony-handled, their blades sharpened to a lethal degree. The knives were presently undergoing tests at the forensic laboratory. And Lenny Price, having remained reticent throughout, was stewing in a cell at Silver Street Police Station, where he would remain until the results of those tests became known.

Lizzie Thornton, after much coaxing from Mia, had eventually let go of her hero and was now fully dressed at the library, where Ruth Findlay was lapping up the drama with all the rapacious enthusiasm of a bystander at a sex orgy.

Lizzie, however, was a broken woman. She now knew that her vision of a shared future with Johnny Lee could never be. 'Crazy bitch' and 'ugly broad' – not to mention the other, more explicit, terms that had spewed from his mouth; the meanings of which Lizzie could only guess at – were not the words of a man in love. Even she knew that.

The CID team was presently enjoying a late lunch in the police canteen while they awaited the call from forensics.

'Pricey can keep shtum 'til the cows come home,' said Wells, through a mouthful of fried sausage, 'but we've got him and he knows it.'

'One down and one to go,' said Mia, toying with her uninspiring salad.

Wells nodded. 'Where's the laptop, Jack?'

'On my desk, sir.'

'You did everything I asked?'

'Yes, and I gave it a good wipe down, just to be on the safe side.' Jack took a sip of his tea. 'Oh, and the tax office returned my call about Sheila Reeves. They've been liaising with the benefits agency and found even more discrepancies. Looks like she's been on the fiddle for years. Anyway, I've handed it over to uniformed, sir.'

'Good.' Wells pushed aside his empty plate and was mentally debating the merits of a pudding when a harassed Sergeant Levers burst through the door. He slumped into an adjacent seat, red-faced, striving to catch his breath.

'I've been looking everywhere for you lot. All your mobiles are off.'

'Are they?' said Wells, feigning surprise. 'Sorry, mate.'

'Where's the fire?' asked Nick, grinning.

'No fire, son, but we've got the Beddows kids in reception bawling their eyes out.'

Mia shot him a worried look. 'Nathan and Amy? Who brought them in?'

'A middle-aged woman … grey-haired … respectable. She just dumped them with a load of cases and took off. She asked me to give you this, Paul.' He handed Wells a white sealed envelope on which 'CID' was printed in black ink. Then he left.

Wells tore open the envelope and pulled out two sheets of good quality watermarked paper, one side of each covered by a juddering scrawl. He read the words a number of times, his jowls all the while settling into a joyless lour. Wells surveyed his team.

'Christ Almighty,' was all he said.

CHAPTER NINETEEN

As Mia watched Wells's face settle into an incongruous mix of excitement and extreme loathing she could hardly bring herself to pick up the letter. But she did, and read out to the others:

For the attention of DCI Wells

My name is Julia Mandley. I am of sound mind and I swear that the contents of this letter are the truth.

I promised you on the phone that I would keep my darling grandchildren safe, and that is why I have brought them to you. Amy will never be safe with us. I let her mother down so very badly, but I won't make the same mistake twice.

My husband started sexually abusing Rachel when she was barely six years old. She confided in me often – a small child frightened and confused – and each time I chose to ignore her. I was in thrall to Robert, terrified of his temper, and it was easier for me to pretend she was making it up. As Rachel grew older she became taciturn, enduring the abuse with a strength far beyond her years. She concentrated on her studies, probably seeing a career as her only means of escape.

Our home was hell to live in, but it was a hell of my own making. When Rachel told me she was pregnant I could no longer ignore the truth. But instead of helping her through that abominable mess I threw her out, told her never to come back again. Robert thought she'd been taken. He was inconsolable for months. He'd lost the love of his life, his reason to exist.

Nathan is a beautiful, quiet and utterly adorable little boy, but my husband can hardly bear to look at him. I assumed it was because he reminded Robert too much of Rachel. I was still in denial, you see. But not anymore. Nathan is Robert's son, the consequence of his sinful ways, and a constant reminder of all that he has lost.

Amy is an absolute joy, and as yet unsullied. But Robert has already started to groom her and I cannot allow him to succeed a second time.

I wish I could give you concrete evidence of my husband's twisted activities, Chief Inspector, but I cannot. Any claims I made would be torn to pieces by him in an instant. Robert is an extremely intelligent man. But he is also a MONSTER *and must be stopped.*

I fear that Rachel was not his only conquest and I advise you to look in the old stable block on the perimeter of our property. Robert has entertained his many friends and 'their children' in that block for years. I have always been forbidden entry, and Robert keeps the keys locked in his briefcase at all times.

I have not cried for Rachel this past week – I gave up all rights to be her mother many years ago – but if you do find her, Chief Inspector, please tell her that I am so very sorry.

I can go now, safe in the knowledge that my two angels will come to no harm. I just pray that God will have mercy on my soul.

Yours, in truth

Julia Mandley

They were silent for many moments, each one lost in their own grisly thoughts.

'Do you reckon she's going to top herself?' said Jack.

Wells grimaced. 'I bloody hope not.'

'So Nathan's his boy,' said Mia. 'God, that's awful.'

'Lucky he wasn't born with four eyes and three noses,' said Jack.

Mia gave him a threatening glance and then took in a sudden sharp breath. She turned to Wells. 'Sir, what if Mandley's taken Sky? What if he's abusing her again?'

The DCI returned the letter to its envelope, his clumsy fingers a reflection of his seething fury. 'Get down to those kids,' he said to her. 'They'll have to stay here for the time being. Get a couple of officers to sit with them, and meet us at Mandley's house when you're done.'

As Mia grabbed her shoulder bag and hurried off, Nick said, 'Shall I get a search warrant, sir?'

Wells nodded. 'For the whole of his property – house, stables, all of it. Get one for his office as well, just in case we draw a blank. And hurry, Nick. If the sick bastard has got Sky, the quicker we find her the better.' He turned to Jack. 'You're coming with me, mate. Lenny Price can sweat it out in the cell 'til we get back.' Wells's face settled into a sneer. 'I dunno, this morning it was rabbits ... now we're after a fucking snake.'

'I hadn't thought of Mandley having Sky,' said Jack.

'Me neither,' said Wells. 'He was quick to come forward when he saw the poster, and he was nowhere near the manor when she disappeared – or so I've always assumed.'

They were outside the Old Rectory, Mandley's sumptuous home, peering into the diamond-leaded windows for any signs of life. So far all was as it should be – no bodies hanging from rafters or slumped in a drugged stupor over the settee – but they were all too aware that Mrs Mandley could be breathing her last in any one of the upstairs rooms.

'Hurry up, Nick, for Christ's sake,' Wells muttered.

Before leaving the station he'd instructed uniformed to locate Mandley and inform him of a break-in at his home – a ploy guaranteed to deliver the lawyer straight into their hands – but they were to leave it long enough for Nick to arrive with the warrants.

As if summoned there by the sheer strength of his desperation Wells turned to see Nick's car cruising through the tall iron gates and pulling up sharp in the neat block-paved parking area. He was out of the car in a flash, running towards the house, search warrants held aloft.

'Right,' said Wells. 'Who's any good at breaking down doors?'

'No need for that,' said Jack, already extracting a credit card from his wallet. 'I'll get it open. No problem.'

Within seconds the door was swinging on its hinges.

'I'll pretend I didn't see that,' Wells said, with a thankful grin.

They'd hardly had time to start on the downstairs rooms when Mia arrived. Straight away Wells instructed Nick to go with her and look for the stable block.

The Old Rectory was a large house with many rooms. Leaving Jack to continue his search Wells bounded up the stairs and threw open each door as he travelled along the lengthy landing.

He found Mrs Mandley in a back bedroom. She was sprawled across the neat three-quarter bed, its lilac-patterned counterpane now dark with the blood from her slashed wrists. The wounds had ceased to gush, the blood already congealing. An awfully bad sign.

There was a cut-throat razor near to her right hand, an empty tablet bottle on the bedside table; its label informed Wells that she'd swallowed a codeine-based painkiller of a high dosage. But how many tablets had she taken? Not the whole bloody bottle, he silently prayed.

While he felt for a pulse at the side of the woman's neck Wells allowed his gaze to take in the room. Pop star posters graced walls painted pink to complement the tie-dyed curtains at the window; cheesecloth-covered boxes and other hippy paraphernalia; A-level syllabus textbooks and romance novels. A place for everything, and everything in its place. Exactly as it was in Sky's caravan.

Rachel's bedroom. It had to be. Whose idea was it to leave the place untouched? Wells pondered. The guilty mother? The perverted bastard of a father?

The woman's neck still held a vestige of warmth, but Wells couldn't detect a pulse. He phoned for an ambulance and dragged the dead weight on to the floor where he proceeded to administer cardiopulmonary resuscitation, his repeated plea for her to breathe muttered in time with each downward thrust.

And then a commotion started downstairs. Robert Mandley had arrived, was berating Jack for calling him home under false pretences. Wells was reluctant to abandon the woman, but the CPR was having no effect and he couldn't leave Jack on his own with the lawyer. The poor sod would be mincemeat in no time.

Wells fled down the stairs, pulling a pair of handcuffs from his jacket pocket as he did so.

'Mr Mandley,' he said, dangling the cuffs before the man's eyes. 'Hold your hands out, you naughty boy.'

It took the weight of both detectives to pin Mandley down as the handcuffs were clicked into place while a jubilant Wells read him his rights. The DCI put in an urgent request for uniformed to collect the man; they wanted him safely installed in the nick while a thorough search of the property could be resumed. And as Jack watched over him from a fair distance – the furious lawyer was breathing fire – Wells hunted out Mia and Nick, the keys to the stable block jangling in his jacket pocket.

The house stood on a substantial plot – far larger than Wells had anticipated – but eventually his eyes fell on a long rectangular building. And as he ran towards it a high-pitched mechanical whining started up, the sound increasing in volume as Wells speedily approached. Nick was slicing through one of the doors with a chain-saw, Mia keeping to a safe distance, hands over her ears.

'It'll be easier with these,' Wells shouted, holding up the keys.

Mia caught sight of him, said something to Nick, and the loud whining ceased.

Wells brought them up to date while he jiggled a key in the lock.

'She's dead?' said Mia, clearly shocked. 'How did Mandley take it?'

'He couldn't give a shit,' Wells huffed. 'He was more concerned about me having these keys. Which makes me

226

think' – he grunted as he applied more force, turning the key at last – 'that we're on to a winner.'

As the door swung open all three were forced back by a terrible stench: organic matter left to rot in the overheated airless space.

Wells and Nick went in first, Mia trailing behind with a tissue clamped over her mouth and nose. The windowless room was dark and Wells flicked the light switch, illuminating a scene from hell.

Sky was slumped in a far corner, held there by thick wall-mounted chains attached to both wrists. At least they assumed it was Sky. She was virtually unrecognizable from that smiling beauty in the snapshot. Her long hair was now matted and dark with sweat; her filthy clothes stiff with vomit, faeces and urine. A thin, stinking, maggot-ridden mattress lay beneath her.

'God, she's dead,' Mia whimpered, as Wells bent to check.

'No, she's still breathing,' he said, grappling for the mobile in his pocket as he straightened up. 'Jack, when the paramedics arrive send them straight to the stable block. If they keep to the road they'll soon come across the entrance. One of us'll meet them here. And don't fuck about, mate – Sky's still alive, but only just.'

There was nothing they could do for the girl. She'd gone way beyond first aid. While Mia waited for the professionals to arrive Wells took Nick on a search of the building. The rest of it had been knocked into one huge room with tiny film sets in each corner: a child's bedroom; a school classroom; another small area covered in sand before a blue backdrop; a kiddies' playground. They found easy chairs and video cameras; a well-stocked bar and American-style fridge; a large wardrobe containing clothes of every conceivable style for the provocative child of today. Everything, in fact, that might appear on the discerning paedophile's wish list.

'Vice'll be clocking up a load of overtime,' Wells remarked gruffly.

CHAPTER TWENTY

DCI Wells returned to Silver Street on a high.

They'd left the Old Rectory and its stable block in the capable hands of uniformed and forensics. And Robert Mandley was in the cells, where he'd remain until a suitable time could be arranged with the magistrates' court for a remand hearing. He wouldn't be hurting any more children. And his friends wouldn't either, once the gorillas in the vice squad hustled him into talking.

Sky was safe and swiftly stabilizing in Larchborough General Hospital's intensive care unit – a mere five-minute walk away from the morgue where Julia Mandley's body was taken after the paramedics' frantic efforts to revive her had failed.

A good result. Apart from the suicide. Shakespeare was well chuffed.

And when he found the forensic report on Lenny Price's knives waiting for him in the office, Wells – his system still pumping adrenalin – was eager for a showdown with the musician.

Price had been dragged to interview room number three – his indignant howls shattering the silence of the sleepy corridors – and was seated at the table, moody and defiant, when the DCI breezed in with Nick.

Wells tossed the report on to the table. 'Know what that is?'

Price eyed the black folder then treated him to a hostile look.

'It's your ticket to the slammer,' Wells said, grinning broadly.

Nick did the necessaries with the tape machine while the DCI slipped out of his jacket and sat facing the man. After a long moment Wells turned to the officer at the door, still grinning. 'This bloke was famous once, mate. Before you were born, of course, but….'

He left the sentence hanging, waited for some reaction, but the musician merely fell back in his seat, staring gloomily at the door.

'Why did you kill Cathy Cousins?'

'Who says I did?' Price countered, his accent slow and silky.

Wells tapped the forensic report. 'This does, mate. It says Cathy's blood was found on your knife, along with skin cells matching her DNA. It says rabbit blood on the knife corresponded with a stain found on Cathy's T-shirt. There were also a couple of partial fingerprints on the handle that were compared with Cathy's and – guess what? – they matched.' He pulled a face. 'Says a lot, doesn't it?'

Price shrugged. 'Doesn't say I did it. Somebody else could've used the knife.'

'Sorry, mate, but apart from Cathy's partials yours were the only prints found.'

'So? The guy could've been wearing gloves.'

'Good try,' said Wells, nodding. 'Look, you're up to your eyes in shit. Just accept it and confess.'

Price shifted his weight in the chair. 'I want my attorney.'

'The duty solicitor's already on his way,' said Wells. 'You wait 'til he's here – your Lieutenant Columbo's got nothing on me when I get started.'

'No, I want the band's attorney. Tell Johnny to fly him over.'

The DCI sucked in a long breath. 'I don't think Mr Rogers can spare the time, to be honest. I reckon he wants this over and done with asap.' Wells laughed. 'He couldn't wait to show my uniformed colleagues your hunting gear.'

Panic suddenly showed in Price's eyes. 'Johnny?'

'Yes, mate. Something tells me he's had enough of "li'l ol' England". Can't think why.' Wells turned to Nick. 'DI Ford, kindly tell Mr Price what we found on his clothes.'

Nick opened up the folder. 'For a start there was a large amount of pollen on the trousers.'

'And did it match the pollen found on Cathy's T-shirt?'

'It did, sir. Also, there were thirty-nine blood splashes found in total and these were an exact match with Cathy's type B positive blood.'

'Anything else?' said Wells, his amused gaze still on the man's face.

'Yes, sir, forensics found a number of Cathy's hairs tangled up with the jacket buttons and a smudge of her lipstick on one of the sleeves.'

'Pretty strong evidence then, DI Ford.'

'Rock solid, sir.'

Wells aimed a disarming smile at Price, his eyebrows raised in a query. 'Anything to say, sir?'

Price said nothing, his stricken look telling the detectives he was still trying to assimilate the knowledge that Johnny Lee had sold him down the river.

'Right, here's the plan,' said Wells, thoroughly enjoying himself. 'You tell us why you killed Cathy and we can get off early for once.' He glanced at his watch. 'Make it quick and you'll be shown to your cell in time for supper. No rabbit, I'm afraid. Fish and chips on Fridays, with a nice yoghurt to follow.'

Price's suntanned face suddenly blanched. He kept swallowing as bile rose in his throat, fidgeted in the chair while his mind raced. 'Fuck,' he said.

'There's a vegan option, if you prefer,' said Wells, deliberately misreading the man's distress.

'Shut the fuck up,' Price yelled. 'It wasn't my fault—' Shock registered on his face, as though the words had leapt out of their own volition.

'What, the girl threw herself on to your knife? Seventeen times?'

'Oh Jesus….' Price cradled his head in his hands, his long frame bent over the table.

Wells shared a glance with Nick. 'What happened, Mr Price?'

The musician fell back in the chair, choking back the tears. 'I was so freakin' tired, man. We'd been working on new songs all night.' He gave a tetchy huff. 'I was, anyways – Johnny was asleep on the couch. People don't know this but … all them songs Johnny composed over the years?' He jabbed a finger at his chest. 'I wrote them, man, they're all mine. And do I get one dime in royalties? No, sir. All the work I done for him, all the years I've been loyal, and I'm still on a freakin' salary.'

Wells said, 'My heart bleeds for you, mate, but hurry up and get on with it.'

Price lunged forward. 'You wanna hear? Then let me tell it my own way.'

Wells held up his hands, nodded for the man to continue.

Price fell back, his fiery gaze on the DCI. 'Johnny came to about six, said he was hitting the sack. But I had to go kill that day's dinner before I could get me some sleep.'

'You'll have me crying in a minute.' The words were out before Wells could stop them, Price's self-pitying tone the red rag to his bullish nature. 'Sorry, mate, carry on.'

Price's eyes narrowed momentarily, but he continued. 'I'd got me about three or four rabbits and was heading back when I found the kid outside the gates. Jesus, she was hot – *real* hot – and I suddenly wasn't tired no more. I said hi, started my babe talk, but that kid – she saw the rabbits in my bag and gave me a look that'd stop a stampede, called me a killer, threatened to report me. I laughed, said them little guys gave Johnny the energy to fuck and now I wanted me a taste. I tried to kiss her but she threw me off, said she didn't want nothing to do with me.

'I was horny, man. And, hell, she'd let Johnny, so why not me? I was feeling her up, trying to coax her, and then the motherfucker bit me.' He held up his forearm, showed the detectives an oval wound on his wrist, its edges a livid purple. He shook his head. 'I was so freakin' wild. I said, you wanna see how I kill your little friends? And before I knew it I'd got the knife and shoved it in her belly. She looked at me, like she couldn't believe I'd done it, and then sorta crumpled.'

'Was she dead?' asked Wells.

'No, she was making these weird sounds. Man, I was shitting my pants. I knew I had to get her out of sight so I dragged her into the field. I needed to think. Only, I couldn't 'cause she was making them freakin' noises.' He looked away. 'So I finished the job.'

'Why destroy her face?' The man hesitated, suddenly coy. 'Mr Price?'

He started chewing on his lip, reluctant to go on. 'This ain't gonna sound good.'

'You think the rest of it does?' Wells spat.

Price hitched himself up in the seat, started pulling at his shoulder-length hair. 'The kid was lying there, still warm. A little bloody maybe, but—' He shrugged. 'I decided to have me a piece now she couldn't say no. So I stripped her and unzipped my pants, but I couldn't do it 'cause her eyes were open, like she was looking at me. Anyways, there was a rock nearby.' That shrug again.

Wells's lips curled back. 'You bastard.'

'I didn't fuck her,' Price added hurriedly. 'A car pulled up – that ugly broad's – so I grabbed the kid's stuff and got the hell out of there.'

'You're aware we found the T-shirt,' said Wells, righteous contempt darkening his eyes. 'Where did you ditch the rest of her clothes?'

Price frowned as he stared at the DCI. 'They're with my things. You said Johnny handed them over.'

Wells tried for a bashful look. 'He didn't actually, sir. I dare say we've got them by now though.'

'But, the report....'

'Oh, that,' said Wells, smirking. 'We made it up to get you to talk.' He turned to Nick. 'Nice bit of ad-libbing there, DI Ford. The lipstick on the sleeve was inspirational.'

'Thank you, sir.'

Price rose up. 'Hey, that ain't right....'

'What *you* did isn't right.' Wells glared at him. 'Look at you, sitting there like a teenage bloody hippy. You must be older than I am.'

'Rock and roll, man,' Price muttered. 'No law against it.'

'True, but there's a law against killing young girls, and you're nicked, mate.'

A knock came on the door and the duty solicitor bustled in. 'Sorry I'm late, Chief Inspector.'

'You're just in time,' said Wells, getting up to stretch his legs. 'I do believe your client's ready to make his statement.'

CHAPTER TWENTY-ONE

'But why can't they stay with Phil?' said Mia.

'Because they'll be better off with a foster mother,' Wells countered.

'Says who? Sky would want them with Phil.'

'You're probably right, but as they've put her in a clinical coma while she heals we can hardly ask her, can we?'

The team was back in the CID office, all loose ends nicely tied – very nearly, anyway. The Beddows children were still downstairs and Mia wanted them to go to Philip Hunt, a sharp detour from normal procedure.

'Come on, sir, you know it makes sense.'

'I said no. Now leave it.'

'But why? They'll be with Phil when Sky gets out of hospital.'

'He's not equipped to look after them. Those kids need professional help, somebody who's properly trained.'

'No, they don't. They need familiarity, sir. They need their own beds, their own things. What they *don't* need is another strange place to get used to. They've had enough of that this week. And Phil's not alone, don't forget. His parents'll be there as well.'

The DCI hesitated. He was remembering Hunt's delightful mother with the sparkling eyes. She'd be an absolute joy to be around. No doubt about it. He looked at his DS.

'How's your mother doing?'

Mia frowned, unaware until then that she'd been holding her breath. 'Fine,' she said, shrugging. 'Why?'

'I haven't asked for a while. I'm sorry.' Wells heaved a sigh. 'Shakespeare'll have a fit,' he said, almost to himself.

Mia shot him a hopeful look. 'When has that ever stopped you, sir?'

A moment of contemplation, and then the DCI nodded. 'OK, they can stay with Hunt, but only until you find a suitable foster mother.'

'Thank you,' Mia said, grinning. 'And I *will* get on to social services, sir ... probably.'

'Take them now, before I change my mind. Nick, you go with her. I want Hunt to know it's a temporary arrangement and I don't trust Mother Teresa here to make that plain.' Wells headed for the coffee machine. 'And, hurry up. As soon as you get back we'll call it a day.'

They arrived at the caravan site in time to see Sheila Reeves being forcibly removed from her gypsy van by two no-nonsense female officers. A male colleague followed behind, returning his notebook to his breast pocket. Billy Reeves stood in the van's doorway, his pink plaster cast now as grubby as his teary little face. An elderly man was behind him, hands on the boy's shoulders; *his* face showing bewilderment and shock.

Nick approached the male officer. 'What you doing her for, Mark?'

'Benefit fraud. The fat cow's been using different names, claiming for kids she hasn't got. Cost us taxpayers thousands,' he sneered. 'Not any more though.'

Mia wrapped her arms tightly around Nathan and Amy as they watched the woman vainly resisting all attempts to get her into the area car. Those poor children were badly traumatized. They needed stability, normality; not more scary stuff like this. During the drive from the station they'd remained ominously quiet. Even the news that their mother was safe in hospital and would soon be home had failed to bring a smile to their faces. Mia was seriously worried.

But then Phil and his parents rushed from their caravan, arms outstretched, and those young faces were transformed. The children struggled from Mia's grip and sprinted towards the adults, laughing and crying as they surrendered themselves to a series of hugs and frantic kisses. Mia stood watching them, a broad grin splitting her face. And she stopped worrying. They were going to be all right. They were home.

'Is it true? You've found Sky?'

The voice startled Mia. She hadn't heard anyone approach. She spun round to see Roy Barlow, hands in his pockets, penitent and strangely cowed.

'Yes.' She gave him a cordial smile. 'And she's going to be fine.'

'Thank God for that.'

Mia nodded towards a pile of luggage stacked outside his caravan. 'You off?'

'Nothing to keep us here now … according to my wife.'

'I think she's right, actually.'

He acknowledged the statement with a nod. 'Our American friends are coming with us. The others, well, they'll be making their own futures.'

Mia stared into his forlorn face, noted the trembling chin, the watery eyes. 'Take my advice, Mr Barlow: be thankful for what you've got because, believe it or not, you're a very lucky man.'

'Are you and Kelly studying the same script?' He tried for a smile but couldn't maintain it. 'Tell Hunt he's lucky as well. Will you do that?'

Mia gave his arm a reassuring squeeze. 'Take care, Mr Barlow.'

As she watched him walk away Phil approached her. 'We didn't get thrown into jail then.'

Mia laughed. 'No, my boss is full of surprises.'

'Why?' he said, frowning suddenly. 'Why would a man leave his daughter to die?'

Mia looked away, her gaze centred on the parched landscape. 'We're not sure, but we think Sky might have threatened to go public about certain things.'

Phil waited for her to continue, but she didn't. 'What things? Was it to do with the pictures?'

'It's not my place to say, Phil. If Sky wants you to know she'll tell you. Just be glad we found her – OK?'

To Mia's surprise Phil wrapped her in a fierce hug. 'Thank you. Thanks for everything.'

'We'd better go,' said Nick. 'The weekend starts here.'

Phil grabbed his hand, held it between his own. 'Have a good one. You deserve it.'

As they approached Nick's car, Mia said, 'You forgot to tell him this was only a temporary arrangement.'

'No, I didn't. You were right. This is where they belong.'

'Nicholas Ford,' Mia spluttered, 'you do have a heart after all.' She gave him a sideways glance. 'Think you'll ever have children?'

That heart she'd just mentioned gave a sudden lurch as Nick's thoughts returned to Sophie Violet's ashes in their cold grave for all those long months. But, strangely, he found that the pain her memory usually evoked was lessening, becoming easier to bear.

'I've got to find the mother first,' he said, with a wry grin. 'What about you?'

Mia looked back to where Phil was hoisting Amy into the air and spinning her around, the girl's delighted screams deafening. See, she told herself, happy endings are possible. Why shouldn't she wish for one herself?

She gave Nick a smile. 'I can always hope, can't I?'

THE END

THE DS MIA HARVEY SERIES

Book 1: Desperate
Book 2: Obsessed

Please join our mailing list for updates on
DS Mia Harvey, free Kindle crime thriller, detective,
mystery books and new releases.

www.joffebooks.com

FREE KINDLE BOOKS

Please join our mailing list for free Kindle books and new releases, including crime thrillers, mysteries, romance and more, as well as news on the next book by Patti Battison! www.joffebooks.com

Thank you for reading this book. If you enjoyed it please leave feedback on Amazon or Goodreads, and if there is anything we missed or you have a question about then please get in touch. The author and publishing team appreciate your feedback and time reading this book.

We're very grateful to eagle-eyed readers who take the time to contact us. Please send any errors you find to corrections@joffebooks.com

Printed in Great Britain
by Amazon